NOVELS BY BURT WEISSBOURD

Callie James Thrillers
Danger in Plain Sight
Rough Justice

Corey Logan Thrillers
Inside Passage
Teaser
Minos

In Velvet
a thriller set in Yellowstone National Park

Danger in Plain Sight

"Here's what happens when you enter Mr. Weissbourd's world: You can't get out. You will be astonished not only by the colorful, playful, lethal characters, you will be hooked into a plot that laughs at whatever else you thought you were doing today. Callie and Cash, beauty and the beast, and the characters that swim through their world are each a gem of humanity observed."

—**David Field**, screenwriter and former head
of West Coast Production United Artists

"Weissbourd delivers a polished page-turner about terrorism, money laundering, and the price of sins rooted in avarice."

—*BlueInk Review*

"From the author of the brilliant Corey Logan Trilogy, *Danger in Plain Sight* is the latest thriller from Burt Weissbourd and his finest novel yet. Weissbourd has created an entire genre—*Seattle Noir*. Callie James and her son, Lew, are indelible characters. I devoured the novel in a single night—and I think you will, too."

—**Jacob Epstein**, writer and executive story editor
Hill Street Blues, writer *LA Law*

"A woman gets in touch with her inner action hero in this bracing thriller."

—*Kirkus Reviews*

Inside Passage

"A narrative that is relentlessly taut and exciting."

—Foreword Reviews

"*Inside Passage* hit all the hallmarks of a great read… Riveting story from the first paragraph."

—Nightly Reading

"The family dynamics and insights to human behavior had me reeling…Juicy, fascinating stuff."

—The (Not Always) Lazy W

"*Inside Passage* is a great thriller and the restaurants you include as part of the story: Canlis, El Gaucho, Tulio, Queen City Grill, Wild Ginger, are all very sexy places. You really captured our city!"

—**Scott Carsburg**, James Beard award winner
and legendary Seattle chef

"I got completely hooked on *Inside Passage*'"

—**Nancy Guppy**, host of *Art Zone* on Seattle Channel

Teaser

"A stunning, fast-paced thriller."

—*Roxy's Reviews*

"Burt Weissbourd is such a great writer… Such a great book!"

—*So I Am a Reader*

"Weissbourd, a seasoned screenwriter and film producer, has the mechanics down pat. Teaser is a fun, action-filled ride."

—*Foreword Reviews*

"Weissbourd's stellar writing, memorable characters and an extremely well-crafted narrative never disappoint."

—*Discerning Reader*

Minos

"Original, consistently compelling…Minos is an exceptionally entertaining and engaging read from beginning to end."

—*Midwest Book Review*

"These books transcend the expectations of genre fiction to become literature."

—**Jacob Epstein**, writer and executive story editor of *Hill Street Blues*, writer *LA Law*

"Mr. Weissbourd draws you into a world of characters and stories that keep you riveted, and you're pretty sure you are visiting people and worlds that have little or nothing to do with you. But he keeps going deeper, and by the end, he has delivered you back to yourself, a self you may not have admitted to before. Mr. Weissbourd, please keep writing."

—**David Field**, screenwriter and former head of West Coast Production United Artists

In Velvet

"This thrilling novel has a breathless pace that combines science and nature to create nail-biting tension."

—*Foreword Reviews*

"*In Velvet* left me breathless, a bit contemplative, and completely satisfied."

—*Manic Readers*

"Weissbourd's writing reminds me of the great Raymond Chandler mysteries."

—**John McCaffrey**, *KGB Bar Lit Mag*

"*In Velvet* is a thrill from start to finish!"

—*Closed the Cover*

BURT WEISSBOURD

DANGER IN PLAIN SIGHT

A CALLIE JAMES
THRILLER

BLUE CITY PRESS
ISLIP, NY

RARE BIRD
LOS ANGELES, CALIF.

THIS IS A GENUINE RARE BIRD | BLUE CITY PRESS BOOK

Rare Bird Books
6044 North Figueroa Street
Los Angeles, CA 90042
rarebirdbooks.com

Blue City Press
62 West Bayberry Road
Islip, NY 11751

Copyright © 2022 by Burt Weissbourd

REVISED TRADE PAPERBACK ORIGINAL EDITION

PREVIOUSLY PUBLISHED BY BLUE CITY PRESS IN 2020

All rights reserved, including the right to reproduce this book or portions thereof
in any form whatsoever, including but not limited to print, audio, and electronic.
For more information, address:
Rare Bird Books Subsidiary Rights Department
6044 North Figueroa Street
Los Angeles, CA 90042

Cover Design by Lisa Fyfe

Printed in the United States

PAPERBACK ISBN: 9781644282984

10 9 8 7 6 5 4 3 2 1

Publisher's Cataloging-in-Publication Data available upon request.

For Dorothy Escribano Weissbourd

PROLOGUE

CASH WAS HUMMING, A fiery local singer's version of Willie Nelson's "Crazy." In his mind, he was picturing this fine-looking, vampy gal singing her heart out. Yeah. Cash sang the words now—walking down the alley, smoking a premium Havana and feeling breezy, at the top of his game. Crooning a final chorus, he stepped under a French-blue awning with *Le Cochon Bronze* written on it in beige script. He unlocked the back door to the restaurant. Four steps led up to a landing and an old cherrywood Dutch door that swung into the restaurant's big, bright country kitchen.

When Cash cleared the kitchen door he stopped, tense—afraid he'd passed through the gates of Dante's twisted northwest Hell. Buying time, he stubbed out his half-smoked Havana in the drain of the black cast-iron sink, then carefully set it on the counter. "Frosty"—his pet name for his boss—had eight of his ancient Japanese ivory carvings lined up on the long prep table. They were rare nineteenth-century erotic netsuke (because their kimonos had no pockets, people used netsuke to suspend bags from their sashes), and of course she had them lined up just so, all in this neat row. Orderly, like everything else in her restaurant. Which was kind of funny since there must have been six or seven different sexual positions on display right there. The one with the moving parts was sweet, better, even, than he'd hoped for.

And there Callie was, crimson spots darkening her cheeks to the color of beet borscht, wanting to scream but talking instead in that quiet, deliberate, chilly way she had. "Terry, how could you do this? How? What were you thinking? Damn it, Terry."

She was the only one in the world who called him Terry. He still wasn't used to it. "I didn't do anything to you."

"You're smuggling into my restaurant. My restaurant. Where I live…My home."

Cash raised a large, weathered palm, as if gentling a frightened animal. "Easy. Hey. Whoa. No one was hurt."

"I trusted you. *I* was hurt."

He looked at the netsuke on the worn maple table. They'd been hidden in her regular order of Chinese vegetables from Vancouver. He should have known that she came downstairs when she couldn't sleep. "But you weren't hurt," he finally said. "And you can trust me not to hurt you." Which was, he thought, the whole point.

She closed her eyes, opened them again. Cash thought he could see little beads of sweat on her brow.

He took a step forward. He was big—six feet, two inches tall, 240 pounds. Hard and intimidating. When he smiled, though, when he did that, people felt better. "You have to admit, they're very cool. Did you see the one that moves?" He leaned over, demonstrating how the carved figures could make love. Smiling again.

The Chinese cabbage caught him square in the head. He was around the table, pinning her arms to her sides, before she could grab a hefty bamboo shoot.

"Please don't touch me."

Cash could feel her shoulders trembling.

"Please don't touch me," she repeated.

"Try a slow breath," he suggested. When she ignored that, he stepped back. "Callie, please. Hear me out. No one knows. No one has to know. No one was caught. I won't do it again."

"Wrong. I know. You're caught. And you can't just act like nothing happened."

"Okay." Cash nodded. "I'm sorry."

"And I'm sorry, but the police have to know."

The lines in his big face deepened. "Listen. That would be bad." His tone changed. "Really bad for me."

"I'm sorry, Terry, but this isn't like a tasteless prank or hitting on women half your age when you're tending bar. Smuggling is illegal, a federal crime, and ivory is banned in the United States. If I don't report it and you're ever found out, they can close my restaurant."

Cash took a breath, looking around. Her kitchen was a warm-feeling space. Copper pots, ladles and cast-iron skillets hung on pegs above the stove and in a nook between cupboards. His eyes came back to Callie's. "Please slow down. Reconsider this," he said, dead serious now.

"I trusted you, and you took advantage of me. My restaurant is all that I have—"

"Okay…this one time, can you try to let this go? You don't need to lay some Callie James all-or-nothing homespun morality on me. No one was hurt. This is a restaurant, not a holy place."

"Say your buyer, or your supplier, is arrested next year and gives you up—I could lose everything. Think about this: the restaurant is all that I have for me and my son."

Cash scratched his uncombed sandy-colored hair. "Look. I'm asking for a favor here. We can agree that you *don't* know about this. It'll never happen again, that's a promise. Please don't do something we'll both regret."

Callie took another breath, and near tears, she repeated, *"Try a slow breath?"*

"It was meant as a helpful suggestion. Callie, I'm in a jam. I was ripped off on a very big deal, and I owe more money than

I have. Truthfully, right about now, money really matters. Can you understand that?"

For a second, he thought he'd reached her. Then she picked up the phone. "Yes, and I'm sorry, but it doesn't change my dilemma." She dialed 911, gave them the name of the restaurant.

Cash closed his eyes. "How can you be so—I dunno —unforgiving?"

"Please spare me the critique."

He pointed a twisted, twice-broken forefinger at her. "Then spare me the righteous, mean-spirited, silver-spoon-up-the-ass moral rectitude."

She looked out the window, tried to ignore him, turned back. "When you get out of jail, don't ever come back here."

CHAPTER ONE

Two years later

Callie wasn't sleeping much. It was a chronic problem, and lately, it was getting worse. She often found it harder to sleep when she was doing well. She knew that much—and no more.

At 6:00 a.m., she'd taken a shower, thrown on jeans and an out-at-the-elbows, navy wool sweater, then she dragged herself down the back stairs to the landing and finally through the Dutch doors to her restaurant's kitchen. She often made her breakfast surrounded by the burnished hardwoods, the copper pots, her three-quarter-ton, eight-burner, black-iron stove and the hand-painted, sea-blue-on-white tiles she'd found in Portugal. She'd eat at the long maple prep table with a view that sloped over the alley and down the hill to the waterfront below. She could watch the people go by without being seen.

She liked being in the restaurant kitchen and in the restaurant; it was *her* place. Everything was as it should be, just so. Here, she wasn't so anxious. The restaurant was soothing—she'd discovered this empirically, on many edgy mornings—especially after a sleepless night.

She'd carefully chosen light wood for the tables and chairs, dark mahogany floors, white linen tablecloths and oak-brown Italian leather for the booths along the back. Ten years ago, she'd found the long brass-and-mahogany bar at a tiny café in rural France. The owner had run off to Morocco with a buxom, back-packing Lakers girl, and his wife had put his bar up for sale that very day. Callie had hurriedly shipped the magnificent bar to

Seattle, intact, before she'd even chosen the site for her restaurant. She'd never looked back. She bought a warehouse on First, north of the Pike Place Market, and three years later, she opened Le Cochon Bronze. She named her restaurant for the market's prominent bronze pig, Rachel. A smaller replica of the proud pig stood beside her canopied entry. Callie called her pig Lulu, after a girl she'd known at cooking school in Paris.

She ran long fingers through her shoulder-length blond hair, glancing through the open kitchen door toward the staircase that wound up to the loft bar. The L-shaped second floor was cantilevered out over the booths along the back. It was accessed from the entry by a gently curving mahogany stairway with handsome black-iron rails. The loft had been her idea, and it had turned out so well that it still made her smile.

Callie made herself a double Americano, sat back down. Blue-eyed and fair-skinned, she was a classic Northwest beauty. People said it was hard to read what was brewing beneath her cool Nordic exterior. From time to time, her reserve was punctuated by an outspoken observation, and Callie was secretly pleased to offer these measured hints of heat stirring under the surface. She had her goals, her routines and her priorities. She worked at staying steady: progressive, practical and positive. She didn't honk, she didn't jaywalk, she insisted that the rules be fair, and she played by them.

As she sipped from a large, colorfully painted mug, Callie liked that in this place, at least, she knew what was what.

She watched a homeless teen checking out her garbage in the alley. With her left hand, she rubbed the back of her neck and thought about Lew, her thirteen-year-old son. Lew was asleep upstairs, and since it was Saturday, he'd sleep in. Callie went through her checklist of Lew worries, as she did every morning: Could he get a B in advanced algebra? Was Lakeside, his elite private school, too much pressure? Did he have a girlfriend? Was it bad for him to eat dinner in the restaurant kitchen? (It was the only way she could sit with him, and she wanted that time together.) And so on. As she did most mornings, after completing her checklist she decided that he was good—yes, he was fine.

She'd worked hard to get it right with Lew. She'd decided early on that she had to be there for him, so she made the effort. Since she wasn't a talker, she did what she knew how to do—holidays, hand-sewing his carefully-chosen Halloween costumes, soccer games, patient, as-needed help with homework, even elaborately planned trips to Disneyland. Whatever time she took away from her restaurant was for Lew. Like her restaurant, their relationship made her happy.

When she was ready, Callie opened her laptop and began her own checklist, the things she'd do herself, and for herself, before opening her doors for dinner.

❖❖❖

José, the busboy with the stud in his tongue, was checking his watch, while Elise, a slender server with a complex love life, was making animated hand gestures and loudly whispering sexually graphic French insults into her cell phone. Will Jackson, Callie's gracious, Charleston-born host, general manager and sommelier, had his eye on their new dishwasher, Jean Luc, a hockey player from Quebec. "He breaks beer bottles on his forehead," Will was telling her. "I saw him do it." Will could be outrageous while keeping a straight face. She tried to ignore him, but his stories were often true.

It was 4:05 p.m. and her people were on. They could look at whomever they pleased, say whatever they wanted, so long as she was ready to open her doors at five. And at *her* restaurant, ready meant perfect. They knew that; that was the deal. Period.

Callie stood back, watching the September sun break through the clouds, pushing a burst of light through a cherrywood picture window with large, square mullions. The sunlight warmed the floors, gleamed in the long-stemmed wine glasses, highlighted the rails that gently curved up to the bar, and just as suddenly it was gone, washed out by another milky cloud.

She adjusted the recessed lights, then she was in the kitchen, checking in with Césaire. He nodded, ready, as he gave her a taste of his signature hot pear sauce for the seared foie gras. Césaire was atypical, a low-key chef. When things got tense, even crazy, he just stayed calm. Césaire ran his kitchen as well as Will ran the dining room or Jill managed the bar. Callie had chosen her people carefully, and they understood her program. And they stayed. On her way out, José caught her eye, tilted his head—he wanted a minute. She met him near the south-side window.

"Can I step out for an hour, please? I got to meet Angela at the Planned Parenthood. Five o'clock. That's five sharp. Elise will cover for me."

"On your day off."

"My day off? Wednesday? Is impossible."

"Fifteen minutes. And you work late tonight. And José, when you get back, keep your mouth closed. Every single second. Breathe through your nose. I don't want my customers to even think there's a nasty silver stud in your mouth. You know that if you take it out, it'll heal—close right up—overnight. Think about that—it's an open wound."

"Thank you. I always breathe through my nose. Thank you." José squeezed her arm as he took off his apron.

Callie nodded. His unmarried sister, Angela, was pregnant, unsure what to do. Callie knew something about that. She'd considered having a child in France fourteen years ago. She was twenty-seven years old, just married and deeply in love. She still remembered the day that she caught Daniel Odile-Grand, her husband of seven months, with another woman.

She'd gone for a long walk afterward. On that walk, she decided that she wasn't ready to have a child with him. She also chose to tell him that she'd leave him if he ever cheated on her again. It was a painstaking decision: she loved him, in ways that were, for her, often incomprehensible, and sometimes so intense it was hard to bear. After less than a year together, she couldn't even picture a life without him. Three months later, Callie caught Daniel with the same woman. He asked, in his disarmingly sincere French way, if their marriage could be *overt*, that is to say, open.

Callie went home to Seattle—heartbroken—where she filed for divorce. That same month, she discovered that she was pregnant. She told Daniel after their son was born. He came to Seattle. They had a horrible fight—how could she have their child without consulting him?—and she decided that she'd raise Lew alone. She hadn't seen Daniel since. Even with regular psychotherapy— she frowned, rueful; therapy had been, for her, endless and anxiety producing; talking about herself, her feelings, argh, nails on a chalkboard—it took years to put him behind her, to move on.

Callie glanced at her reflection in the front picture window before she did her rounds to check the flowers. She was wearing a black skirt and a patterned black-and-white silk blouse she'd found in Milan. She looked good, she thought, as she turned to check the tables inside. Routinely, she forced her head back into the restaurant. It was Saturday night, and that's where her head belonged.

She worked to focus. This was her time, walking through the tables, checking the flowers, the settings, the music, even the angle of the setting sun. A special evening for each and every guest. Unlikely, she knew, but that's where she set the bar—*her* standard for *her* restaurant. She planted herself at the front door, fingers lightly tapping the top edge of the old maple lectern where she kept her leather-bound reservation book. She looked out over the restaurant, picturing in her mind how given moments of the evening might turn. If one of these snapshots felt too noisy, or too crowded, or too chaotic, she'd adjust her seating plan until she was satisfied. She wasn't prescient, but she got it right more often than not.

She took an iPad from the shelf in the lectern, and at ten to five, as always, Callie reviewed the chart with Will. As always, he wore a black suit with a colorful silk bow tie. Tonight, his tie had beige polka dots on a French-blue background. Though he'd never say so, she was sure he'd had the bow tie made to match the awning over their entry.

They adjusted a few late seatings, and then she went to work at the door. Sue Reynolds and her guests were pleased to be seated by the window. The Tomlins were in from Bainbridge Island. Bill and Marge were lawyers, and they dined out litigiously. They asked for endless substitutions, then invariably sent things back. She sat them in a quiet booth.

Callie glanced up at the loft. By six o'clock, the bar would be crowded. She headed up the staircase. The loft was large—deeper than it seemed from below. It easily accommodated the long bar, with room for seven small tables along the railing.

In the far corner, beyond the bar, was Callie's table. It was set back, unobtrusive. From her corner, she could see the length of the bar and look out over the restaurant. Once the evening was well underway, she'd sit alone at her table, enjoying the varied life of her restaurant.

At the bar, Callie said hello to several people she recognized, then told the Simpsons that their table would be ready in minutes. She was distracted by a young man who put his hand on Jill's arm as she rounded the bar with a tray of drinks. Jill nicely asked him to let go. When he put his hand on her waist, Callie was right there, deftly moving it away.

"And who might you be, sweetheart?" He was a little drunk. And he was English. His accent was irritating.

"I'm Callie James." Callie extended her hand. "I'm the owner, and I'm pleased to welcome you here."

"Jimmy. Jimmy Pearson. Buy you a drink, Callie the owner?"

"No thanks. Here's how it works here, Mr. Pearson. If you touch a woman who works for me again, you'll be asked to leave."

"Go on." Jimmy looked feisty.

"This is my place. Those are my rules." She held his eyes.

Brian, a busboy and occasional bouncer, had materialized behind her.

"Rules? This is a fucking bar, lady." People turned.

Callie smiled, chilly.

Before Jimmy knew what was happening, Brian was leading him out the stairway behind the bar, down to the alley.

"Bloody bitch," he yelled from the stairway.

Callie ignored that as Brian firmly closed the door behind him.

At the bar, Jill nodded thanks, and all was right with the world. That is, until Callie looked downstairs and there, standing in her doorway, was—unmistakably—Daniel Odile-Grand.

After fourteen years, she'd still recognize her ex-husband any-where. He wore blue jeans, a black tee shirt and—could it be? Yeah—that same beat-up brown leather jacket. He looked older: he'd be fifty-six, she realized, fifteen years older than she was. But he looked good—tall, tan and lean. He'd always looked good. Damn it.

Why was he here? He wanted something, she knew that much. Something hard to do, that he couldn't get from anyone else. Callie considered turning him away. It would be a scene, she was sure of that, and she didn't want a scene at her restaurant on Saturday night. She decided to wait before calling Lew. Tonight, he was staying overnight at his best friend's house. If she called him, he'd be here in a flash. She'd see what was what before making that call. This was going to be hard.

She watched Will greet Daniel. Daniel wanted Will to do something—to find her, she was sure—and when he wanted something, he expected to get it. Will had no idea who Daniel was, but he'd met impatient, imposing Frenchmen before. She could see how he was leaning in, confiding his little secrets, hanging on Daniel's every word, making him feel important. Daniel was becoming aware he was being managed, and it was making him even more insistent. She could imagine his do-you-know-who-I-am stuff. And she could imagine just what Will would say later, deadpan—"Sweet pea, why does this good looking Frenchman, who seems to know you, think he invented cunnilingus?" Will would say it, too. Straight-faced. Callie closed her eyes, ran thumb and forefinger along her brow. She had to admit it; he had this French-man pegged.

Callie caught Will's eye, made a slight motion with her hand. Will led Daniel up to the bar and seated him at Callie's corner table. Callie came over.

Daniel stood. "You look good," he said, trying to kiss her cheek.

She sidestepped, avoiding him. "Wait here," she instructed, and then she was gone, down the stairs, to tend to her restaurant. She needed time to steel herself before she could possibly deal with this intense, complicated man.

Callie busied herself with restaurant business. A cancellation caused her to rearrange some of the seating. When Césaire ran out of the poussin, she helped him organize a squab substitution. Elise gave her an earful about the Tomlins, who'd sent back the last poussin—the bird was unevenly cooked, they insisted. No, they wouldn't accept a substitution. Callie went to their booth. She didn't have the energy to negotiate tonight. When she graciously offered to treat them to their entrées, Bill and Marge triumphantly agreed to the squab. She caught José coming out of the kitchen with his mouth open and told him that the awful stud better be gone tomorrow.

During a lull, Will came over to the front door, where she was greeting customers. He waited until she'd seated them and returned to the lectern. Will looked up at Daniel. "He's the one."

"What?"

Will whispered, "He invented—"

"Stop it," Callie interrupted, stifling a smile.

He answered the phone, took a reservation, looked back at her. "So?" Will waited. "Who is he?" And when she didn't respond: "Sweet pea...just who is your fetching, cocky Frenchman?"

Callie almost smiled. She envied Will. Envied the way he savored the details, envied his hand-painted bow ties. More than anyone she knew, he enjoyed every single minute of his waking life. He'd been with her since day one, and at work, the littlest things were still important to him. It was how he kept his finger on the pulse of her restaurant. And how he took such good care of her. She adjusted his tie, needlessly. "Okay. That's Daniel Odile-Grand, the brilliant, artlessly egotistical, left-wing journalist."

"The what?"

"He's the French journalist who writes those unsettling articles *explaining*—" Callie hesitated, suddenly aware she was pressing her thumb and forefinger to the bridge of her nose. It was, she decided, like pinching herself—yes, it was real; Daniel was in her bar and yes, he'd actually written those particularly provocative articles. "*Explaining*, occasionally praising, Islamic terrorists in the Middle East, Southeast Asia, Central Africa. He describes why they do what they do. He's written about ISIS, Al-Qaeda, the Taliban, to name a few, and most recently, he wrote about the Islamic State fighters in the Philippines."

"I read one of the ISIS articles. Yes, he's brilliant—though vaguely reminiscent of the toxic intellectuals of the antebellum South defending the indefensible—but then there's the attitude, the inflammatory language—" Will made a sour-lemon face.

"In English."

"Cross Marie Antoinette and Yankee General Sherman—"

She took his hand, shushing him. "He's also my ex-husband. I'm not sure why he's here. I may need your help. And keep a lid on it."

"This is so hot. I can't believe this. You want me to call Lew?"

"Wait and see. I'm working up the nerve to talk with Daniel."

"Get on it, honey. I'm here if you need me." Will gave her hand a little squeeze and sent her on her way.

Daniel was drinking Armagnac, her most expensive, she was sure. She knew just as surely that she'd end up paying for it. Callie sat, facing him. She signaled Jill, who brought her a tepid San Pellegrino water with lime. Callie took a sip. "Okay. I'm working. Let's get this over with."

"Callie, you are even more beautiful," Daniel said. He made a sweeping gesture with his hand. "And your restaurant, she is fantastic…formidable."

"Please save that."

"I was too young. And you—so head…So headstrong." Pronounced *edstrong*.

Callie said nothing. He'd been too young? She was fifteen years younger than he was.

"How is our son?"

Our son? He's thirteen years old, and he's never met you. "He's fine. Before we say another word about Lew, though, tell me—why are you here?"

"Okay. Yes, this is fair…I am on a story. *The story* of the modern terrorist world. Money laundering. Arms dealing. It is very big… énorme." He shrugged. "So they try to kill me."

"Right. Of course." She remembered how he used to hide his articles in their freezer, in case some imagined adversary came looking for his work or set their apartment on fire.

"I am not joking. Four years ago, money went offshore. Weapons went to terrorists, I am certain. Then Amjad Hasim, an arms dealer, he is killed, and I find nothing. So last year, I try again to follow the money. In Paris, I was beaten, threatened with death. Since I am here—it's only four hours—I lost them, but they'll try again. In Seattle, I am unknown. I trust no one—" He raised his glass. "Sauf toi…My life is in danger. I have limited money. I need a place to stay for two days, maximum. Then I am gone."

"You need protection, call the police. They don't have to know who you are."

"Police? In Paris, the police say it was a mugging. They do not understand. They are not, you know…sympathetic." He pursed his lips, nodded tersely. It was French punctuation: something important was coming up. "They hate me since I expose the corruption."

"I didn't know that you did that."

"Mais oui. Absolument. And here, your police are useless. They think every Muslim is a terrorist. They can't tell a Sikh from India from a Syrian from a Palestinian from a dark-skinned Israeli—"

"Uh-huh." Memories washed over her. What she didn't understand—even now—was how she'd ever accepted his egotism. Sex, she supposed—with Daniel, it was like being caught in an undertow, carried insistently out to sea. And youth. She'd been so hopeful. And Daniel, when he was focused on her, was so delightfully charming, so articulate and intellectually able, and, in his way, so intensely in love. Unlike anyone she'd ever known, he could sparkle, light up the night sky like a shooting star. Daniel raised his voice, aware she was distracted. It brought her back.

"And what do I tell them? I have no proof. Just give me the two days and I'm gone. It would be a chance to talk with you—to, as you say, *catch up*—and I'd like to meet my son."

"You had your chance for that." Five years ago, Daniel had called, coming through Seattle. He arranged to meet Lew, then he didn't show.

"My dear, life is compliqué. Agh…" Daniel raised both palms, both eyebrows. "She does not always work out as we wish. I wrote my boy, apologizing. And now I am here."

"He waited up for you until three in the morning. He fell asleep on the windowsill. You stood him up. You got around to writing him two weeks later." The postcard was still tacked to Lew's wall. Thinking about it made her mad. "Just seeing you brings back a raft of unwanted memories. Daniel, you can't just waltz back into our lives and…I'm sorry. This is too hard." She was tearing up, losing her composure. She stood, working to stay calm. "Please…Please leave."

Daniel spread his arms, palms up. "Callie, fourteen years is a long time. Excepting one brief call, no contact—you even returned my letters unopened. A price, a dear price, has been paid." He nodded. "I propose we put the past behind us. I need help. I've changed…I'm ready to try again."

"*You're* ready?" Somewhere inside Callie, a dam gave way. "Fourteen years ago, I would have done anything for you. I loved you that much. You married me—I still don't know why. When I caught you cheating on me, I thought my life was over. When I caught you with that same woman again, you told me in your best sincere way that you weren't ready for marriage. Daniel, you washed your hands of me." She was leaning over now, in his face. "Do you remember what you said? Do you? You said you wanted to be 'intégré et complet' before committing to one woman. Later, you were angry with me, in that egotistical way of yours, for having Lew without consulting you. You said that you didn't ask for—nor, truthfully, want—the responsibilities of a child. You gave up on me, and your son, a long time ago."

"You are too hard." He leaned in, frowning. "Too hard and—what is this word?—yes. Unforgiving."

She was upset and angry now. Still, this word, *unforgiving*, rang a distant bell. "Just leave. Please." She pointed. Brian, her bouncer, was hovering.

Callie followed Daniel down the front stairway. As he neared the door, something came over her. Perhaps it was the thought of explaining to Lew that his father had been here and she'd turned him away. Perhaps it was a last, lingering memory of her first, her only, great love. She watched Daniel walk through her front door, past her little bronze pig. Callie grabbed her purse and angrily followed him out. A light rain was drizzling, and the street was a slick, gunmetal gray. From under the canopy she called his name. He turned toward her. "Here, take this," she said. Callie dug into her purse. She handed him all of her money: almost a hundred and fifty dollars—singles, tens and twenties.

He frowned again, took the cash and walked into the street, into the rain. She watched as he tried in vain to hail a taxi. He waved his hand angrily as one passed him by. It was just like Daniel to walk into the middle of the street and expect the cabs to line up. Callie was relieved, though, that he was leaving.

She turned back toward the restaurant. Inside, it was warm, lively and festive. Through the wet, steamy windowpanes, Callie thought the scene looked like a lovely Impressionist rendering of life well lived.

"Callie," Daniel called from the street, where he was still trying to hail a cab. When she turned toward him, he called out, "Adieu," and threw her money at her. It was a Daniel-sized gesture.

As he turned back, the speeding black pickup truck struck him in the side. It was a bone-crushing collision that sent Daniel flying through the air and crashing through the restaurant's front window.

People screamed. Callie was suddenly breathless. She couldn't focus. Broken glass was everywhere. Singles, tens and twenty-dollar bills floated through the air and scattered across the sidewalk, where a crowd was already forming. And inside—

Inside, her restaurant was a shambles, bedlam. Daniel lay sprawled across the Reynoldses' table; his left arm and leg were angled in a stomach-churning way; blood was streaming from his face. The Reynoldses were standing there covered with glass and spattered with blood. Plates and glasses fell to the floor as people stood, moving away from the body or rushing for the front door. They bumped into one another, jostling tables and chairs. Was it a terrorist event? Callie heard someone ask. A few patrons had ducked under tables. Callie just stood there, trying to process what had happened.

Will came running out, trying to get the license plate number of the hit-and-run driver. But he was too late; the pickup was long gone.

It was, Callie decided, a nightmare, a dark, unyielding vision of her world gone mad. That was her last thought before she passed out under the French-blue canopy with the name of her restaurant scripted on it in beige.

CHAPTER TWO

When she came to after the accident, Callie was propped up across from Will in a booth inside her restaurant. She looked around, apprehensive. Daniel was being packed into an ambulance and the police were everywhere. Will explained how he'd given Daniel's name to a police officer, and they'd called it in. Apparently, Daniel had made it onto several lists in the US Homeland Security database. The police had called the FBI, who would be heading to the hospital to talk with him. When Will left, one of the cops—an older detective, sixty at least, with a worn, creased face and crew-cut gray hair—sat opposite her. Politely, Detective Santer told her that, occasionally, he'd read Mr. Odile-Grand's articles about Islamic terrorism, the causes, the objectives, and so on.

Callie grimaced. She looked around her. Every time she got near Daniel, horrible—unimaginable—things happened.

"You know this guy?" he asked Callie.

"Uh-huh." She watched her staff, amazed at how quickly they'd cleaned up, cleared out her restaurant, then restored some kind of order.

"You agree with him?" The guy cracked a gnarly knuckle, taking in everything, she was sure, though he seemed vaguely bored.

"He understands and writes about things that most Westerners don't even think about. He says things about the origins, the reasons for terrorism that people need to hear, but I haven't agreed with him in fourteen years," she said truthfully.

"Good."

"I know. His articles—" She saw that she didn't need to finish. Callie shrugged. She didn't write the damn things.

"He's done worse. According to our database, he's friendly with lots of terrorists."

"He interviews them. He tries to understand why they do what they do. It doesn't mean he likes them." She pressed her thumb and forefinger to the bridge of her nose, feeling the start of a migraine. Why was she defending him? Guilt. She had nothing to feel guilty for, damn it. "He says people are trying to kill him."

"Maybe. Witnesses said it might have been an accident, hit-and-run."

"He turned and threw that money at me. Otherwise, he'd be dead."

The detective shrugged, rubbed his knuckle. "The Feds are interested in him; they'll decide how to handle it."

"They debriefed him in Paris, after a trip to interview Al-Qaeda leaders. It was four or five years after 9/11. I was still with him. It didn't go too well." She lowered her head, massaging her temples now with her fingertips. "Will they help him?"

Detective Samter frowned down at her, grim-faced. "You like this guy?"

No. The way he asked it, though, she realized it was not an idle question. Callie thought about what to say. She felt somehow responsible for what happened to Daniel now. She'd ignored his plea for help—Lew's father—and he'd almost been killed. It wasn't an accident, either, she knew that much. Callie glanced up. "He's the father of my child," she reluctantly admitted.

"Uh-huh." Samter scratched his head. "In that case, lady, send him home as soon as the doctors release him. I'll be honest—lots of good cops died on September eleventh. SPD, the Feds, they'll never forget that terrorists did that. And they'll know that your ex recently visited the territory controlled by ISIS in Syria. I read that, after, he refused to be debriefed by the Feds and the CIA. He antagonized them, called them incompetent imperialists."

Callie sighed, nodded; that was Daniel, all right.

"They'd love to get their hands on him, try again, so they'll find a reason to lock him up. In prison, he could get hurt...And if someone wants to kill him, he's an easy target inside. Get him out of the US. He doesn't belong here."

They watched the ambulance pull away, lights flashing, siren wailing.

Callie stood, ignoring the rush of head pain that threatened to make her pass out again. "Thank you, Detective," she said, extending her hand, "When I can, I'll talk with him about that."

***

Will and the staff covered the destroyed front window with flat-tened cardboard boxes, held together by staples and duct tape. It was 1:00 a.m. before the window was sealed. The police were long gone and the restaurant was empty. Will locked up the front, then went looking for Callie. He found her sitting at her favorite spot in the kitchen, head down on the long maple prep table.

"We're okay." He put a hand on her shoulder.

She raised her head. "They tried to kill him. He told me he was in danger. He said he needed to hide. I didn't even believe him."

"He'll live."

"The police and the FBI, they hate him."

"So?"

"They're going to throw him in jail. He's hurt. He's afraid of prison. And it's not safe for him. He won't be able to manage."

"Just how big is this guy's reputation?"

"Do you ever read the *New York Review of Books*, the *Guardian*, the *Economist*—"

"Honey, unlike you, *I can sleep*."

"Right." She sat up straight. "He's got an international following among left-leaning intellectuals. The point is, he's met quite a few terrorists. He often interviews them before they're well known. Recently, he wrote about terrorism in Somalia and the Philippines. Several years ago, after he visited the Islamic State to interview ISIS leaders, the FBI and the CIA wanted to debrief him, but he denounced them both." She nodded; it was even worse than the detective had made it sound. "He said the FBI were stupid, racist and inept. That the CIA had as much chance of infiltrating a terrorist cell as breathing underwater. For good measure, he added that the jihadists, as a rule, were more sensible than the members of the Freedom Caucus in Congress...You get the picture?"

"They're going to throw away the key."

"Yes. If only I'd helped him when he asked..." She took his hand, feeling low again.

"What's come over you?"

"I handled this badly. All he wanted was a place to stay. Will, he could have been killed...He said I'm unforgiving."

"Unforgiving? It's all right to hate your ex."

"He's Lew's dad," she said, suddenly teary. "That's what I've been thinking. What if he'd died? What would I tell Lew? That his dad was dead because I was an unforgiving bitch?"

"Callie, that's way too harsh..."

She ignored him. "What *do* I tell Lew?"

"You tell him what you always tell him, the truth. And then you all will work it out...Now, you need some rest. This will be easier to sort out in the morning. And in this godforsaken gray city, it'll surely keep till then." Will bowed slightly as he offered his arm to help her stand. "I'll lock up."

"Thank you," she said softly. Callie took his arm, got up slowly, then went to the Dutch door that led down four stairs to the landing where she'd take the other staircase up to her apartment.

Will opened the door for her. A Southern gentleman, he always waited at the foot of the stairs until she was safely inside. Approaching her apartment door, Callie decided that she'd visit Daniel at the hospital tomorrow morning, try talking with him again. That decision made her feel better.

At her door, she stepped back. Something wasn't right. She could see where the lock had been forced open. Had the police looked in her apartment? Someone else? Why?

She waved for Will. He came up quickly, motioned her back, then slowly cracked the door. He looked inside, and with two fingers waved her in. "You have a problem," he said.

Looking inside, she saw a man's body lying on her carpet, his legs sticking out from behind the couch. She stepped in, looking more closely. "Oh Jesus," she said, recognizing Daniel, passed out on her living room floor. A cut on his face had reopened. A pool of blood was slowly spreading on her white, woven Berber rug. She cried unexpectedly, relieved he was alive.

"You going to call the police?" Will asked when she stopped crying.

Callie shook her head. She knew she couldn't call the police. She also knew that she would help Daniel—for Lew and, though she didn't fully understand why, for herself, too.

"What a time to turn squishy."

Callie clicked into restaurant mode. "We need a doctor, right away. And Daniel needs to be moved."

CHAPTER THREE

The ferryboat ride from downtown Seattle to Bainbridge Island took thirty-five minutes. It was a beautiful ride, even on a cloudy day. When the sky was clear, snow-capped Mount Rainier loomed in the south, the Olympics rose in the west, and the Cascades framed downtown Seattle to the east. As you began the crossing, the ferry left Coleman Dock, Ivar's Acres of Clams, a spiffy little fireboat and a hodgepodge of high rises behind, cut boldly northwest across the shipping lanes, then continued steadily toward the fir-green shores of the island. When you turned into Eagle Harbor, you entered another world. Bainbridge was pretty near perfect, said many of those who lived there.

Avi and Christy Ben-Meyer lived on the south end of the island. Their lovely home was on Bean's Bight, a pleasant, winding road that meandered through a gentle landscape dusted with tasteful, spacious homes like theirs.

Christy and Avi had come a long way to live on Bean's Bight. Christy had been born in Butte, a freckle-faced, hardscrabble Montana girl. When her parents died in a car crash, twelve-year-old Christy was sent to live with her great aunt in Seattle. Blue-blooded Auntie Baker shipped her straight away to Lakeside, the fancy private school, and instilled in her an unrelenting ambition to be something she wasn't. Later, Avi, a keen and ruthless Israeli-born Argentine investor, helped her realize her ambitions.

Avi began his off-the-radar investment company in the late nineties in Buenos Aires, Argentina, where his uncle, Nachson, had a lucrative niche law practice. Nachson, who preferred to be called Nathan, represented companies and people who wanted to trade assets in international markets. He was a method-of-payment specialist, able to trade machine parts for oil, computer chips for sandalwood, even medical equipment for sugar cane. Nathan would choose gems, gold or almost any other commodity or currency as the method of payment.

Nathan represented traders, importers and exporters, large and small. Significantly for Avi, Nathan's clients also included Mexican cartel bosses, arms dealers, real estate magnates and Latin American military leaders. What Avi brought to the table was his God-given investment acumen, four years with the most prestigious Israeli investment house and — at Uncle Nathan's suggestion — three years of banking experience in the Cayman Islands. By 2001, he'd invested and laundered money for an Afghan drug lord, the beneficial owner of a sugar cane plantation empire, and a well-connected Middle Eastern arms trafficker. All of whom had been carefully vetted through Nathan. Avi never had more than fifteen clients, and the minimum investment was fifteen million dollars, of which he took three percent a year as his fee.

Christy and Avi met at a technology investment symposium in Palo Alto in 2006. He was thirty-nine, she was twenty-seven. Christy had a hunch about him from their first encounter. And after their first intimate evening together, she knew she had it right— this refined gentleman was plainly the devil's own instrument. Exactly what she'd been looking for.

Avi, who had a history of dating, then leaving, younger women, knew after just one night that his frustrating search for a life partner was over. Christy was the one—the sinister soul mate, the brazen, unapologetic lover he'd longed for. At last.

In '07, they were married. He moved to America, eventually becoming a US citizen by marriage. With Avi's financing, they started the Northwest Capital Group in Seattle—a meaningful piece of the next iteration of his business. He hoped to provide new, secure identities for carefully selected clients who would pay for it handsomely. Northwest Capital would invest their legal income from safely laundered money.

Twelve years later, at fifty-two, Avi was even more elegant— white hair a little too long, handsome and gracious. Since meeting him, Christy had turned her rangy cowgirl looks to her advantage. At forty, she was tall, auburn-haired and lithe. In elite Seattle circles, Avi presented himself as politically progressive. Though he still invested and laundered money for arms merchants, generals and cartel bosses, he liked to tell how he'd been a personal friend of Fidel Castro, and of course, Golda Meir. Though "Goldie" died when he was fourteen, their families had stayed close. A connoisseur of fine wines and younger women, he still avidly pursued his taste for fine wines, but since his first evening with Christy, he'd never dallied with another woman.

While Christy sat in their beachfront den, monitoring tomorrow's Asian markets, Avi paced in the outbuilding that housed their offices. Maurie Fischer, the chief executive officer of their various companies, sat at the conference table. "And the car accident?" Avi asked. When Maurie shrugged, Avi repeated his question softly. "And the car accident?" The softer his voice, the angrier he was. He added, almost in a whisper, "We eat at that restaurant."

Avi sat down beside Maurie at the conference table, watching his old friend. He knew Maurie was mentally walking through the problem and its solution, step by rational step. For Maurie, a lawyer and a CPA, the world was still a logical, if disorderly, place. Avi waited, patient, while Maurie cleared his throat. Maurie suffered from sialorrhea, commonly called hypersalivation. This ailment was caused by medication he took to treat his glaucoma, and Maurie had to spit frequently. He kept a spittoon handy, especially at stressful times. He spit into it now.

Avi had found Maurie in LA. He'd heard that Maurie's small accounting firm had done work for the Teamsters' pension fund, even for Sinatra. People said he could multiply five numbers by five numbers in his head. The first time Avi and Christy met him at a deli in Santa Monica, Maurie was wearing plaid Bermuda shorts and a peach-colored golf shirt. He told Avi right off that he was no "clotheshorse."

In '09, just before Maurie became the third partner in Northwest Capital, Christy sat him down for a candid conversation about fashion. Characteristically blunt, she told him that she didn't give a rat's ass if he looked like a garish, color-blind golfer, but sadly, this wasn't LA, and his casual attire would attract unwanted attention to Northwest Capital. Since then, Maurie had worn a black suit and a button-down white Oxford every working day.

Maurie tapped his partner's arm, ready. "Okay, the local help mishandled the incident with the hit-and-run. They were assigned to kill the Frenchman. They failed. It was, therefore, my fault for using them." He nodded; the ducks were lining up. "Already, I'm bringing in my best professionals. Very able, smart young people from LA. They know Odile-Grand escaped from the hospital. They know he's hiding. We've already created our plan to find him."

Avi didn't respond.

"Callie James is the ex-wife. We know she's the first person he went to see in Seattle. We suspect that he contacted her when he left the hospital. At the very least, she will have a way to find him. The California help will ask her for that information. If she doesn't provide it, they will insist, as only they can do it. Perhaps she will cooperate. More likely, she'll make it a police matter. Either way, we are satisfied. Once Odile-Grand is in custody, our work is child's play."

Maurie cleared his throat, spit into his spittoon, then sat back, ducks in a row.

Avi looked out the window. Maurie would handle this, ably. So what was bothering him? With a thumb and index finger, he traced his eyebrows. It was the mere existence—the fact—of this problem that was so troubling. As Avi had grown older, he'd focused his attention carefully on his most important priorities. He'd let other interests lapse. As such, he could no longer anticipate Latin American politics, nor trade their currencies profitably. He'd even accepted that his English would never be perfect. But Amjad Hasim had been, for a long time, his most important priority—Avi knew that he'd made no mistakes. He'd crossed every t, dotted every i. He and Maurie had hit their marks just so. So how was it even possible that several years later, everything they'd accomplished might be at risk? Bad luck? Coincidence?

He did not believe in luck. He loathed coincidence.

Avi looked at Maurie, wondering how best to impress the importance of his concerns. Go slowly. Very, very slowly, he concluded. God, he reminded himself, is in the details. "My good friend, so far Daniel Odile-Grand does not know the most important aspects of what he's stumbled upon. He may know that Hasim was selling weapons, he may even know where some of his money went. But that's all. Furthermore, in this country, because of his outspoken articles and unpopular assertions, the authorities are not collaborating with him or even paying close attention to his ideas. They surely dislike him. Your strategy of putting pressure on his ex is sensible, but risky. If people around him are hurt unnecessarily, especially a former wife—" He ran a hand through his long white hair, taking time to choose his words. "The status quo will shift against us. The Frenchman will receive far more attention. He will be taken more seriously by the press and the police."

Christy came in, blowing Avi a kiss. Her stride said she had something going on and she wanted to talk, but it was also clear that she'd read from the expression on his face that he was in the middle of something important. They managed a complex communication without a word. She sat at the table to wait.

"I'll take precautions," Maurie said, nodding.

"After all of our precautions, this French journalist tied Amjad Hasim to Ares Limited," Avi noted. His brow knitted. "We're concluding our retirement next year. We've already retired Ares. Maurie, how, please, is this threat possible?"

Maurie frowned. "A fluke. Four years back, he was doing some story about weapons disappearing. That story died when Hasim died. Then a couple years later, the French guy's doing a separate story about money laundering, and he learns about hacking. Apparently, he never forgot about his interest in Hasim, because as far as we can tell, he decided to use his newfound skills to track Hasim's money. From there, he got to Ares."

"This is totally unacceptable."

"I understand. Not to worry."

"Not to worry? We were told we were done with him in Paris, last year."

"Yes, I thought so."

Avi leaned in, speaking softly, deliberately. "I refuse to believe in coincidence. I question even an unlikely convergence of events. A man happens upon Hasim's connection to Ares. He writes about missing weapons, money laundering. That same man has an accident at a restaurant where we are known…" He touched Maurie's arm. "These are points in a line. Properly extended, that line could lead to us. It must be erased. *Without a single further point of connection.*"

"Mistakes have been made." Maurie shrugged; a fact was a fact. He blew his nose into a red-and-white-checkered handkerchief that he returned to the pocket of his pants. "I'm sorry for this."

Avi leaned back, sorry that he'd had to be so very hard on his friend. Okay, he'd delivered his message; it was time to soften the blow. "Perhaps life has simply pitched us a French spitball. In any case, you mustn't take this personally. Mistakes have been made, yes, but I agreed to Hasim."

Christy came over, rubbed Avi's shoulders. "You're too hard on yourselves. The both of you. Maybe God would be that perfect. *Maybe*."

He reached back, held her hand. "Thank you." And to Maurie: "In His absence, can this—this boil—can it be lanced discreetly?"

"The California help we've called in is experienced, able and untraceable. They'll get the information we need from Callie James, or drive her to the police, without killing her." At Avi's dubious look, Maurie leaned in. "You are perhaps overly worried and preoccupied with unpleasantness. 'Boils'?" Maurie pursed his lips. "My friend, pretend I am a pastry chef. You ask me, will the crust be light and fluffy?" He raised a palm. "The crust will be light and fluffy. Not to worry. It's what a pastry chef does."

CHAPTER FOUR

Callie was at the door, listening to her doctor friend, Mary. Every so often she looked over at Daniel, who was resting on the couch in this small apartment in Eastlake. A friend of Will's had an acting job in LA, and Will had a key to his empty apartment. Whenever she looked at Daniel, Callie wondered if she'd lost her mind.

At the emergency room he'd been taken to after the accident, they'd put over forty stiches in Daniel's torn body: the car and the broken glass had left cuts from calf to cheek. He'd joked to her and Mary that, naked, he looked like an American baseball. They'd set his leg, which was broken in several places, then put on a cast. His left arm was fractured, bandaged and in a sling. As Daniel had vividly explained, once he was settled in his hospital bed, a nurse asked if he was ready to talk with the FBI. Daniel requested a reprieve of half an hour. During his rest time, he asked the policeman sitting near his door to take him to "la toilette," then explained in some detail how he needed help with his "business." The man, who was reading sex ads in the *Stranger,* said, "Hell no," then pointed down the hall.

Daniel had slowly hobbled off, leaning on his crutch. He made a scene of getting into the bathroom. When he saw that the policeman was once again reading his paper, he came out, deftly turned a corner, then quickly left the hospital through a side door. In the parking lot, he paid a young woman forty dollars—he hadn't thrown all of Callie's money at her, after all—to drop him at the north end of the Pike Place Market, not far from Le Cochon Bronze. He'd entered through the back door to the landing where one staircase led to the kitchen, another to her apartment. He pulled his broken body up the stairs to her apartment, forced the lock, then collapsed on the floor, "spent," as he put it.

Callie had woken up Mary, who worked at the Pike Place clinic and lived nearby. She'd known Mary since college. Mary had agreed to meet them at the Eastlake apartment, where she'd stitched Daniel back together again.

Before she left, Mary explained that Daniel should stay in bed for at least two weeks. At the door, she leaned back in and confided, "Callie, I never do this."

"This is new for me, too, and I'm holding on by a thread." Callie kissed her cheek, let Mary out. She turned to Will and her ex, who'd already begun to dislike each other. "You can't move for two weeks, minimum," she told Daniel.

"Here?" Daniel looked around again. "I die."

"You have a better idea, chief?" Will waited. "The authorities are looking for you, aren't they?"

"If your police find me, I am up the shit creek, for sure."

Callie grimaced.

"You could go home," Will suggested.

"No way. The story, she is too big. And I am this close." He raised his unconstrained right hand, his thumb and forefinger almost touching.

"Let me ask you a question, maestro." Will stood over him now. "If you stay, won't these same people who are after you try and find you again?"

"They try if I leave or if I stay. I am only safe if I have my story. If I can write about, document, their corruption, their money laundering, their weapons dealing...the politicians, the police, will have to take action."

Will shook his head. His face was grave when he looked at Callie. "They'll come to the restaurant. Callie, they'll come looking for you."

When Daniel shrugged, he winced. "This is possible. Yes. They found me at your restaurant before, so they have capable, well-trained people. Yes, these people could come back to the restaurant."

Of course they could. And how would she manage that? "What do I do if someone comes to the restaurant asking about you?" she asked, starting to worry.

"You say you do not know." Daniel nodded. "To everyone. At the hospital, I disappeared. I was careful. No taxi, no bus, no trace. I was especially careful that the woman who drove me couldn't identify the restaurant from where she left me off. I vanished. Poof," he added, with a snap of his fingers.

"And when they threaten her?" Will asked sharply.

Daniel raised a palm, unfazed. "Think about this—you can truthfully explain that we haven't been friends for fourteen years. You insist that you do not know where I went, and you hope that I never come back."

Callie frowned, her worries now becoming palpable. "What if they threaten Lew?"

"If you help this man, you'll have to hide Lew." Will raised his voice, irritated now.

Daniel ignored Will's tone. "Yes…yes, I was going to suggest this. Hiding him would be prudent."

Callie scowled. "This is scaring me," she snapped.

Daniel knit his brow, then offered, "Callie, if they frighten you, and it becomes too much for you to bear, just tell me, and I will find a way to divert them, then disappear."

"How will you do that? And where will you go?"

"I'll cross these bridges if, and when, I must."

"Cut him loose now," Will advised. "These are killers. They'll hurt you to find him." Will saw her expression and added, "He's a big boy and, as you know, he's been in danger before. He says he can disappear."

She thought this over, watching Daniel. Then she turned to Will. "No," she said evenly, "I can't. He has nowhere to go. The police aren't an option—that detective, Samter, he told me that in prison, the people who did this can kill him—"

"Sweetie, my God, this kind of risk-taking is not like you. Five hours ago, you threw him out of the restaurant. Now, you're hiding him and putting everything you have in peril. What are you thinking?"

"I'm not sure…I'm really not…I'm still furious with Daniel, but I did understand one thing tonight—I want him to live to meet his son. I owe this to Lew." And it surprised her as much as it surprised Will. Only Daniel saw it coming.

"Merci, chérie," he said. Daniel tilted his head toward her, his expression actually tender. "Merci."

◆◆◆

A half hour later, they were still mulling over what to do. "I need help for my story," Daniel was saying. "Someone to be my legs, my eyes and ears…You understand? Yes?"

Callie ignored Daniel. "*We* need help if any of these danger-ous people come back to the restaurant," she said to Will.

Will nodded. "Good help. Someone who fits in and won't alarm the customers."

"Yes. I was afraid of that."

"I'll need the computer, the headset for the telephone, and takeout menus, Chinese, Mexican—only the best—"

"Zip it, Daniel," Callie said, running a thumb and forefinger along her lips. "Private detective?" she asked Will, hopeful.

"Who do you trust? Besides, it's not what they do."

"Security company?"

"Those big guys with guns?" Will made a face.

Callie let this sink in. "Shit," she said. "You're right."

"You know who we need?" Will said.

Unfortunately, she did. "Shit," Callie said again.

◆◆◆

It was weird, she knew, but when bad things happened, Callie could sleep. At 9:00 a.m., after four and a half good hours, she went down to the kitchen to prepare breakfast and wait for Lew. Her contractor was out front, supervising a temporary window repair so she could open at five. Since she'd woken from her deep sleep, she was confused about what had happened, what she'd done, why she'd done it, and what she'd do next. She was overwhelmed, and all she knew for sure was that she was feeling helpless and inept.

The detective, Samter, had called, wanting her to know Daniel had taken off from the hospital. He asked her to be in touch if she heard anything from him. She didn't like lying to policemen. It made her feel shifty, and vulnerable. But in the midst of her confusion, she had one touchstone: It was not okay to hurt anyone at her restaurant. Especially Lew's dad.

She still wasn't sure what to tell Lew. She'd called him last night and explained that there'd been an accident at Le Cochon Bronze, that the front window was broken. She assured Lew that she was fine, that he shouldn't worry, that she'd see him in the morning. What she didn't tell him was that his father had been struck so hard that he'd come crashing through her artfully mullioned picture window. The one she'd designed herself, laying the masking tape in squares across the frame until she'd sized the panes just so.

Callie was on her second Americano—and still unsure what to tell him—when her thirteen-year-old son came bounding through the kitchen door. He was tall and good-looking, like his dad. When he was happy, he had this wonderfully contagious enthusiasm. He had her blond hair, fair complexion and robin's-egg-blue eyes. People said he looked like her, except, as Will put it, "the blinds are up, and the air conditioning is off."

"Jeez, Mom, it looks really bad out front," Lew said, then gave her a quick hug.

"How was the sleepover?"

"Fine."

"*Fine* meaning what?"

"We watched *Animal House*. It was gross, very cool. Then we ate pizza, played video games—he's got *Overwatch*—and talked on the phone with girls."

"Sounds fun," she said, hesitating.

"What's up?"

Callie watched his expression change. Lew was keenly sensitive, and she could see he was on to her confusion. She answered his question truthfully. "That man who was hit by the car last night…I think they were trying to kill him."

"Trying to kill him? Is he okay?"

"He's going to be fine. Sit down, honey, there's more to tell." She waited until he was on the stool beside her. Callie put an arm around his shoulder. "The man was your dad."

Lew sat there for a minute, thinking this over. "Was he coming to see me?" he finally asked.

"Yes, he wanted to see you." She nodded, glad that this was true. "He'd also come to see me. He wanted my help. I refused."

"You what?" Lew stood, his face getting red.

"Slow down. It's okay. I'm going to help him. I'm helping him now."

"Okay. Good." And excited now: "When can I see him?"

"Soon," she said. Lew was still so eager to connect with his dad, in spite of so many disappointments—he'd even collected some of Daniel's articles in a scrapbook. His resilience was one of many things she loved about her son, and for the moment, she allowed herself to hope that a genuine relationship with his father was still possible for him.

Callie heard the kitchen door swing open. Was Césaire here early? He had a key. But when she turned, a young man and woman were walking through the Dutch door. Customers? Maybe they'd seen the contractor working out front and decided to try the back. Weird, and less likely still, they were sun-tanned. He was blond, handsome, tall and fit. She was blond too, a blue-eyed, California girl. Had to be. Her hair was cut short and it framed a model's angular face.

They were late twenties, she guessed, and they wore expensive-looking tailored suits. They seemed to be a pair, though a pair of what, Callie wasn't sure. They could have been world-class litigators, high-powered sports agents, even CEOs of Fortune 500 companies. They were attractive, even striking, though their faces were hard. "Sorry to interrupt," the man said, "but our business is urgent. I'm Gray, and this is my associate, Kelly." They shook hands with Callie, nodded politely at Lew.

"What's so urgent?" Callie asked, wary.

"We're looking for Daniel Odile-Grand. We have business." Gray was the talker. "He was in an accident last night, and he disappeared from the hospital. We have to talk to him."

FBI? Unlikely. Even on TV, she'd never seen Feds in Italian suits. No, she knew just who these people were—the dangerous professionals she'd been worried about. The people hunting Daniel. They were earlier than she'd expected.

She didn't even look at Lew. "I don't know where he is," she said.

"Perhaps you could find out," Gray said, his hard tone making clear that the pleasantries were over. "We'll be back tonight. After you close. I think you can find him by then." He paused, let that sink in. "As I said, our business is urgent." They left through the restaurant; she heard the contractor wish them a good afternoon as they went out the front door.

"Creep city," Lew said.

"Uh-huh," Callie agreed, setting her hands on the edge of the maple prep table to keep them from trembling. Gray had threatened her, she knew that, but it wasn't the kind of threat that she could take to the police. And if she went to the police, Daniel would pitch a fit, and of course, the police would lean on her. Then, as that detective warned her, they'd bring Daniel in and find a reason to lock him up. Yeah, she was afraid again, feeling helpless.

Callie checked the Dutch door and the back landing. No signs of forced entry. On her way back in, she glanced up toward her apartment. The door was open. She cautiously went up the stairs.

Her apartment was as comfortable as her restaurant. She'd used the same old hardwoods, Italian leathers, and so on, then added a white, woven Berber rug and colorful fabrics for her simple, country-style living-room furniture. There was a lovely view of the South Sound from the window. But at the door, her face fell. Her apartment had been searched. *Tossed*, she thought, was the vernacular. They'd emptied every drawer in every room. She turned when she heard Lew shutting the door behind him. His eyes were wide, his face, angry.

Callie's cheeks felt flushed. She made a gesture with her hands that included the mess in their usually orderly apartment. "Damn it. This is nasty, a warning."

"It's bad, really bad, Mom…What can we do?"

"Do we want to help your dad?" she asked, a real question.

He looked around. "Yeah, we do."

She looked around, too, irrationally relieved that she'd been able to remove Daniel's blood from her carpet. That would have been too visceral a reminder of what these people were capable of. "Are you afraid?"

"Well, yeah," Lew answered truthfully.

"It's important, then, to be sure. Why do you want to help him? What's he ever done for us?"

Lew hesitated. Standing there, his face stormy, he was thinking about how he'd answer her question. She'd seen him like this before, and Callie knew he'd wait until he sorted out just what he wanted to say.

When he was ready, he began carefully, "I do know some of how I feel," he paused. "When I think about it, what he's done for us isn't the only thing that matters. We don't have to like him, or to be like him. But if he needs our help, we should help him." Lew's eyes met hers. "He's my dad, and he's in trouble…C'mon, Mom, what more do you want?"

She put a hand on his shoulder. "Okay. You're right. We'll see him when it's safe. In the meantime, I'll tell you what I know. But for now, can you stay with a friend?"

Lew nodded. "Are we in danger?"

"I don't know. Maybe." She hesitated. "Enough to take precautions."

"You need someone to help you," Lew said. "Someone tough."

"Uh-huh."

"You know who can do it?" he asked pointedly.

This was becoming a sore subject. Even Lew knew what she should do. "Yeah, honey, I do," she said, resigned.

And Lew was right, Cash was her only option. She'd just have to swallow her pride and talk to him. Will knew where to find him. She'd admit her mistake, express genuine remorse, then be ready to overpay.

As hard, as distasteful, as it would be, she had to hire him before those people came back tonight.

CHAPTER FIVE

Callie didn't know why they called this place the Dragon. The so-called club was on a side street between Pike and Pine. The entrance was unmarked, and she'd unknowingly walked by it twice. She finally had to ask this aging biker where it was. He spread tattooed arms, made a don't-put-me-on face—then, when she politely asked again, he pointed out what appeared to be a bleak, abandoned storage facility. Razor wire was coiled on top of the fence in front. "You go in through the alley. It's on the third floor." When she actually went into the alley, he followed her. "Lady, you sure you want the Dragon?"

"Yeah."

"It's not a Chinese restaurant. Maybe you're confused."

"I wish."

It was 9:00 p.m. Late enough so the Dragon would be up and running. Callie had come from her restaurant. It had been a quiet but reassuring night—regulars had come out to support her—and she was able to leave early. Under a long, black leather coat, she wore a light-gray cashmere sweater and a silk skirt.

"People like you don't go in there," the aging biker offered. "Dragon's not your all-ages kind of deal."

She understood his concern. "I have to find someone. I'll be okay, thanks," she added.

"Takes all kinds," the biker said, mostly to himself.

She watched him leave, then went through the alley door. Inside it was cold and dark; one exposed light bulb hung at the second-floor landing. She stopped there. At her feet were empty beer bottles, litter, and what she thought was drug paraphernalia. Upstairs, she could hear the music. It was dreadful. Two guys wearing shiny black vinyl overalls came up behind her, checked her out. She ignored them.

Callie took a minute, bracing herself, organizing her ideas, sitting on—no, stomping on—her rising anxiety. Three girls came down the stairs. They pushed right by her, as if she wasn't there. One of them had a silver ring through her nose attached by a chain to another ring in her earlobe. Callie considered leaving. What good could come of anything that made her feel like this?

She paused on the stairs, then started up again. She didn't have a choice. Gray and Kelly would return tonight after closing, and they'd want answers. That gave her until about 1:00—to be ready for what, she wasn't sure. The only man she knew who could take care of this for her was inside.

According to Will, who'd actually spoken to him, Cash was working nights as the bouncer, helping out a friend who had refused to pay protection to local thugs. Maybe that was true. Maybe. Cash's life had always been a mystery to her. He'd been at her restaurant nine months before she caught him smuggling in the ivory carvings. She still wondered if he'd taken the job only because he thought it would be easy to sneak things in. Will, who liked Cash and had kept in touch with him, said the erotic netsuke had been pre-sold for more than $200,000. Half had been paid in advance.

The betrayal still stung. Let that go, she chided. Just let it go.

Cash was, she reminded herself, the only man she knew who could actually help. He was tough; he'd been around violence. And he was smart, in an unassuming, pragmatic way. She'd once watched him work through the thorny riddle of the cannibals and missionaries. Will had posed it to him at the bar, during a slow moment. Cash had moved three cannibals and three missionaries across the river in a rowboat meant for two, without the cannibals ever outnumbering the missionaries on either shore. He'd solved it on a napkin, by trial and error, in less than three minutes. What he could do, she'd realized, was hold a vast, complicated picture in his head. And he could manipulate variables within that picture.

According to Will, "Cash" got his name creating then executing complex import/export deals without putting up his own money. He'd moved Iranian rugs out of Morocco into Spain, then on to New York City; Burmese jade through Japan to Seattle; premium cigars from Cuba (which, to her horror, he smoked behind her bar) via Mexico; and so on. She'd hired him knowing about the smuggling, but Cash had sworn that those days were over. A seasoned restaurateur she admired had even provided a reference.

When she found the contraband in her vegetable shipment, she knew instantly that she'd been naïve. Maybe he'd been in a jam and needed money, as he'd said, or maybe he was a chronic offender who'd used her and her restaurant for at least one of his illegal schemes.

Still, there was a part of her that had cringed with recognition when Cash accused her of being righteous. When he worked at Le Cochon Bronze, he came on time, he did what he said he'd do, and he wowed people at the bar. She had to admit that her servers, her kitchen staff and, most importantly, her patrons just loved him. No one ever understood why she let him go. Another restaurateur had told her to lighten up, that good bartenders were rarely knighted. "Erotic netsuke in the fiddlehead ferns," Will had mused. "That's sweet."

Cash could help her with the people hunting Daniel; she knew that. He'd worked in the netherworld of smuggling, maybe even money laundering. And if he agreed to help—if—she knew that she could count on him. Although he was a scoundrel, and a womanizer, he kept his promises—according to Will, his word was the glue that held his multi-tiered deals together. Callie reasoned it was some kind of honor-among-thieves thing.

She wondered if he felt even a little guilty about how things had gone down with her. Maybe he'd see helping her as a way to settle up.

A beer can rolled down the stairs, landing near her feet. Who was she kidding? Cash was a scam artist, a professional smuggler. He was probably bringing pirated video games, or mobile phones, or stolen gemstones or worse into this wretched club. From Hong Kong via Panama or something. He'd help her for money, and he'd make her pay. Right.

Two slow breaths, then she took the remaining flight of stairs. A group of people were clustered around the door to the club. She drew some looks as she stepped in line. Inside, it was dank, foul smelling and dingy. She saw distant smoke—there were wood fires in pits beside the stage, a fire department violation for sure. She watched the smoke rising, working its way up, being drawn into two large vents set in the ceiling. All of the windows were covered with dark curtains. The only decorations in the old warehouse were two strobe lights hanging from the ceiling.

At the far end of the room was a makeshift platform. On her side of the platform, she saw something that looked like an improvised, oversized aquarium. Yeah. Oh my God…Yuck, she thought. There was a long, fat snake inside. On the platform, between the fire pits and the smoke, a scraggly local band was performing some kind of loud, raw music that she simply couldn't fathom. As far as she was concerned, they could have called this place the Dump, the Slum or—though she didn't know how this word broke into her normally well-policed consciousness—the Crapper.

She was scanning the perimeter of the space when she saw him. He hadn't changed. Big, rough around the edges, still oddly charismatic. And his hands—scarred, weathered and misshapen, the hands of a mason or a commercial fisherman. That's what had made it so unexpected when, behind her bar, he'd mixed and moved drinks with the light, easy touch of a piano player.

When he'd tended bar for her, Cash had worn a subtly pin-striped blue wool vest, one of three she'd found in Italy. He wore it over the white shirts she'd bought especially for him. Above the bar, that was as far as he'd go. Below the bar, he wore blue jeans and running shoes every night.

Tonight, he wore a wife-beater undershirt. On the front was a band she didn't know, doing things she didn't want to know about. She hadn't realized that he had a tattoo on his shoulder—some kind of army thing—or that he was so well muscled. Though he'd never talked about his past, she knew he was from Seattle, and that he'd served overseas.

Cash was talking with a group of maybe six young people. They were a hard punk crew: leather, chains, piercings, the works. She inched closer, hearing him say, "Gentlemen, you're welcome at the Dragon, but I'll have to check you out."

"Check out what, man?"

"No alcohol, drugs or weapons in the club."

"Shit. We're not messing with anyone. We just want to hear some music."

Cash smiled; he understood. "Nothing personal. It's my job. I need the money."

"That's cool," one of them said.

"No fucking way that prehistoric fuck is touching my shit," a fat guy with a Mohawk proclaimed.

Cash stepped right in his face. "Please reconsider that."

The fat guy met his eyes, looked him over. "Pops, don't fuck with the bad dog." He slapped a blackjack against the palm of his hand.

As the creep tried to push past him, Cash maced his face.

Callie couldn't believe how fast it happened. Just like that, the big guy was on his knees, gasping. She saw the little canister in Cash's palm. Was that a skull-and-crossbones logo? Jesus. Three other guys had materialized around the group. Some kind of backup system. They had—yes, those were nightsticks. Each of them looked off, chilling. These were dangerous-looking men. She'd bet that they were Cash's friends.

A tall, sinewy one took over. He wore a leather vest over his otherwise naked torso. There were at least four scars—they looked like bullet holes—on his upper body. In seconds, the boys were out the side door.

She turned her attention back to Cash, hoping he'd see her, make this easy. He had. But he wasn't having any. He looked right at her, giving no clue what he was thinking. She had no choice but to make her way through the crowd.

"Terry, may I have a word with you in private?" she asked.

Cash didn't answer, but he was still looking right at her.

The band was so loud, she couldn't tell if he'd heard her.

"Terry?" she said again, louder.

"Who da fuck is Terry?" one of the bouncers yelled, as he returned to his position near the door.

"Cash," she yelled.

Cash's expression never changed, but he took her arm, led her to the side door.

"Terry?" the man yelled after them, laughing. "You named Terry? Shit. You named Terry?"

◆◆◆

The side door was locked from both sides, and Cash used his key to open it. It opened onto a landing for the back stairs. The band was on a break now, but the recorded music was still loud—and, Callie judged, breathtakingly bad. This landing, too, was graffitied and thoroughly trashed. There was a condom near her foot. Callie carefully stepped over it, looked at him, said, "Hello, Terry."

Cash didn't answer.

She forced herself to hold his gaze. "I need your help," she said. "I'll pay for it."

Cash silently pointed his twice-broken forefinger toward the stairs.

"Please hear me out. I need your help at the restaurant."

Now, his mouth fell open in disbelief.

"I'll pay you well."

He made a cross with his fingers, backing away.

"That's not funny...Look, it's not easy for me to be here," she said truthfully. "This is serious. And you're the only one I know who can help. And yes, I overreacted to your stunt at my restaurant. I'm sorry for that. Bottom line—I'll pay five thousand dollars a week for you to tend bar."

He made a wry face. "What happened to 'when you get out of jail, don't ever come back here'?"

"Okay. I'll eat that. But my ex-husband showed up at the restaurant, and someone's trying to kill him. They've...they're threatening me, too, and they're coming back tonight, after closing. They want me to turn him over. I sent Lew to a friend's, but I need..." She trailed off.

"Callie James with an ex who's trouble?" Cash shook his head. His sandy-colored hair was short and tousled, clean but uncombed. "I would have thought you only dated philanthropists or altar boys."

Okay, she deserved that. "You ever hear of Daniel Odile-Grand?"

Cash shook his head.

Callie recapped the story. When he asked why she didn't just call the police, she squirmed a little, but she explained the situation and her reasoning. And retelling it, she was pleased that her thinking still seemed sound and her actions right.

Cash heard her out, then said, "Are you out of your mind?"

She bristled, but held down her anger. "It's out of character, yes, but I think it's the right thing to do."

"Your moral imperatives still send shivers down my spine."

Callie changed the subject, hoping to take the edge off her past mistake...And sidestep her new wave of anxiety. "You never went to prison after I turned you in, did you?" She knew he hadn't. Will thought Cash must have made a deal with the customs people, given them something substantive, a thing that they needed. He had no idea how he did it, but Will suspected that Cash had recovered the netsuke.

"Damn near."

"You make a deal?"

He didn't respond. Fine, it was none of her business.

"What are you doing at this godforsaken place?" she asked.

"Out of your mind. And still cold as a bottomfish."

"That's not funny. What are you doing here?" she repeated.

"I like the music," he said. And he turned toward the door.

She felt a rose-colored spot developing on each cheek. She grabbed his shoulder. "Damn it, Cash, Daniel's in trouble and he's badly hurt. They tried to kill him while he was leaving my restaurant. I told him I'd help, and I take my promises seriously. You, of all people, should understand that. I know you don't like me. I know that you think I treated you unfairly. And okay, maybe I did. But I'm offering five thousand a week and a change from this dreary place." She waved her hand at the dank, smelly stairwell.

Cash's expression was neutral as he pulled something out of his pocket. "I'll give you some free advice. Send him home. These are professionals. And if they launder money, as he claims, they play by different rules than you do. Cut him loose, Frosty, and save your code of honor for your waitstaff."

"He's Lew's father."

Cash carefully cut, then fired up, a large Havana.

Callie held her ground, barely braving the smoke. She could see his eyes moving; he was thinking, and that was something. She just had to hold his attention. "Five thousand a week, and tips, is good money for bartending, and looking out for me if I need that," she said. "I'll guarantee ten grand."

Cash slowly twisted his cigar. "Not worth the risk," he said. "Or the headache."

Damn it. "Fifteen thousand, guaranteed. But that's my limit."

Another puff, considering. "At some number, it's worth the risk."

"Seventeen five. That's my final offer."

He flicked his ashes to the floor. "Here's what it takes: twenty-five thousand up front. Fifty thousand at the back end. That's seventy-five thousand all in." He added, "This is not a negotiation," when he saw the look on her face.

"Are you crazy?" she yelled over the music, sure she'd misheard.

"Is that a no?" When she didn't answer: "Let's wind this up, then."

"Okay, I'll guarantee twenty thousand."

"Yes or no. Fifteen seconds." Cash checked his watch.

Shit, what was he doing? "I don't have that kind of money."

"I'll hold the deed to your restaurant until you raise it."

She gasped. "Never." What he was doing, she realized, was playing her like a violin.

He turned to leave.

Callie couldn't decide whether to scratch his eyes out or hire him. Reason prevailed. She'd hire him first. She could raise twenty-five, and she'd figure out how to renegotiate later.

Cash opened the door.

"Yes. Okay? Yes, damn it. You're hired." When he didn't even turn around, she grabbed his arm. "I'll need you at the restaurant tonight. Soon. They intend to come after closing."

"I'll want backup."

"They come out of your share."

"Have the deed ready. We'll be there well before closing, say eleven thirty."

"No deed."

"No deed, no deal."

She made a guttural noise. "Okay. Right. Make it as hard as you can."

Cash leaned close. His eyes were a hard glint in the dim stairwell light. "Let's get this straight right now. This is not a game. This is not like working for you. If I do this, I'm in charge. I say a mosquito can pull a plow, you hitch it up. Period. No questions. No rules. Is that clear?"

"Clear as a bell," she said to his back as he headed into the Dragon. For just a second, she wanted to tell him what to do with his cigar, but she didn't.

◆◆◆

Will was atypically anxious. The evening was not going well. Though he'd personally called every party to reconfirm, and to reassure them that the restaurant would be the same as ever, it obviously wasn't. There was a draft from the temporary window, newspapermen kept sneaking in to ask questions and take photos, there had been four last-minute cancellations, and then that young couple had stopped by while Callie was out, asking for her. They looked like out-of-towners—LA, Will thought. Probably movie people, he told her, though he didn't explain why.

"Were they well dressed?" Callie asked. "You know, Armani?"

Will raised his eyebrows. "Armani? Sweetie, hello, it's the new century. Those his-and-hers suits are one of a kind, tailor-made by Italian designers in Beverly Hills. Fifteen K a pop, easy."

"How do you know that?"

He looked at her as if to say, *are you kidding?* "They said they'll be back at closing."

Callie checked her watch. It was close to midnight, and the restaurant was almost empty. People still lingered at the bar. Callie asked Elise, her French server, to take over at the front door. "Cash is due any minute," she explained to Will.

"Excellent." He leaned in. "How? Tell me everything."

She took his proffered arm, giving him the highlights as he led her under the bar to the kitchen.

On their way in, she glanced at the dish pit in the alcove behind the door. The dishes were clean and stacked, the bus tubs put away. She nodded, pleased with Jean-Luc, the new dishwasher. But when she turned to the rest of the spacious kitchen, she squeezed Will's arm so tight that he let out a little cry.

There, at her maple prep table, were Cash and two of the associates she'd seen earlier—the lanky, bullet-hole-ridden bouncer, and a prosthetic-legged Afro-Caribbean man with a buzz cut. This man wore a sports prosthetic leg—gracefully curved black metal attached to the thigh with perforated leather. She'd already seen how the clean geometry allowed him to move quickly and easily at the Dragon.

Cash was offering Césaire's seared foie gras with the hot pear sauce to his friends. Césaire liked Cash, but Callie could see that he wasn't so sure about Cash's associates. The tall one hung back, quiet, methodically sorting through her kitchen cabinets. He had fair hair and odd, roving green eyes. Césaire was speaking French to the prosthetic-legged man, who sampled the foie gras again, carefully, without dropping any on his blousy black silk shirt. "Franchement," the man said, "c'est, au mieux, ordinaire."

"It's, at best, ordinary?" Callie asked, at a loss for words, understanding enough French to know that this barbarian was critiquing Césaire's famous pear sauce.

Cash turned. "Here's the deal," he said. "Andre"—he pointed at his French-speaking friend—"he works with me at the bar. Find a place for Doc downstairs."

Does Andre know how to tend bar? Callie wanted to ask, but she didn't. Now that she was in a better-lit area with Doc, she could see that in addition to the four bullet wounds, he had a jagged scar that ran down his right arm from his neck to his elbow. And his eyes didn't work together. Yeah, that was a problem. She'd never seen a scarier person. How was she going to find a place for him downstairs?

Will read her mind. "He can help Césaire in the kitchen," he suggested. And then, being the gentleman he was, Will introduced himself, shaking hands all around. "Welcome back," he said to Cash.

Cash liked Will. He smiled, relaxing a little for the first time since Callie had seen him. Still, she looked at these men in her kitchen and she wondered what she'd done.

When Doc touched her hand, she stepped back. "Is he Terry?" he asked politely, pointing at Cash. And when she nodded, he added, "Man hides his given name, he often carries the burden of shame. You know?"

"Uh-huh," Callie said, unsure if he was serious or teasing.

"Shame, remorse and—very likely—instability," Doc added.

Doc was the unstable one, she decided.

Cash shot him a look, which Doc ignored, while Will took over, finding a smock and apron for Doc and shirts and vests for Andre and Cash. Andre looked them over, then declined the shirt and vest. Will politely took them back.

After dressing, Cash called Callie aside. "The deed?" he asked.

"It's in my safe-deposit box." And before he could say anything, Callie added, irritated, "You'll have it first thing in the morning. And you'll have my check for twenty-five thousand dollars tonight. You have my word that the check is good. And that the deed is yours."

"That's good enough for me," he said, surprising her.

◆◆◆

At 12:45 a.m., Cash was behind the bar, cleaning up. Andre was wiping down the tables, singing a Creole song and sporting a roguish smile. His prosthetic leg made a distinctive noise on the wide-planked mahogany floor. The restaurant was almost empty. There were still a few people in the bar.

In the kitchen, Doc was alone, tasting sweet and hot Italian pork sausages Césaire had found for him in the walk-in refrigerator. A variety of mustard jars sat open on the table. Doc would take his sausage out of the microwave, inspect it carefully, dip it in one of the jars, take a bite, inspect it again, and then dip it in another mustard. When he began lecturing Césaire about the high fat content of these Italian sausages, Césaire excused himself.

Callie was downstairs at the lectern, texting Lew. She told him about Cash and his tough guys and promised to call him in the morning with an update. Looking up, she spotted Césaire frowning, going briskly to the front door.

At the door, Callie took Césaire aside, asked him to sit with her for a minute. They took an empty table. Callie knew he was frustrated, even angry, and she wanted to distract him. She got right to it. "I've been considering a change to the menu. How about fresh lingcod in the bouillabaisse, and a new preparation—something unexpected, distinctive? Will you think about it? When you're ready, let's talk." There was no hurry. Perfecting a favorite dish on the menu was, for both of them, a deliberate, thorny business—it was far easier to inadvertently nudge a great thing in the direction of good than to inch that great thing toward superb, even heavenly.

She watched his eyes light up. Césaire smiled, the frustration leaving his face. She knew that, for him, this would be a labor of love. There were some things, at least, that she could still fix.

◆◆◆

It was 1:15 a.m. when Kelly and Gray returned. They must have been watching, because they came in as the last patron left. Will showed them to the bar, where Callie was waiting at her table. They sat facing her, different suits this time. Gray wore a thin gold square-link chain around his neck and a matching gold earring—stylish and expensive. Kelly wore a similar gold necklace with a floating diamond solitaire pendant. As Will was asking where their suits had been made, Callie interrupted. "A drink?"

"Another time," Gray said, all business now. "Have you found Daniel Odile-Grand?"

"No, as I said before, I have no idea where he is."

"That's unacceptable," he said matter-of-factly. He turned to his partner, who nodded, regretfully smiling her agreement.

Callie was prepared. Cash had told her to hit her "ice mode" button—a phrase he'd coined for her chilliness when irritated—at any sign of trouble. He'd recognize that and take it from there.

"I beg your pardon?" she replied, classic subzero. She sipped her tepid San Pellegrino with lime.

"As I explained, urgent matters are at stake." Gray waved his hand to include the dining room downstairs. "I'm told this fine restaurant is underinsured."

"Yo, Callie." Cash had materialized behind her, carrying chips and guacamole for the table. "I thought you said we were well insured."

"We are, in fact, well insured," she agreed.

Cash leaned in. His physical presence didn't seem to faze these people. "So we don't need insurance, then, we're fine," he pointed out.

Gray leaned in, too, measuring Cash, finding him wanting. "Listen carefully, cowboy, this is not your concern." He said it slowly, advising a dim-witted child.

Kelly shook her head and spoke for the first time. "No, surely not."

Cash's eyes locked onto Gray's. "Then this is your unlucky day, pardner. From now on, to get to the lady, you go through me." He flashed a shit-eating grin. "Did you call me *Cowboy?*"

Gray grinned ever so slightly. Kelly smiled, picture perfect.

"*Cowboy?*" Cash repeated, frowning now as he emptied the bowl of guacamole on Gray's cream-colored silk suit.

Gray was up, going for his gun. He fell to the floor, writhing, when Andre planted his metal prosthetic in the hit man's groin. Cash already had Kelly's arms pinned at her sides. Andre took her gun from its shoulder holster and trained it on Gray, who was on the floor, covered with guacamole.

"Let this go," Cash told Gray. "You don't want a war. Not with me."

"Nice suit," Andre added, and lifted Gray's gold necklace with the black metal toe of his prosthetic leg. "Love the bling."

CHAPTER SIX

One of the reasons why Avi and Christy Ben-Meyer had chosen Bean's Bight for their home was because many of those who lived in the neighborhood were connected, one way or another, to the Country Club. The Country Club consisted of eighteen stately homes, some still owned by fourth-generation descendants of the founders, with commonly owned acreage at Restoration Point, the southeastern tip of Bainbridge Island. This unique 230-acre communal retreat was originally conceived as summer homes for Seattle's elite—typically, established banking and lumber families. Now, many of them were used year-round. Decisions at the Country Club, including who could buy a home if one ever came up for sale, were made by club members. The community didn't allow mortgages, and since the number of homes on the communal property was limited, relatives and would-be members occasionally bought on neighboring Bean's Bight instead. Over the years, many of those on Bean's Bight had come to be included in Country Club functions. Some, however, were not.

Christy and Avi had bought five acres on the Bight five years ago, and within a year they were regulars at the Club. As owners of Northwest Capital, they were already known in this circle.

To design their home, they'd chosen a local architect, well known for his understanding of Northwest design traditions. When he told Avi that the wood stove would go where he said it would, Avi politely fired him, and hired another architect, also well known for his understanding of the area. Together, they created a 4,000-square-foot Northwest classic. It had cedar siding, clear fir posts and beams, stained oak floors, fir paneling, a Vermont Casting wood stove, a river-rock fireplace, sweeping views of Puget Sound and Mount Rainier through the windows of their two-story great room, and so on. People said the house enhanced the local landscape without being pretentious—high praise, indeed.

Tonight, Avi and Christy sat by their river-rock fireplace, looking out at the South Sound. They were watching the Bremerton Ferry powering past Blake Island. Its windows were little white squares gliding relentlessly through the black night. To the east, a Japanese container ship slowly navigated the shipping lane toward the Port of Seattle.

"The horse is still in the barn, babe, relax," Christy offered. "The setback at the restaurant can't touch us." She was aware of Avi's black mood.

"Is Maurie too old? He said his LA people were able."

"Callie James found good help. Maurie can handle that."

"We're supposed to conclude our retirement in less than nine months. We've already liquidated some of our holdings."

"All good. As planned."

He touched her thigh. "He's not like the others. Amjad Hasim brokered weapons from the Soviet stockpile. He moved them from Russia to Afghanistan and on to various buyers, including terrorists. The consequences should anyone ever connect us to him…"

"He's long gone. Where are you heading with this?"

"Among many transactions, he sold at least two enhanced nuclear suitcase bombs." Avi watched her. He loved how her mind worked. *Steel trap* was the American term, *a steel-trap mind*. All he had to do was give her a starting point.

When she got it, Christy pursed her lips.

"Yes, the world changed on 9/11," Avi acknowledged. "The point is that anyone who can trace Amjad's activities would be one of the few people who can actually answer the question 'just what are certain specified terrorist groups capable of now?'"

"Hmm." Christy nestled her head against his shoulder.

"If it's known that we worked with him, all the resources of the federal government will be used against us. Although nothing could be proved in a court of law, our assets will be frozen, and we'll be put under a microscope. Retirement, including liquidating our considerable remaining business holdings, would be impossible."

Christy ran her fingers down the back of his head, lightly caressing his long white hair. "Can't have that."

"No," he agreed.

◆◆◆

"I'm needing more mango juice," Andre yelled to Callie.

Callie was coming upstairs, watching Cash and Andre get ready for the restaurant to open in an hour. "This is a French restaurant. Why don't you learn what we do?"

"I know what you do, lady. What you do is boring, *understimulating*." Andre nodded; this was a fact. "I've worked bars in Vientiane, Marseilles, Tangier, Port-au-Prince; bars where life is lived, where silver-spoon little worlds like yours are rocked, then kicked to the curb."

"Knock it off." Her patrons said Andre was a good listener. Why, then, didn't he listen to her? "Just serve what's on the bar menu. We don't offer a drink called the Bronze Pig—"

"Can I help it if your fancy, bored customers want something new? If they turn on to the exotic tastes of Indochina, North Africa, the Caribbean?"

Callie just looked at him. He wore his blousy black silk shirt and one gold earring. "A guest asked me what you put in her Pig. At first, I didn't know what she was talking about. When I put it together, I didn't have the nerve to tell her that you made this garbage up as you went along."

Andre set a short, fat glass on the bar. "Lady, I'll mix you a *Pig* right now."

"Stop it," she snapped. She put a hand on her bar, tried again, "No thanks. Two favors, gentlemen." She waited until Cash turned toward her. They'd settled into a routine of not speaking to each other unless it was necessary. "Try and keep your shirt buttoned, Andre. My bar isn't the appropriate place to show your tattoo. And don't call me lady. I know a dog named Lady."

Cash turned away, lit up a large Havana Cohiba Esplendido. He was wearing the shirt and vest that Callie had bought for him. Even she had to admit he looked good, which, at the moment, irritated her even more. She made a face. "Terry, if you'll spare me a minute of your precious time." Precious is a miserable understatement with what I'm paying you, Callie wanted to say. And since *I'm* paying, lose the friggin' cigar. Instead she asked, "What's the hourly rate for seventy-five thousand dollars per week?"

"One thousand eight hundred seven fifty an hour," he shot back.

"Hmm. Good for you, huh?"

"Sadly"—he leaned over the bar—"this is not close to over. And if the gals want to see Andre's hot tattoo, what do you care?"

"Hot tattoo? The man has two women having sex on his chest."

"Right. That's a hot tattoo."

"I don't want him showing it at my bar."

"If you look closely, they're Vietnamese women, I think. Nice looking."

"You're not listening," Callie said, louder than she meant to. She bit her lower lip. The teasing was making her feel antsy and irritable.

That's when Will brought the cell phone upstairs into the bar. "You know who. When I turned off the cell, he started calling the restaurant every ten seconds."

Callie took the phone. "Once you've left a message—just one message—don't keep calling me here," she said, ice-cold. "Yes, I'll have someone look in on you tonight… Yes, Mary will come by tomorrow, check your stitches…" She tried to be patient. No luck. "Daniel, right about now, no one wants to hear about your story… How about cat food and Diet Sprite?" She clicked off the phone. Will and Cash exchanged a high five.

"I'll take his phone away," Cash added, matter of fact.

The routine at her restaurant had changed. It was Wednesday afternoon, 3:00 p.m. Time to gear up, everything just so.

Right.

In the kitchen, Doc was playing his boom box. Some kind of hip-hop music. He had his mustard jars spread on the table, and wild game sausages—elk, venison, pheasant and wild boar— stacked neatly beside the microwave. He had two of each sausage: one plain, and one with additional ingredients, such as elk sausage with pears and port wine, or wild boar with cranberry. He'd bought the low-fat game sausages himself. Doc had found the wine cellar and helped himself to a fine cabernet that he was enjoying with his sausages. Césaire, almost always easygoing, had threatened to quit if Doc was in his kitchen tomorrow.

Jean Luc, the dishwasher, had just found a hockey game on Andre's TV (which sat on the bar now) to watch until they opened. For the moment, Andre's chest was covered, but last night, she'd caught him, shirt open, mixing a Bronze Pig for a fancy Eastside woman. It had "herbs" in it—uh-huh. Callie thought the woman was stoned when she left the restaurant.

Will, who in his usual fashion had managed to get everyone's story, had told her that Andre was born in the French West Indies and lived for a time in New Orleans. As a young man, he put in five years with the French Foreign Legion, then spent another five years bouncing around as a bartender—Marseilles, the Caribbean, New Orleans—homeschooling himself in military history, strategy and tactics. Eventually, he found work as a mercenary, then worked off and on as a tactical military consultant, before meeting Cash in North Africa.

Andre and Cash had worked together at God only knew what for the past eleven years. When she asked what they did, the answer was always the same vague word, "projects." She didn't understand how a man with Cash's able mind could be like he was. How he chose his friends. How he thrived on high-stakes, high-risk projects. Will said he'd made quite a lot of money smuggling, until she turned him in and he had to stop. She tried to imagine what it meant to be a very smart, very able smuggler. She couldn't. She wondered if it was hard for him to stop. Thinking about that, she started feeling uneasy, then vaguely guilty about what she'd likely cost him, so she went back to the matters at hand.

The one good thing was that after Cash and Andre had literally dragged Kelly and Gray down the stairs and out of the restaurant, Kelly and Gray had not been back in two days. On the other hand, those two days had lasted about a month. Cash wouldn't even let her see Lew. He insisted that she send him someplace where the people after Daniel would never be able to find him. She'd worked it out. Lew was now backpacking—off the grid in Oregon—with his best friend, Andy Rosen, and Andy's dad. They'd already left. They didn't even know yet where they'd be. Ed Rosen was expert at wilderness trips, so Lew was safe. Lew loved backpacking, and it would keep him happily busy, not to mention distracting him from the problems at home.

Cash allowed her just one phone call before they left yesterday—and no emails or texts, period, were allowed while Lew was gone. Cash made the call for her with one of his burner phones. She told Lew how Cash and his two men had successfully driven off the threatening couple he'd met. She told him that Ed knew the rules, and if she needed to talk with him, Cash would contact him on the satellite phone Ed carried in wilderness areas.

Lew made sure that his dad was safe, then made her promise to let him know if anything else happened to him. Finally, he said in his honest way that he was ready to take a break. They both understood that he'd be safe, and right about now, that meant a lot for both of them.

Callie feared that life would never be the same. Her restaurant had already changed. It was not quite so orderly, or predictable, and that made her uneasy. She'd opened Pandora's box, let the genie out of the bottle, taken the road less traveled, whatever. And it didn't suit her.

Worst of all—though she wouldn't admit that even to Will—Cash was growing her bar business. He and Andre worked the bar like they were born to it. She'd been worried that Jill might resent the extra vacation. On the contrary, she not only understood why Callie was limiting bartenders, she was in every night, watching these guys work. Jill peppered Andre with questions about a variety of Asian drinks. Late last night, Jill confided to Callie that she was thinking of a trip to Laos. Vientiane. Yeah.

The ground Callie stood on was shifting, wobbling, at least, and she felt disoriented and low. Her restaurant was supposed to open in two hours, and she was drifting. She wasn't sure how to regain her focus. She turned toward the bar. "Terry," she said crisply.

"Yo, Frosty," Cash called over the sound of the TV.

"Don't call me that." She tilted her head toward her table, an invitation. She pointed at his cigar, raised her eyebrows.

Cash set his cigar aside, came out from behind the bar. She met him there. He handed her the tepid San Pellegrino with lime he'd poured. "I've been thinking," she began.

"Is this another one of those shape-shifting deals?"

"What?"

"You know, like when you change from hating the sight of me to desperately wanting me to work for you."

"Please stop it." She couldn't take any more teasing. "Please. This is too hard for me. I miss my son. You've turned my restaurant upside down. People are calling Le Cochon Bronze *the Bronze Pig*. Or just *the Pig*. After Andre's drink. Daniel is so worked up about sitting still that I'm afraid to answer my own phone. Césaire's about to quit. And Andre and Doc don't even listen to what I say in my own restaurant."

"Guys like Andre and Doc don't often hang out at fancy French restaurants," Cash said. "Callie, they don't care what people think. They have their own way of seeing things. It's what makes them good at protecting you."

"Is that supposed to make sense?"

"Let it go, Callie. Their eccentricities won't hurt you. Just let it go."

"Does Doc have to play that loud music?"

"He's almost deaf. Doc was badly beaten in Angola. He was carrying diamonds for me. Since then, he plays his music pretty loud."

"I see. Okay…And Andre? I couldn't prove it, but I think he's getting all these Eastside ladies high."

"Andre's a hard guy, a former mercenary. He's also very smart. Speaks five languages, he's a self-taught military tactician. And he's bored. He's amusing himself while he protects you and yours. And if the bad guys ever come at you, you'll want Andre at the bar forever and you'll happily drink Pigs for the rest of your life."

"I guess." She made a sour face. She didn't understand this man. He had a feel for people. And what he said made some kind of weird sense. The guy understood these off-the-wall things, and when he explained them in that soft voice, it was like they were plain as the nose on your face. But they weren't even close to obvious; they were screwy, twisted, outside of normal thinking. Is that why he made her so uncomfortable? She didn't know. "Terry, I'm scared all the time. It doesn't help that you won't even let me leave the building." She started to reach a hand across the table, then pulled it away. Touching him made her tense up. "I need this to be over."

"So send Daniel home to Paris."

"He won't go, or he'll come right back. He's tracking laundered money and stolen weapons. He believes that the key to what he's been working on for four years is right here in Seattle."

"Cut him loose, then."

"What if they find him and kill him?"

"That's possible. No, that's likely."

"He's Lew's dad," she said, a whisper to herself.

"If you want to be out of this, you have only one other option— go to the police."

"We've discussed that. You know I can't do that. He'll likely die in police custody, so that's not even an option." She hesitated. "There's one thing, though. I'm thinking…" She let it trail off, started over. "Can you move him? Don't tell me where."

Cash looked at her, curious.

"I'm afraid I'll tell them. Or that I'll tell that detective—"

"Why would you tell?"

"I'm not so brave as you and your friends." She wasn't afraid to admit it. "And I don't have the stuff to lie to Detective Samter forever. He's been calling daily. I want to tell him the truth." She looked at him. "I think we're different in that way."

"You think I like lying?"

She considered that. "No. I think you can do whatever you have to do. I think you have a much broader repertoire of tolerable behavior—that is to say, behavior you find acceptable—than most people. In fact, more than anyone I've ever met."

Cash shook his head.

"Am I right?"

"About you or me?"

"I know I'm right about me," Callie said, smiling.

"I certainly tolerate a broader repertoire of behaviors than you do. It's why your bar business is improving. People don't feel like they need to be a certain way."

She felt the heat on her face. "Why is it that every time I try and talk with you, you end up pointing out my limitations and giving me advice?"

"Because your limitations," he said carefully, "are slowing us down, and lately, you need lots of advice."

She wanted to slap him. She couldn't. Hell, she hadn't even slapped Daniel when she caught him cheating for the second time. She closed her eyes, opened them, took a slow breath. "Right," she said tightly. "Look, what I need now is to focus. Get back to work. I keep thinking they'll make some move, you'll handle it, and this will be over. It has to end soon. I'm worried and uncomfortable. Tell me what to do."

"Okay. I like your idea. It's in the works already, but I'll speed it up. We'll move Daniel tonight. I'm not going to tell you where he is."

"Good."

"Once he's moved, I want you to think about letting this go. You could tell the police you don't know where he is, which would be the truth, then tell them about Gray and Kelly and let them go after these fancy creeps."

Callie considered this. "Will Daniel be safe?"

"He'll be well hidden. But he won't be safe if he keeps trying to report his story. If he surfaces, they'll find him."

"He'll go after it as soon as he can move. In fact, he wants to talk with you about helping him. He's been on a borrowed computer, going over his old files, reviewing every money transfer he believes he can connect to Amjad Hasim."

"I won't touch it."

"I can't make him back off a story. No one ever could."

"Uh-huh." Cash touched a scar on his hand. "Look, I don't know your ex. But the guy you say he was writing about, Amjad Hasim, I met him in Amsterdam, eight or nine years ago." At her surprised look, he shrugged. "I get around. But you think Andre and Doc are scary? Hasim looked at you like a mongoose sizing up a cobra. When he opened his mouth, you expected foam, spittle, but no, he was articulate. The guy could be silky like a politician or coarse as a carny, and he was always very smart. Callie, if whoever hired Gray and Kelly was connected to Hasim, and they really want Daniel, we can't stop them. We can't stop them by playing defense, anyway."

"I don't understand."

"This game can be fast or slow. So far it's been slow. Probably because they intend to kill Daniel without anyone noticing, or anyone paying much attention, anyway. Ask yourself why they didn't just shoot him in front of your restaurant. They want him to die accidently, or disappear, and they don't want anyone asking why. They're being very careful. That's why you've been okay so far."

"How do you know this?"

"Think about it. It's not easy to locate a man on the run, just hours after he arrives from Paris. It's harder still to set up an 'accident' as he's coming out of a restaurant that very evening. Whoever's behind this has resources—money, information, professional contacts. And by now, they've surely found ways to hurt you. As well covered as you are, there's always going to be some way to hurt you. If you want Gray and Kelly to back off, we have to go after them. Find out who they work for, find something to trade, make a deal, or make them understand that the price for what they want isn't worth it. We can't do that playing defense."

"I don't like this idea. I hired you to keep Daniel and my restaurant safe. Not to go off on some kind of macho last-guy-standing-wins deal."

"You're not listening."

"No," she said, gritting her teeth, "you're not hearing what I'm saying."

Cash squinted, his face hard. "We're wasting our time."

"I agree. And what's worse, you make me feel more and more helpless…and hopeless."

"Callie, you didn't hire me to make you feel good. You're up against very dangerous people. There's nothing you can do to change that reality. They don't live in your world or play by your rules."

"If you were them, Terry, what would you do?"

"I'd burn down your restaurant, or hurt someone you cared about."

"You're scaring me." She felt her lips pinch between her teeth. She didn't need this. "Damn it, Cash."

"I'm sorry to be the bearer of bad news, but you have reason to be scared." When she didn't respond, Cash frowned, looked away. "I'll move Daniel tonight."

❖❖❖

Cash was shaking a martini. It was 11:00 p.m. and people were still lingering in the restaurant. The bar was going strong. Drinkers were lined up three deep, watching Andre and having a good time. The top two buttons of Andre's black silk shirt were open. He was mixing a Blue Mist, explaining how he'd discovered it in Vietnam. It was made with gin or vodka, a blue cordial (curaçao), various juices and a French Marc de Bourgogne or other eau de vie, depending on his mood. He added a touch of a spice he kept in the pouch hanging from his belt. Something sweet from the Mekong Delta, he'd explained. Cash wondered what would happen when Callie figured out that Andre's pouch was attached to one of his erotic netsuke.

He glanced over to where she sat at her table, sipping her San Pellegrino. He'd found himself watching her surreptitiously when she was around. She was so uptight it made him tense just to look at her. Every time he tried to make a joke, she got this icy thing going, and he was afraid she was going to call the police again. When he touched her, even if it was an accident, the woman started, like an involuntary twitch.

This time, he thought, she had reason to worry. The money being spent on Daniel was just too much. Cash was pretty sure Daniel didn't know just how heavy the threat was. He'd grabbed a tail, unaware there was a man-eating tiger attached to it. And just who was this enraged tiger? And why was he or she so worked up about Daniel? Why go to the trouble to make his murder look like an accident? Why not just kill the guy? Who would care besides Callie James, this odd, pretty much unconscious woman?

For Christ's sake, she barely spoke to Daniel for fourteen years, then, out of the blue, she decides to risk everything for the guy. Cash smiled. That was Callie all right. That was the one thing he understood: Callie James and her incomprehensible rules, her homespun morality. He'd seen how her fierce, often righteous sense of fair play could turn rigid, and sour as vinegar. And he worried that it could become a dangerous liability at the worst possible time.

Cash reviewed in his mind just what Daniel was hoping to write about—Amjad Hasim, money laundering, weapons smuggling, terrorists…learning about any one of those things could get him killed. But there was something even more sinister at work here. He'd touched some nerve, woken a sleeping dragon, and the dragon wouldn't stop until it went back to sleep, satisfied.

Cash had watched a South African trader deal weapons to Syria, knowing they would be passed on to terrorists. He'd liked the Afrikaner, Jaco. Jaco had been one of Cash's diamond sources. He'd advance diamonds to him for complex deals, knowing that Cash would make him whole, plus a little vig, once the deal was done. Cash's friend and mentor, Izzie "the Macher," a big shot from New York City, tipped Cash off that Jaco should stay away from the Syrian weapons deal. When Cash cautioned Jaco, he said he'd be careful. Soon after the weapons were delivered, Jaco was beheaded, his body eaten. After, it was said, the dragon went back to sleep, satisfied.

No, Cash didn't want to know what Daniel had unleashed. It was bigger, far more dangerous, than he imagined. He pushed it out of his mind. This whole deal didn't pass the smell test. Unh-un.

Cash was preoccupied, looking over the bar, when he saw Kelly and Gray come up the stairs. He watched as they found an empty table and sat down.

Cash came over. "Suit clean up okay, young fella?" And when they didn't respond: "What can I get you?"

"Diet Coke," Gray said.

"Working, huh?"

"You're a funny guy, huh?"

"More of a friendly guy. Let-bygones-be-bygones kind of fella."

Gray went right on. "You're the big-enchilada kind of fella. So we thought we'd talk with you. Chew on this, hot shot: You help us find Daniel Odile-Grand. We'll pay you a hundred and fifty thousand. Here's fifty K." Gray took out an envelope, set it on the table. "Call it earnest money. A hundred and fifty K ain't chump change, cowboy. We'll want that address tonight. We'll keep you out of it."

Cash took the envelope, opened it. The money was all there. "Are you attractive young people confused?" He checked the money again. This was not what he'd expected. But it was interesting. "I work for the lady."

Tonight, Gray wore a diamond earring with yet another expensive tailored suit. He fingered the earring.

For the first time tonight, Kelly spoke. "For a couple of minutes, you could work for us, too." She smiled, vaguely flirtatious. She wore a black cashmere suit over a simple white sweater. There were diamonds surrounding the face of her watch. It had a thin gold band.

Cash could feel Callie's eyes on him from across the floor. He leaned his elbows on the table. Kelly was nice looking—hard, cool nice looking. And well muscled; she'd flexed when he held her arms to her sides. She was working now, using her assets. He decided to encourage her. Cash grinned his grin. "I'll think about this," he said. Letting them think they were getting along solved one of his problems. He'd be in the clear until the meeting. Enough time to move Daniel. He took the money. "Meet me at three a.m. at the alley door."

"Forget the Diet Cokes," Gray said on their way out.

◆◆◆

At 1:30 a.m., Cash let himself into Daniel's Eastlake apartment. Callie had called to explain who Cash was, but nevertheless, this was an uneasy encounter. "Are you protecting Callie?" Daniel asked, looking up. He was sitting on the couch, working on his borrowed laptop.

Cash nodded.

"I hope you're worth whatever you get paid for this."

Cash didn't respond. He already didn't like this guy. But he guessed that they were both smart enough to avoid an overt conflict.

"I'm moving you," Cash said right off.

Daniel ignored that. "I'm glad you're here. I need your help."

Cash ignored that as well. "Get your shit together. We're out of here in three minutes."

"I want you to find out about InterCap. InterCap was somehow connected to Ares Limited. There was an office in Seattle. They were getting funds from the Cayman Islands. I have—"

Cash took Daniel's right ear, twisted it, pulled him to his feet. Daniel at his best—uninjured—was no match for Cash. "Just listen and do what you're told." He looked at the man's sling, then handed him his crutch.

"Redneck...Espèce du connard," Daniel cried out, as he tried to bite Cash's arm. "Callie used to have the good taste in men," he managed to snarl. "Never a low-life peckerwood, like you."

Cash twisted the ear until Daniel was squealing, then he whispered in Daniel's other ear, "If you say another word, I'll gag you." The Frenchman was good looking, he could see that. The kind of guy a young Callie might make a mistake with. The kind of guy who could make her distrustful. He watched him, wondering how Callie had ever managed his demands, his fervor, his certainty. "Hah...of course," he eventually declared. "*You're* why Callie can't sleep."

Half an hour later they were at the Dragon, where Cash locked Daniel in the little apartment he kept on the top floor. It had a bed, a light, a small refrigerator, a hot plate, and a bathroom. One of Cash's bouncer friends had already taken Daniel's cell phone, and the apartment had no landline. When Daniel protested, Cash took some duct tape out of his jacket pocket. That shut him up.

"You'll be safe here, and you won't bother anyone," Cash explained, after he'd shown him the facilities.

Daniel lifted a hand. "May I speak?"

Cash nodded.

"You don't scare me. I have been attacked by more dangerous men than you—"

"I'll bet."

"You interest me, however. I understand from Callie that you have experience with moving money across borders." Daniel opened his laptop on the bed then turned it toward Cash. "Please, let me give you a taste of what I'm finding. Suppose I were to tell you that Amjad Hasim moved hundreds of millions of dollars before he died."

Cash didn't respond. The way he saw it, Amjad Hasim had had a very dangerous communicable disease, like the Ebola virus. And this virus had surely lived on after its host died. Why would anyone poke around something like that?

"It went in pieces from various accounts belonging to a company called Ares in Russia, Morocco, and so on, to the Cayman Islands, where I lost it. In Seattle, a company named InterCap received funds from the same bank, the Cayman Islands Bank of Trade—"

"I want no part of this."

Daniel looked up from the screen, surprised. "Please, monsieur...hear me out."

Cash left, locking the door behind him.

◆◆◆

At 3:00 a.m., Kelly and Gray were waiting at the alley door. Gray was sipping from a can of Diet Coke; Kelly flashed her perfect smile. Cash stepped into the alley prepared to pass along an address for Daniel. His plan was to give them the apartment Daniel had just vacated. Andre and Doc were already waiting there. They'd get the jump on the couple, then work on them for a while, make them sweat. Cash would eventually interrogate them himself, get whatever information he could. Best case, he'd find out who they worked for, see what it would take to strike some kind of deal for Daniel's safety, then send them home. He didn't have high hopes, but it was better than waiting around for something to happen.

He hadn't told Callie the details of his plan. He'd simply said that he had an idea and he hoped to strike a temporary truce. Buy some time. He told her that he'd fill her in tomorrow morning. He suggested that she get a good night's sleep, take a sleeping pill. He didn't want her to worry.

What he didn't expect was that sunny, well-dressed Kelly would punch a jab stick into the back of his neck and inject him with a knockout drug—right there in the alley—before he said word one. He never even saw it, expertly mounted under the sleeve of her cashmere jacket.

They cuffed his hands behind his back and hauled him up the four steps to the kitchen door. When he woke up, his head was throbbing, and he was tied to a chair at the prep table. Cash had been gagged with his own duct tape. No, they weren't interested in what he had to say about Daniel.

"You still a friendly guy? What was it? 'Let-bygones-be-by-gones kind of fella'?" Kelly asked. She touched an envelope on the table—she'd found their money in his jacket pocket—then she tightened the tape across Cash's mouth. "I like it, you and me talking like this." She leaned in, mouthed a little air kiss.

Gray was watching. He finished off his Diet Coke, set down the can.

"Here's the deal, killer," Kelly said softly. "We have to talk with Daniel Odile-Grand. We are prepared to do whatever is necessary to find him. We know something about you. Upon reflection, we believe you didn't intend to help us. In fact, we believe your purpose is to thwart us. Thwart?" Kelly raised her eyebrows—she was no dumb blonde—and winked at Gray. She liked her work. "However, we believe that you can still help us. Yes, you're the fella who will make the most convincing statement. Our point, our message, if you will, will be taken seriously. Your employer will lose confidence in you, grow fearful. And the authorities are likely to understand your misfortune. After all, smugglers, washed-out soldier boys, even cowboys, often come to a bad end." She made a face—*sorry*—then turned to Gray. He was restless. "Check the fridge, see if they got more diet coke," she suggested.

All business, Kelly took off her black cashmere jacket, hung it on the back of a kitchen chair, and took a fourteen-inch garden hose, carefully crafted for this work, from her leather bag. While Gray went to get another Diet Coke from the fridge, Kelly set her diamond watch and earrings on a table near the stove.

Cash went through his options. Andre and Doc were at the apartment, waiting. They'd wait for an hour, if need be. The restaurant was closed. Callie was sound asleep upstairs. They'd blindsided him—played him for a fool—he had to admit that.

Maybe he was too old for this.

Kelly beat Cash methodically, professionally. She inflicted visible damage, using the length of garden hose, which was filled with sand, on his head, face and upper body. Cash passed out the second time she brought the hose down on the back of his head. When they were satisfied they'd made their point—frighten Callie and let her know that the hired help wasn't going to cut it—they untied Cash and dumped him on the floor of the room-sized walk-in refrigerator. Kelly gave directions as Gray piled cold seafood, uncooked meats, and all of Césaire's sauces on top of Cash, making a large mound on the floor. Then he emptied the shelves of the braised veal osso buco, marinating duck confit, bone-in beef short ribs, beluga and osetra caviar, hotel pans filled with prepped fish, even the pallets of oysters, clams and mussels.

Cash was still breathing when they left him buried under the pile of raw fish, sauces and meats. Just barely.

◆◆◆

The phone call from Andre woke Callie from her sleeping-pill-in-duced sleep on the sixth ring. 4:00 a.m. Jesus. She was groggy.

After a beat, she managed, "No, I have no idea where Cash is...For God's sake, it's dark out...Okay, okay...I'll check down-stairs...Yes, I'll stay on the line."

She threw on a robe and made her way down the back stairs. The fish smell was palpable the moment she opened the kitchen door. She groaned, picturing money swirling down a drain. Some-one, Doc or Andre, she'd bet, must have turned off the walk-in. There was no other way to account for that smell. It was the mussels, she guessed; they always went first. "Did you guys touch anything in the walk-in?" she yelled into the phone, angry.

"Walk-in?" Andre asked.

"It's a big refrigerator. Against the west wall of the kitchen."

There was a pause while Andre asked Doc a question. "Doc keeps his wild game sausages in there," Andre explained.

"You put game sausages on the meat shelf?" He must've hit the wrong switch, turned off the fan. Well, that explained the smell. She'd bet on it.

"Lady, don't worry about anything except Cash." And when she didn't answer, he added, "Find Cash. Okay?"

Looking around the kitchen, she said, "Cash isn't here." The smell, however, was even worse.

"Check the walk-through deal. Hurry up."

"Of course I'm checking the walk-in. Jesus, it's not even all the way closed. And it stinks of fish, thanks to you geniuses."

"Listen carefully. Whatever you find, don't move him. Keep the phone on. We'll be there in ten minutes."

Callie asked, "Why?" Then she set the phone on the maple table.

She breathed through her mouth and pulled the heavy refrigerator door fully open. When she stepped inside, it was dark and hot and fetid. She held her breath. When she managed to turn on the light, she gagged. Someone had trashed her entire fish and meat supply. Piling it all in a great heap. All the things she kept refrigerated—fish, meat, everything from foie gras to cavier, raw oysters to lamb shanks. And her sauces. Then they'd turned off the fan and the refrigerator. Even worse, to make their point, they'd found her space heaters—she had one in the ladies' room, another by the entry—and turned them on the pile of raw fish and meat. The stench was awful; it would soon be unbearable. She didn't think it could get much worse—and then she saw something move.

Yeah, she was sure that a king salmon had shifted. Then she saw a calf's liver quiver. She heard a low groan as something emerged from the pile.

She screamed when she saw Cash's face.

CHAPTER SEVEN

"Don't call me again," Mary whispered. They were in Callie's bedroom, and Mary was working on Cash. He was lying in her queen-sized bed, drifting in and out of consciousness. The bruises on his swollen face were dark blue, red, even purple. In her mind, Callie likened his head to an over-ripe, rotting eggplant. She felt immediately remorseful—the dreadful image had come to her against her will. She forced herself to focus, carefully watching Mary, who had put in fourteen stitches so far—on his scalp, face and ears. She had perhaps that many more still to do. She'd already reset and taped his broken nose. Aside from several cracked ribs, the rest of his body was bruised, but nothing was broken.

"He should be examined at a hospital," Mary said.

"Can't do that," Callie said firmly. She was saying what she'd been told to say, unsure why she had to say it. She applied a cool rag to Cash's forehead. He was still drifting, not really awake. Mary had given him a powerful narcotic to help with the pain. Callie hadn't stopped worrying since she'd found him.

Doc and Andre stood in the corner of the room, watching Mary work. Every now and then, Doc would come closer, point something out. It was Doc, in fact, who'd insisted on a potent painkiller. When he asked Mary to check Cash's inner ear, take blood and urine samples, then check liver and kidney functions, Mary asked, "Do you understand what you're asking?"

"I've been beat up," he said.

"And that makes you qualified?"

"Taught me what was what."

"Qualified to practice medicine?"

"Medicine's not hard. Evading duty payments on medical equipment brought into Seattle, that's hard."

Mary shot Callie a look. *Who are these guys?*

"I can't begin to help," Callie confessed. "They're from another planet." She pointed at Doc, who wore his leather vest and no shirt. "They call this one with the bullet holes Doc. Figure that."

"Or try asking," he quietly suggested. And before she could snap at him, he offered, "I was a corpsman, part of a medical unit in Vietnam."

Mary looked him over. "Can you help me stitch him up?"

"I think so, yes."

So just like that, there he was, working on one side of Cash's face while Mary worked on the other.

And for the first time, Callie realized that this sinewy, quiet man had to be more than sixty years old.

Will, Doc and Andre had all arrived within ten minutes of her discovering Cash in the walk-in. She'd called Will right away while she waited for the others. When they arrived, Doc and Andre had taken charge. They'd laid Cash on the table, checked him over carefully. With hindsight, she could see that Doc had known what he was doing. He'd said right away that Cash would be okay, even though he didn't look okay to her.

When the men were sure Cash wasn't in trouble, they laid out the rules: no hospital, no police.

Orders, not suggestions. Will counseled her to follow their "advice"; this was their work, he explained, and plainly, they were experienced. They asked her to call her doctor friend, and moved Cash upstairs on a stretcher they'd fashioned from one of her walk-in refrigerator shelves. Will said he'd take care of the mess in the walk-in.

Later, he told her he'd called Jean-Luc to help him. The dishwasher had walked boldly into the refrigerator, seen the stinking pile and said, "Smells like fish, eh?" As he began the cleanup, Will thought he heard him singing in Quebecois French, something about the girls from Newfoundland.

◆◆◆

The phone call came at 9:00 a.m., thirty hours after the beating. Cash, still Mr. Know-It-All, even with that awful face, had predicted it. He said that they'd give Callie a chance to stew about it. And God knows, she'd done nothing but. She kept seeing him buried under the stinking pile in her walk-in.

Will answered the phone, buzzed her from the kitchen. "Callie, for you," he said. "We'll be right up."

She was sitting beside Cash, adjusting a wet cloth over his eyes and brow. After sleeping off and on for about ten hours, he'd been able to talk, and had confirmed that his injuries were not nearly so bad as they looked. Though his eggplant face was pretty grim—bruised, misshapen, crisscrossed with stitches—he'd have no lasting effects. He'd stayed up for several hours, then slept for another ten. When he woke up again, he was hungry. Callie made chicken soup. Still a little punchy, Cash said that a broken nose would add character. Under the circumstances, Callie hadn't taken the easy shot; they'd consider his character another time. He'd refused more medicine. But every time she looked at his face, she was frightened. If they could do this to him, the man who was supposed to protect her, they could easily do worse to Césaire, to Will, to her, even to Lew...These people could hurt *anyone* she cared about. She'd held on to that, turned it over in her mind most of the past day.

Callie touched Cash's face gingerly as she picked up the phone. She was somehow responsible for this, a guilty feeling she couldn't shake. "Callie James," she said.

"I understand you had a problem with your walk-in refrigerator." It was Gray, his upbeat voice and take-charge manner unmistakable.

Callie put the phone beside Cash's ear, and then she leaned in so they could listen together.

"The walk-in's a taste, a little amuse-bouche. Next comes the main course, the entrée, if you please."

Cash tapped her arm. They'd prepared for this. "I want to talk," she said. "When can we meet?" Just speaking to this man was hard, really hard. She had to work to keep her voice from quivering, cracking.

"We'll call at noon." Gray hung up.

She could feel the sweat on her brow, at the small of her back. She couldn't do this. Meet these people? Un-unh. She looked at Cash's face. "I'm calling the police," she said.

Will, Doc and Andre were all in her bedroom now. Cash pressed thumb and forefinger to the bridge of his broken nose—they'd been over this ground—and looked at Doc.

"To what end?" Doc asked, polite.

"Look how they hurt him. People can't just do that."

"He'll live," Andre pointed out.

"He could have died."

"If they wanted to kill him, he'd be dead," Doc said.

Callie stood, then started pacing, working to hold herself together. Even these mercenaries were patronizing her.

Cash watched her pace, then sat up in bed, wincing. "They beat me up to frighten you," he said, his voice soft, gravelly. "They *want* you to go to the police."

"What if I tell them I don't know where Daniel is, like you said?"

"Too late for that." Cash propped another pillow behind his head. He took a sip of water, readying himself for this conversation. "You can't call the police about the beating and not bring me into it."

"So?"

"If the cops lean on me, I'll tell them where he is."

"You? Why?"

"I did a deal to stay out of jail. They can send me away anytime."

"What?" This was out of control. What had she done? "Thank you, at least, for telling me."

Another sip of water. "Your work, Frosty."

"Does that make you feel better, huh?" Smart-ass. At least he was himself again. "I bet the police cramped your smuggling style."

Cash frowned. "You have no idea."

Callie nodded, shaking her head. Wanting to ask him more.

He saw her look. "Just let it go."

"Okay…What are you going to do?" she asked.

"Payback," Andre said. Doc nodded; this was an easy call.

"Are you crazy?" Callie felt dizzy.

Cash took a drink of water. "Callie, you have a decision to make. Go to the police or do exactly as we say." He took another drink. "If you choose the cops, I'll keep the twenty-five, walk away." He started a shrug, grimaced instead. "I may still go after these people."

Callie was pacing now, taking slow breaths. "This is like some terrible movie."

"Not necessarily," Andre countered. "Remember the beating that Brando took in *On the Waterfront*?"

"Stop it," she snapped.

Cash went on. "If you choose us, we'll take 'em out, try and strike a deal with their boss. They're not going away unless we make them."

"What does *take them out* mean?"

"Fuck 'em up," Andre said. He was tapping his prosthetic leg on her hardwood floor.

Callie was pacing circles now, working at breathing. Was she seriously about to endorse violence against these people?

Cash went right on. "If you choose us, I'm going to talk with Daniel—I have an idea how he could help me make that deal." When Callie looked at him, he said, "One of my guys is watching him. My guy has a burner phone. There's no chance of us leading them to him." He shot her a hard look. "Callie, this is what you hired me for." He shifted his weight on the bed, groaning softly. "And I don't want to have this conversation again."

Callie stopped pacing abruptly. She felt like she was neck-deep in quicksand, sinking slowly, inexorably. She wanted to scream. Instead, she rubbed the back of her neck, hard, hurting herself, working to stay in control.

And then she was back on what he'd said, how he didn't want to have this conversation. And all of a sudden she was really angry, upset. "You don't, huh?" She glared at him. "Terry, I'm paying you more money than I have. I ought to be screaming at you." She stepped closer. "But Jesus, how can I yell at you when you look like that? I mean, you were supposed to *fix* everything. Now this is so screwed up. You are so screwed up." She made a fist, squeezing tight, trying to stop her emotions from welling up. "I mean, if you're so goddamned smart, why are you lying there, looking like an overripe eggplant?" She whipped around. "And Andre, stop that horrible tapping." She felt a tear. Jesus, she was crying.

"It's not screwed up," Cash insisted, raspy and irritable. "It's moving forward. Stopping these people is not a deal you walk away from after a little amuse-bouche."

"What the fuck is that, anyway?" Doc asked.

"When the chef offers you a little taste of something before dinner begins," Will explained. He continued, hoping to defuse the tension. "Like lobster broth with foie gras oil, or a quail egg with a touch of caviar."

"I lived in France," Andre said. "Shit like that never happened to me."

Callie wiped her tears with the back of her finger. "You never said it was going to be so hard. And I can't put anyone else in danger—not Césaire, not Jill, nor you, Will. I can't do any of this. I just want it to stop."

"Cut Daniel loose," Cash suggested. "Give him up to your detective. Your hands are clean."

"Then Daniel's dead."

"Possibly," Cash acknowledged. "On the street, in prison, he's easy to find."

"I can't take that chance. And I can't just turn you and your guys loose to—what was it?—take 'em out. No, *fuck 'em up*."

"What in hell can you do, lady?" Andre asked.

"Shut up, Andre. Just *zip* it. You're less sensitive than a flounder. Terry was almost killed at my restaurant. I can't let this go on." She was afraid she'd start crying again. Or that he'd start tapping again. She was shaking her head. "It's *my damned restaurant*…"

"Terry?" Andre said to Cash, smiling just a little.

Doc looked at Andre. "Flounder?"

Andre's smile faded.

"Callie, let's step outside your restaurant, hypothetically. Where these people live, rules are made opportunistically." Cash's voice was gentler now. "I know that country. That's why you brought me in. That's why I signed on for this. That's why you're paying me so much money." He paused, resting. "What happened to me, it's a risk I willingly took. Yes, they got the jump on me. But this is nothing, a feint, a jab, a tease. I'm banged up, yes. But it's no big deal." He sat up, to make his point. "It's our move now. It's show time. I'd like to finish this. Make up your mind." He leaned back on his pillows, already tired out.

Callie was chewing her nails, a thing she rarely did. "You're scaring me, you know," she said to Cash. "I want to talk to Detective Samter."

Cash handed her the phone.

A piece of a nail came off in her teeth. She took the phone, then snapped, "Why are you doing this? Why? The money?"

Cash nodded. "Yeah, that's it."

"That's all?"

Cash thought about this. "Well, in spite of you, I like your son...Maybe I can help him have a chance to get to know his dad." He shrugged. "But mostly, it's money." He watched her, steaming, staring at the phone. "So, did you make up your mind yet, Frosty?"

She threw the phone at the wall. "Just make this situation go away. Please." She left the room.

"That's a yes to your plan," Will explained.

CHAPTER EIGHT

No one ever imagined that Christy would come so far. She'd been a gangly, awkward adolescent. Lakeside, her elite private high school, was not an easy place if you weren't part of the popular crowd, and she didn't meet their marks. In an unkind subculture that rated everything from God to grasshoppers, Christy was ranked at the very bottom. So she was an outcast, teased and excluded. She finally found her niche as a driven, overachieving workaholic. She clawed her way to Stanford, where she earned an MBA in five years. Until she graduated, she was focused like a laser. It was 2002 and technology was happening. She got a job at a Seattle-based tech investment firm.

She didn't mind swimming upstream. In her shrewd, laconic cowgirl way, Christy was relentless. Still, a few years into her career, she was stuck: at her firm, she couldn't get closer to the real money than the low-level Microsoft executives or the secretaries with stock options. Even worse, in a community that wanted people to go slow, hide their ambitions, avoid conflict, and play by the old-school rules, Christy didn't fit in. She was this rangy, aggressive woman, outspoken in a way that went right for the jugular. She bluntly said things that weren't always easy to hear, and she rarely, if ever, felt shame. All of these characteristics were disliked in this conflict-avoidant, unexpressive culture. So, as gifted as she was at understanding financial matters, at identifying unexpected investment opportunities, she was firmly exiled to client Siberia—research. In her darkest moments, she reminded herself to stay focused on just one thing: to get where she wanted to go, serious money was her *only* option. So she was waiting.

Avi was what she'd been waiting for.

Avi left Israel for a banking job in the Cayman Islands at twenty-seven. At thirty, he emigrated to Buenos Aires, where his uncle Nathan lived and had a thriving law practice.

The thing about Avi was that he was uncommonly able in an unassuming way, charming, and so understated that most people, except Christy, never knew that he had strong feelings and an intense emotional life. He was also a worrier, which was, for him, a double-edged sword. He mastered his anxiety by crossing every t and dotting every i so meticulously and thoroughly that he was almost mistake proof. He rarely suffered a misstep.

By the time Avi met Christy, he and his uncle Nathan had established a solid investment portfolio and money-laundering repertoire. The international investment fund Avi created for his private investors, European Capital Management, was an offshore shelf corporation—as such, it was largely on paper and had virtually no activities. ECM itself had several wholly owned subsidiaries, all offshore shelf corporations as well, including Ares Ltd., Global Trade, Fulcrum Ltd. and InterCap Ltd. All of the corporations had a single corporate shareholder who was an unidentifiable subsidiary of the bank. The result was that all of these entities could do business worldwide, and no one would ever know the true beneficiary of the transaction.

To facilitate moving money discreetly, Avi partnered with one of Nathan's oldest clients, an international real estate investor, and together they formed Global Real Estate Ltd. (GRE). Avi's partner was the public face of the company, which owned commercial and residential properties in Vancouver, London, New York, Miami, LA and Hong Kong. Avi supplied the capital, discreetly, through

Ares and InterCap, while his partner chose, then managed, the properties, for fifteen percent of the profits.

The way the money laundering worked was this: ECM invested money for Avi's clients in Ares Ltd., which in turn invested in InterCap, which then invested in GRE, which used the funds to purchase property. As such, a Colombian drug dealer or a Soviet weapons smuggler could untraceably invest ill-gotten money in a new office building in LA or buy a condo in Miami.

When he met Christy, Avi was already thinking that the future, for him and for his clients, was in the USA. He was working on a simple idea, a way to move their money to America safely. And a way to give a handful of his wealthiest clients a fresh start—a new identity and clean cash that they'd never need to launder again. Most importantly, Avi, ever concerned, could sit back, relax, and enjoy the fruits of his labor without constantly looking over his shoulder, worrying about his powerful clients' well-being. Northwest Capital Management, still a gleam in his eye, would invest their legal income from GRE. It was, he reflected at the time, the final iteration—a chance to wind down, enjoy the rewards of his remarkable success and, eventually, pursue his hobby. He'd grown interested in American wines. He imagined owning his own vineyard, in Eastern Washington, perhaps.

But now, just when he thought all the loose ends were tied up, that relentless French journalist was trying to reopen the story about Haslm. If he wasn't stopped, he could open Pandora's box, put all of their meticulous work at risk. Already, it was making them rethink their carefully planned retirement schedule.

As the sun dropped toward the Olympics, he and Christy were sipping a Reynvaan Family Vineyards 2012 cabernet, watching the reflected light, pinks and reds, shimmering on Mount Rainier. The tide was in, and a purse seiner was setting its nets not thirty yards in front of their beach. Christy wanted to shoot holes in the little fishing boat.

"Put a couple bear slugs in her hull. Sink that seiner where she lies," Christy said. "Then we can talk about my buoy."

Last fall, one of the fishermen had cut off their pretty red-and-white buoy. It sat about forty feet out at low tide to secure their boat in the summer. Apparently, it was getting tangled in their nets. She was still mad about it. "They have to earn a living," Avi suggested. He'd never understand how she could stay mad for such a long time about such a little thing.

"Fox has to eat. Doesn't give him the right to kill my damn chickens."

Avi was reminded of an Americanism he particularly liked: *You can take the girl out of Montana…*He smiled warmly. She *was* a Montana girl. He went fishing with her every summer near Bozeman. The country reminded him of Patagonia, only there were so many more people. He loved to fish, though he wasn't very good at it. Christy was a natural. She routinely caught four fish to his one.

He watched her pout now. She was worried, he decided, had to be. "I'm not sure I take your point. Nevertheless, I will buy you a new buoy in the spring. I will chain it such that it can't be easily cut. And then we shall see how the seiners set their nets."

"I'll be watching like a hawk. I want a sign, too. A warning sign on that buoy. Let them know that if they fuck with it, I'll shoot. I will, too. I swear to God."

"You shall have it." It occurred to him that she might be as worried as he was. "Maurie said we should have our situation resolved soon."

"*Now* would be good."

"He's optimistic. Apparently, the ball is rolling."

"Who else knows how we handled Hasim?"

"No one." He watched her staring out the window and was grateful he wasn't fishing on that seiner. She furrowed her brow, pursuing some idea. He could see by her expression that she had hold of it like a pit bull. When she had her idea, she lit a Marlboro, took a long, slow drag.

"Let's put someone else on it. Another level altogether. Let's pay the freight for a proven man hunter." She paused, another pull on her cigarette. "World-class. Just in case."

She *was* as worried as he was. Good. "Maurie called Casper Pinder. He's in Seattle, standing by."

"Perfect."

He raised his wine glass. "To interesting times."

"Yep." She touched her glass to his, pensive. "And suppose we eat out tonight?"

He laughed, a soft low chuckle. "And pray tell, where might we eat?"

"Le Cochon Bronze."

He leaned in, lightly kissed her lips. "Perfect." Avi put his arm around her, holding her close. What was it about this woman that made him so happy, that satisfied him so completely? Part of it was their uncommon sexual compatibility—their sex life was unpredictable, stirring and brazen. For an understated, painstaking man, it was exhilarating to feel unrestrained, even audacious. For a man who felt no shame or guilt about his nefarious work, it was unexpectedly exciting—a dizzying counter-intuitive leap on some twisted continuum—to enjoy guilty pleasures, to, for an instant, taste shame. They somehow did this for one another. And how she appreciated him. Their chemistry was electric, their communication, wordless, instantaneous. Devilish became racy became naughty then finally fabulous. And after, she always, always made him laugh.

He looked down. Christy was watching him, smiling, reading his mind.

CHAPTER NINE

The call came at noon, exactly. Cash watched Callie pacing nervously around her bedroom, waiting for Will to buzz her on the telephone intercom. Andre and Doc were in Callie's living room, standing by. Cash, propped up on her bed, was frowning, worried. This plan depended on Callie. It was their best chance precisely because she was so anxious, so vulnerable. Kelly and Gray would not be as cautious with her.

He'd been reluctant to use her, he had to admit. But after an hour of sorting through options—just like that, she said that it had to be her. She'd worked it out, her way. When she'd asked if they'd hurt Will or Césaire or Jill next, Cash hadn't seen where she was going. She'd finally said they had to be stopped, that she was the best—no—the only option, and it was the right thing to do, period. Then she said that she couldn't imagine doing it.

Cash thought she was right, in her way, about all of those things. If anyone had a chance to pull this off, it was Callie. But he couldn't see her doing it, either. So he'd spent an hour coaching her—practicing what to say, going over options if they threw her a curve. Various ways to get where they had to go. She understood what she was supposed to do, the objective, anyway. But he didn't know if she was up to it.

Callie answered the intercom. She held the phone near Cash's ear, so that he could hear, too, then pushed the blinking button on her phone.

"I don't want any more problems," she said. She cleared her throat, nervous. "I'm going to see if I can arrange for you to meet Daniel. See if you can work this out."

"That's a good idea," Gray said, upbeat.

Callie hesitated. Cash nodded. "I'm going to have people there," she said, her voice still a little shaky. Then stronger: "I'm not going to let you hurt him."

"Your tough guys?" Gray asked, punching the last words with irony.

"Right."

"Impossible."

"Then we're stuck." This said more surely.

"Certain? That's a life-changing decision," Gray said, meaning it.

She looked at Cash, who was nodding encouragement. He touched her arm; this was the moment of truth.

"Give me something," she insisted. "You say you want to talk with Daniel. I'm afraid you'll kill him. I can't let that happen."

Gray didn't respond.

"Give me a way."

"You can have one of your guys at Daniel's."

"That's a start."

"Why don't you join us?" he asked, upbeat again.

Yeah. Okay. There it was. Gray's chance to hold her hostage. And, Cash had explained, the only way she'd be able to do what they needed.

Her voice was soft, trembling. "I choose the time and place." Callie looked at Cash, who nodded.

"We meet wherever he is. If you don't take us to Daniel, we'll keep you, and trade down." His tone was hard; he meant that.

Callie's hand was jostling the phone now. Cash covered the phone with his own hand to calm her trembling. "You're not hearing me," she said weakly.

Gray ignored her. "Be in your alley just south of the restaurant, near the cross street, in two minutes. Alone." He hung up.

Two minutes. They were smart. Cash gave her a thumbs-up. "Okay. Two minutes is enough." He laid a weathered hand on Callie's arm. She was hyperventilating. "Callie, one last step. You can do this. Remember, you can't get in the car with them." He turned to Doc and Andre, standing by the door. "Good to go?"

"On it." And they were gone, down to the alley.

◆◆◆

Callie opened the alley door, stepped out, alone. She wore jeans, a wool sweater, and her long leather coat. She could hear her heart beating, feel the sweat dripping down her back. It was all she could do to breathe. Jesus God—she closed her eyes, said a silent prayer, then walked down the alley, taking measured breaths. She stood at the meeting point, waiting.

The Lexus pulled into the alley seconds later. As the rear door opened, Kelly, who was driving, flashed her best smile, and Callie nodded back. Then she did the hardest thing she'd ever done: as she lowered her head to get in the back seat of the car, Callie slid the canister of bear mace from the large right-hand pocket of her coat. She used her body to shield it from view. As she set her foot on the door frame to enter the car, she swung her hand from her side, pressed the black tab as she extended her hand forward, and blasted a long burst of bear mace—Counter Assault, it was called—into the front seat. She screamed—heretofore inaccessible rage—as she fired off the bear spray. Then, as she'd been instructed, Callie threw herself, not into the car but facedown onto the pavement in the alley.

Kelly and Gray opened the car doors—retching, unable to breathe, eyes on fire. Blinded, breathless and helpless, they were easily subdued by Andre and Doc, who threw them to the ground, where they cuffed them, semiconscious, gagging, near hysteria. Andre and Doc hustled them in the alley door, then down to the basement. Doc, wearing a gas mask now, hurried out to move the Lexus.

Callie was still lying in the alley, in shock. She was crying when Andre helped her up. Her nose and eyes were burning terribly. She looked at the canister of bear mace. It was black, and bigger than her entire hand, and so powerful that she was still having difficulty breathing, just from leaning into the car long enough to fire the burst into the front seat.

"Nice work," Andre offered.

She just stared at him, tears streaming down her cheeks. When she extended her hand, it was shaking.

♦♦♦

When she'd renovated the restaurant and her own apartment, Callie had refused to think about the damp, musky old basement in her worn-out old warehouse. Two years later, she'd knocked down a wall and cleaned up the large open space for restaurant storage, mostly wine. At the center stood an oversized ancient furnace, which heated the entire building. She'd had to cover it with some kind of foam because of the asbestos. It was in its own little room, and she'd painted the interior walls yellow, so it wasn't so dreary. She'd left one room untouched. It was a small room in the corner, where she kept paint samples from the dining room, unused wood trim, leftover fabrics, a defective barstool and broken-down restaurant memorabilia she couldn't bear to throw away. Over the years, it had stayed damp and musky. In this room, Andre and Doc had cuffed Gray and Kelly to rings they'd anchored in the north- and south-facing walls, after moving the accumulated paraphernalia to the east and west.

Kelly and Gray stood, arms above their heads, facing each other. Doc explained to them that they would have difficulty breathing for some time because the capsicum in the spray was a bronchial constrictant. Nevertheless, the men gagged them both, though they used narrow strips of cloth so Kelly and Gray could still inhale through their mouths. This kindness was deliberate. Doc was insistent that whatever happened, no one was going to choke to death on his watch. Their plan was to ask Kelly and Gray several key questions, let them know, unequivocally, the urgency of their queries, then give them a moment to digest their dilemma and come up with the answers.

Doc was standing beside Gray, who was feigning control, looking away. "Here are the questions," Doc said softly. "Who hired you? What were you hired to do? What will it take to call this thing off?" Then Doc added, "You get that? Nod." When Gray continued to ignore him, Doc motioned Andre to leave, put his gas mask on again, and fired a pretty good burst of mace in Gray's face. While Gray frantically rubbed his eyes—one, then the other—against his upraised arms, made retching noises, spewed spittle and fought for breath, Doc maced Kelly, too. "Think about those questions. And how, without the answers, the *pickle* you're in can only worsen."

He turned out the lights and left them there, writhing and gasping. At the door, Andre sighed, adding, "Payback, she is one sweet bitch."

◆◆◆

Cash was propped up in bed, feeling pretty good. Andre and Doc had given him their report. So far, so good. Kelly and Gray were considering their questions, considering consequences. He'd see them later. In the meantime, it was time to talk with Daniel. His mind, however, had circled back to Callie.

She'd come through; he had to admit it. What was it about the woman that surprised him at every turn, that regularly defied his expectations? Afraid of so many things, always denying, controlling, doing things in her own overly cautious way. Then she takes a risk that would scare off most experienced risk-takers. Like stepping up with the bear mace—like it's a thing she has to do, going for a root canal or something.

It had taken half an hour to talk her down afterward. At first, she was shaking and crying. She'd screamed at him, blaming him for making her do things she couldn't do. Shouldn't do. But she'd done it anyway. Even if it made her so upset and angry that those little beet-colored blotches spread across her face and neck. She was a riddle he couldn't solve. And it was getting under his skin.

Callie was taking a shower now, washing away any sign of what she'd done, any sign of what was in her basement, ostensibly getting ready to go down to her restaurant. Cash wanted to talk with her—ask questions, see if he could figure how her unpredictable, irritating, often counterintuitive mind worked. If he could just understand the counterintuitive piece, maybe it would help him reason with her. He worried that she was about to do something foolish. That was Callie—a positive step followed by remorse and self-doubt. He turned that over. Maybe not. But thinking about her made his head ache. He'd choose his moment, he decided. Sometime soon. For now, he had to put her out of his mind.

Cash called one of his men at the Dragon, Eric, who was keeping an eye on Daniel. Since meeting him, Eric called Daniel "the doofus." Cash used a burner cell phone, one of several Doc had given him, to call Eric's burner, then asked him to put Daniel on the line.

"Hey Daniel," Cash said, interrupting a string of French obscenities.

"I am a prisoner. I cannot work. Agh…Are you satisfied?" Daniel asked. "Are you satisfied, monsieur?"

Cash started a smile, but it made his face hurt. He grunted instead, then offered, "Daniel, here's something going to pick you up —I took a beating on your behalf."

"I hope they kicked the shit off of you."

Another near smile, another quick retraction. "They did that. Yes."

"You are right. This picks me up." He made some guttural noise. "Oui, énormément."

"Good. Now, here's our business. I caught up with the people looking for you. I'm going to try and get to their boss, strike a deal. Back 'em off. I need your help here."

"You are simpleminded. Unless you give me up, they will not deal."

"That's precisely what I'm going to do—give you up. What if I tell them you'll drop your story, meet with them? I could set a meeting in New York City. Buy some time."

"You can tell them. I will not do it."

"Right." He was not getting through. Nope. "I'm thinking the *only* deal I can make is to promise them that. It's all I have to trade. I need time. The meeting is what we call a head fake. You know, signal one direction when you mean to take another. So yeah, we'll promise that."

"How's this? You can promise them that I will help them kill you when this is over."

Cash took out a cigar. This was going to take a while. "Daniel. Daniel Odile-Grand. You're a forest-for-the-trees guy."

"A what?"

"Never mind." He fired up his Cohiba Esplendido. "Okay. I'm going to go here for what we call the big picture." A slow pull. Cash exhaled. "You're alive because Callie stuck her neck out for you. So far out that she's having trouble making it through the day. My job is to keep her out of harm's way, without losing you. The only reason I don't cut you loose to cook your own goose, or make this a police matter, is that she won't let me. Callie genuinely believes, as only she could, that since you flew through her window, you are her responsibility."

"Yes, yes…*that* is the girl that I married. You cannot know this, but she always had values. Even when I first knew her, she could figure out how and why she felt about something. She would tell me when she didn't like what I was working on, even when she knew it was a good thing—important—to expose. And now, she adds to this talent le courage."

Cash brought this back to the present. "And she pays well. So this works for you and for me. What about for her?"

"I can't walk away from my story. It's what I do…what I care about. For me, the most important thing."

Cash rubbed the bridge of his nose. Set his cigar in the ashtray. "Of course you can't walk away. You couldn't walk away even if you wanted to. It's *too late*. Any way I cut it, you have a target painted on your back. You know something that people want to kill you for. Sadly, you don't even know what it is that you know."

"I know that I am close to finding a complicated system for moving money illegally. I know that Amjad Hasim, and others, used that system for hiding corrupt profits—"

Cash interrupted. "I get that. Say you figure all of this out, publish it. So what? *Why kill you?* There has to be something more. There's a dark secret somewhere behind this. And you have no idea what it is or how to find it. You don't even know who is doing this."

"How do you know what I know?" Daniel raised his voice, getting angry.

Cash took a sip of water, realizing he had to be very concrete, specific, to get through to this Frenchman. "Let's try again. What you and I need to cooperate on here is getting Callie out of danger. *Callie and Lew*, your ex-wife and your son. You have to agree to do exactly what I ask until we get them out of the middle, out of harm's way. Okay?" He listened, hoping for he didn't know what. Nothing. "So…we both know the bad guys won't back off. But maybe we can shift their focus. We'll set the meeting in New York City. I know someone there who may be able to help. He knew Amjad Hasim, did deals with him. I need to get something on these people—to know what it is about Hasim, about his dealings, that they don't want you to learn. I can trade that information for Callie and Lew's safety. If I have two days before the meeting, I have an idea how to do that…"

Cash trailed off, wondering if Daniel was even listening.

"When Callie and Lew are safe," Cash continued, "when I know what I'm dealing with, I'll lay out your options, including if there is any deal I think I can possibly cut for you. Whatever you decide—and if character is destiny, you'll make yet another narcissistic, ass-backward decision—I'll present it to Callie and argue that at this point, this is your call. I think I can convince her that you have choices, and that she's no longer responsible for you. Then you can do whatever you damned well please."

"Ah." There was a silence. "Voilà. I see. You are an American. A realist. Everything is practical." Daniel sighed. Another pause. Then, just like that, he made one of the *agh* noises that preceded the pearl being set before the swine. "There are tribal cultures where, if I enter someone's house, I am their responsibility."

If this tribe had an alphabet, any way at all to understand him, when Daniel opened his mouth he was big-game bait. Cash would put his own money on it.

"Conversely, if by entering the house, I place them in danger—if, as you imply, I have put Callie and Lew in harm's way—they are then my responsibility." He let that sink in. "Forest for the trees. Évidemment. You can take your *head fake*. I hope you can, as you say, *get the goods, back them off*. I doubt you can." A loud, deliberate yawn, then, precise and forceful: "More likely, I'm thinking that you'll get your *bite*—how do you say it?—your Richard, your Johnson, yes, your tiny little *pecker* caught in the zipper...That would be the good time—no?—to look at the *big picture*. Are you following me, you back-asswards redneck?"

Cash laughed out loud, even though it hurt. "Nicely done... End of the day, you are one silver-tongued douchebag."

"Silver-tongued douchebag—what is this? A great orator?"

"Uh-huh, sure. So, will you help?" Cash bet that whatever Daniel said next, it would be preceded by the *agh* sound.

"Agh, I will do as you ask. You have my word. Make your deal."

Cash wondered if he'd misheard. Was that a yes? He picked up his Havana, giving Daniel a chance to drop the other shoe and screw this up. When he didn't, Cash simply said, "Thank you," wondering just what it was that had made the light go on. Lew, he guessed. "Incidentally, your son is a fine boy. I'll arrange for you to see him when this cools off."

"Thank you."

◆◆◆

Callie was at the bedroom door, dressed for hosting dinner in a simple black dress and a white pearl necklace. She'd overheard most of Cash's conversation with Daniel. She'd almost smiled when he'd said the thing about her feeling like Daniel was her responsibility because he'd flown through her window. It wasn't entirely wrong. Still, he understood her about as well as she understood him—and they weren't seeing any of this the same way.

When something bad happened, it was always her fault for not going his way sooner. And of course, after bad news, his way of thinking invariably led to yet another preemptive strike. Which, in turn, kept getting them deeper into trouble.

It was a vicious circle. The way he saw it, she was overly cautious, slow, rigid and contentious. The way she saw it, she'd done things his way, much faster and more agreeably than she'd wanted to, and now—for God's sake—she had two deadly thugs chained up in her basement; she'd just committed her first assault; her overpaid, so-called protector was beat-up, puffy and purple; her ex-husband was virtually a prisoner; some very sinister, unknown people were still trying to kill Daniel; and this uncontrollable, and to her way of thinking, incomprehensible, smartass held the deed to her restaurant. When she'd given it to him the next morning, as promised, he'd taken it away somewhere without even thanking her.

She went over to the bed and put out his cigar, making a sour face. "Did you call him a silver-tongued douchebag?"

"I did."

"Hmm…Did he think it meant *great orator*?"

"I'm afraid to ask how you knew that."

Callie smiled, rueful, then turned serious. "You're playing every angle, aren't you?"

"There aren't many angles to play. I want you out of the middle, and I want to talk to a decision maker. Someone who can cut a deal for Daniel."

He was already figuring out how to help Daniel. She should have known. "You always sound so sure of yourself."

"I know how to evaluate options. But Callie, it's possible that there are none left. Hell, it's probable. I think Daniel knows enough that they'll kill him no matter what. If that's the case, I need you out of it, before this goes any further. That's a different kind of problem. If this doesn't work, it's hardball. And we have to move fast, get ahead of them."

Here we go again. Pressure, sports metaphors and danger. "Can't you ever just back off for a minute, give the other guy a chance to move on, let this go?"

Andre and Doc were at the door, checking on their friend. Andre frowned in response to her question. "Doc, tell sugar here 'bout the scorpion and the frog," he suggested.

"Don't call me sugar."

"Just sayin' you sweet. I didn't call you bitch or burger. And sweet as you are, you especially need to hear this story…it's a fable."

Doc nodded. "Aesop or Bidpai, perhaps African folklore. No one knows for sure."

Callie raised both hands, resigned. "Okay, let's get this over with."

Andre said, "Hit it, Doc." Cash propped himself up.

Doc stepped forward.

"A scorpion and a frog meet on the bank of a stream and the scorpion asks the frog to carry him across on its back. The frog asks, 'How do I know you won't sting me?' The scorpion says, 'Because if I do, I will die, too.'

"The frog is satisfied, and they set out, but midstream, the scorpion stings the frog. The frog feels the onset of paralysis and starts to sink, knowing they both will drown, but has just enough time to gasp, 'Why?'

"Replies the scorpion: 'It's my nature.'"

Callie shook her head. "You guys are crazy. That's ridiculous. Why would the scorpion kill himself? He'd never do that."

"You're not getting it," Cash said. "The point of the fable, and some say it goes back to the third century BC, is that what is fundamentally vicious will not change."

"I don't necessarily agree. Okay?"

Andre shook his head. "Honey, don't argue about the scorpion's nature. What you want to be thinking on is: *Am I the frog?*"

"Of course I'm not the frog."

"Then don't ever give the scorpion the chance to *move on,*" Andre insisted. "He'll sting you, sure as sunrise. *That's his nature.*"

"You can't *let it go,* either." Cash went on. "Unless you plan to cut and run."

"I give up." She couldn't think about this now. She'd put herself in Cash's hands, however reluctantly, and that's where she was. It didn't matter that she didn't like it one bit. Or that he never let up. Scorpion and the frog? Were they trying to get under her skin? If they were, it was working. Callie changed the subject. "Thank you for telling Daniel that you'd arrange for him to see Lew. I told him he'd see his dad when he came back."

"We'll keep that promise."

She looked at him, face all puffed up, black and blue and red and purple. Callie turned to her mirror, checking her own face. She ran a finger along her cheekbone and sighed, feeling low.

"What's wrong now?" Cash asked.

Callie turned toward him. "You're sure you know everything. I'm sure I don't know anything." She fingered her pearl necklace, smiling gently. "We're quite a pair."

◆◆◆

Callie came into the kitchen at 6:30 p.m. Césaire had everything under control. He even had Doc peeling potatoes, a thing that she'd negotiated to mollify him. Jean Luc was telling some kind of joke about girls from Newfoundland, who he called Newfies. It was better, she supposed, than breaking beer bottles on his forehead.

One of the specials tonight was cassoulet with game sausages, a thing that Césaire had reluctantly agreed to try as part of her carefully orchestrated settlement in the kitchen, and the room was filled with the fine smells of garlic, sausage and Césaire's other wondrous seasonings. It made her feel better.

The dining room was full, and Will was at the door, managing easily. She stopped to talk with regulars at table six: the Johnsons' son, Elliot, was home from college, and they were taking him and his new girlfriend out for dinner. There was some tension at the table, and Callie made a special effort to make them feel welcome.

At the lectern, she touched Will's arm. He was on the iPad. He closed it and looked up. "Thank you for taking over tonight," she said to him.

"My dear, you are not irreplaceable, although I must say, you look superb. Particularly under the circumstances."

"Don't remind me."

"Macer by day, maître d' by night," he whispered.

"Stop it," she hissed. In this room, at least, she could make the rules.

"So you know," Will said, "that detective, Ed Samter, has an eight o'clock reservation."

"Nice."

"Be careful what you say. Serving him dinner isn't a felony. But locking people up in your storeroom, especially after you spray them with bear mace, that's likely a gray area."

Callie smiled a perfunctory smile, adjusted his bow tie, then went up the stairs to the bar.

At the bar, Andre was partially unbuttoned, working on some kind of drink with an umbrella in it. Since when did she stock little paper umbrellas at her bar? Jill was giving him a hand since Cash was laid up, and they seemed to be working well together. Jill was tall and built like an athlete, a body builder. She had short, jet-black hair, and tonight she wore a simple black dress, highlighted by a flat-colored silver necklace with an oval-shaped pendant. She seemed to be smitten, which was especially surprising since, as long as Callie had known her, she'd never been interested in men.

Callie made her way to her table, where Jill had her San Pellegrino waiting. She looked across the bar area. Because the loft bar wasn't visible from the street, you had to know about it to find it. Over time, it had become a destination in its own right. It was crowded already, twenty-five to thirty people, more women than men, always a good thing. Many of them were young people who'd have a few drinks and move on for the evening. Perhaps fifteen percent of the bar crowd stayed for dinner. There were female executives and men in leather jackets. She saw two drag queens who came in regularly. They were drinking Andre's umbrella drinks. Sitting on the stool next to them was a man in a blue Patagonia jacket with a neatly trimmed beard and a nice smile. He was sipping a Red Hook and listening to their tall tales.

Down below, the restaurant was humming. Each of her sixteen tables and all eight booths were full. She could hear the ring of silver on plates, the whoosh of napkins unfurling, the unmistakable ping of wine glasses raised in a toast. Dinners were underway: she could smell the sauces and the seasonings. There was always a rhythm to it, an undercurrent she could hear, even feel. Tonight, the dining room was a fine, gentle purr. At the bar, it was louder, edgier.

She thought about the detective. She'd have to talk with him. He certainly wasn't coming for the food. Maybe she could duck it, just act like nothing was happening, or insist that she never mixed restaurant business with personal business. Right. She'd let it percolate, she was thinking, just as she noticed Christy and Avi Ben-Meyer take a seat at one of her bar tables.

Christy and Avi were regulars, in from Bainbridge Island maybe once a month. She'd been at Lakeside with Christy, though Callie hadn't known her well. Christy was a year behind her, and what Callie remembered was this sullen, driven workaholic, set on going to Stanford. Christy pretty much avoided the social scene. And she never seemed to care how she looked. At a school where people paid attention to fashion, Christy was an anomaly: jeans, a plaid shirt with silver buttons, and cowboy boots. In winter, she'd add a wool pullover. And she always kept her red hair cut short. Callie had liked that she was her own person, but she'd felt sorry that she didn't have any friends, and that Christie was all too often the victim of nasty, sometimes cruel pranks.

Callie guessed Avi had changed all of that. As far as she could tell, the charming Argentine gentleman had pretty much brought her back to life. Tonight, she looked great, dressed in—yes—a sleek, long-sleeved Max Gengos black silk blouse and a form-fitting skirt. Christy had the body for it, too, lithe and tall. And her gorgeous auburn hair was piled on top of her head in a way that accentuated her height. Her light-brown freckles were a subtle counterpoint to her stylishness; they made her youthful, even girlish.

Avi, as always, wore a dark-blue suit. In a city that defined casual, Avi defied the conventions. He was distinguished looking and he dressed formally. Occasionally, he dressed down in a dark-blue pinstripe suit, but that was rare. She'd once seen him wear an edgy silver Armani tie, but he explained that it was his birthday, and Christy had bought it for him because it complemented his white hair and made him look distinguished—her "éminence grise," as she put it—which was true. He'd laughed at that, then he lightly kissed his wife's hand.

Callie liked them. They were gracious and appreciative diners, and her servers liked to work their table. What she liked best was that Christy and Avi were not only plainly in love, but they always seemed to enjoy each other's company. Callie envied them that.

Christy Reyes, she reflected, heading toward the bar. Who would have thought?

Christy and Avi were sitting at the bar, looking across the brass-and-mahogany surface at Andre, the new bartender. They turned toward Jill, who was coming their way. "What's with the umbrellas?" Christy asked Jill, when she stepped in to take their drink order.

"Our new bartender makes drinks from all over. He puts the umbrellas in his Blue Mist."

"Blue Mist?"

"A favorite in Saigon, dating back to when the French were in Indochina," she explained, as if it were true. "It's made with Bombay Blue Sapphire gin, curaçao, French Marc de Bourgogne and some special ingredients. We're getting lots of compliments on it."

"I bet." Christy smiled. "I'm just not a risk-taker," she said, politely declining the Blue Mist. "I'd like the Glenmorangie Port Wood Finish. Neat, please."

"Coming up," Jill said. "And the regular for you, sir?" she asked Avi.

He nodded. Avi always ordered a bottle of their best cabernet, whatever Will, the sommelier, recommended.

When she was gone, Christy leaned in. "The bartender's a ringer."

"Yes. He doesn't miss a trick."

"The drink business is a little much." Though she liked the man's clothes, she had to say. His shirt was open. Something was going on on his chest. She'd just bet he had a great tattoo.

"He's bored."

She understood. "See anyone else?"

"Not yet. I'm sure there's at least two more. One in the kitchen, another on the floor or somewhere else."

"Check the messages?" Christy asked. "Maurie—"

"He'll text." Avi checked his phone, again. "Nothing yet."

"He's supposed to have something by six. It's what?"

"Seven ten…We'll give him until morning."

"Come morning, if it's not fixed, I want Casper on it first thing."

"The rules will change," he noted. "To treat an infected foot, Casper amputates the leg."

"Right." Christy pursed her lips, then added, "Right as rain."

Avi stood and extended his hand as Callie came over. She took it in both of hers as he kissed her cheek.

"Welcome," she said. "Your table is ready. You're by the window."

"Thank you," Avi said, as Callie got a kiss from Christy.

"Christy, you look beautiful," Callie said, stepping back. "It makes me happy to see you both looking so well."

"Callie, you are a gracious hostess, a splendid restaurateur, a diplomat sans pareil," Avi said. "And, as always, looking lovely."

Callie bowed slightly. "Did your uncle enjoy the Stonessence Syrah we recommended?"

"Yes, Nathan fell under the spell of this exquisite Washington State red. And he has a discerning palate." Avi kissed the back of Callie's hand. "Merci et bravo!"

Callie bowed again. "Let me show you to your table. I'll have Jill bring down your drinks."

"Can you spare us for a minute, sweetheart?" Christie asked Avi, then to Callie, "A minute? I'd like to ask a personal favor."

"Of course." Callie led her to a quiet corner beyond the bar.

"Avi has a birthday next month," Christy confided. "There's a rare imperial bottle of the nineteen forty-seven Château Cheval Blanc that he's been trying to buy for years. I'd like to give it to him, but I can't find it. Can I ask Will to help?"

"Absolutely. He loves this kind of project. If it's available, he'll find it."

Christy took Callie's hand. "Thank you. Avi will be thrilled."

♦♦♦

Just before 8:00 p.m., Doc fired a burst of mace into the little storeroom. Kelly started retching. Gray cried out something unintelligible. After a second short burst, Gray, the heavy hitter, crumpled.

Doc set up two fans, then opened the door and both dingy windows to air out the room.

At 8:30, he led Cash down the back stairs to the basement. Cash was in good spirits and moving reasonably well on his own. Both of his eyes were still black. His stitches were little black seams in patches of red.

Peering into the storeroom, Cash thought Kelly and Gray looked bad. Not as bad as he did, perhaps, but pretty much wasted. Gray's dark-gray, double-breasted suit and Kelly's smoke-gray pantsuit were wrinkled and soiled by tears, urine and spittle. Worse still, their faces were ravaged: eyes red and puffy, dirty, tear-stained cheeks, still fighting for each breath. The bear mace was a nasty thing, he knew. One time, he'd tried it in the woods, just to see how it worked. It was a windy day and a little gust blew some spray his way, just a downdraft. He'd spent an hour with his face in a stream before his eyes stopped itching and burning. And that was after he learned to breathe again. People like this could manage a beating, even a broken kneecap, but bear mace, that was crazy.

"Hey kids," Cash said, standing in the doorway. "Reap what you sow, eh?"

Cash moved in front of Gray and undid his gag. Gray gasped, taking long breaths. "Yo, amigo," Cash said. "I'm saying let bygones be bygones. I'm thinking even steven." Cash looked over at Kelly—she was taking frantic, heaving breaths, her eyes wild—then back to Gray. "So…answer a few questions?"

Gray took a long breath, wheezing, and nodded, eyes closed tight.

Cash stepped closer, betting that right about now, Gray was ready to rat out his mother. "Who hired you?" he asked.

"We don't know." Almost a whisper. "We get a text." He paused for a wheezy breath. "It gives us a phone number." Another breath. "The voice on the phone…it's scrambled."

"Who's your boss?"

A beat. "Mario."

"Mario who?"

"Don't know."

"What do you know?" Cash nodded at Doc.

Gray shook his head, a plea. "Two-fifty K up front. Two-fifty when it's done."

Cash let that simmer. It was bad, really bad. "Can I talk to Mario?"

"You'll never find him. No one can." Another labored breath. "We never even met him."

A dead end. This guy had nothing to tell. "What were you hired to do? Kill Daniel? Make it look like an accident?"

"Find him." Gray coughed. He couldn't stop. His face turned red. "Find him. He disappears. No mess."

"Who can I talk to? I want to cut a deal."

"I don't know." Another coughing jag.

"Give me that phone number."

He rattled off a number with a 310 area code, then worked to clear his throat. "You'll get a machine. Punch in six-oh-six." He paused, out of breath. "He'll call back on my cell."

Cash found the cell in the inside pocket of Gray's suit, used it to dial the number. When the machine picked up, all he heard was a beep. Cash punched in 606.

The call came in less than thirty seconds.

"Talk," the scrambled voice said.

"I have your people. I want to make a deal."

No response.

"We meet in New York City in two days. I'll bring Daniel Odile-Grand. Until then, you back off. I want a ceasefire."

"Why?"

"I need to talk with someone who can negotiate a truce. Find a way out that works for you and for us. If this continues to escalate, if we can't make the peace, we all get hurt. And I *can hurt you.*" A beat, setting up what was coming. "If you don't agree to this, I'm going to help Daniel with his story. By now, you know who I am. And believe me, I can help with this story. I know how to launder money through offshore shelf corporations. And I worked with a guy who can track that money. We know about Ares, about InterCap. I will pursue Daniel's story until I know just what happened, just where the money went, and where the bodies are buried." He let that sink in. And closing the deal: "Speaking of which, I knew Amjad Hasim in Amsterdam."

There was a long silence. "Deal."

"Will you call off your people?"

The strange, scrambled voice had hung up.

◆◆◆

Callie stopped at Detective Samter's table on her way out of the kitchen. Will had seated the detective in a booth, and he was enjoying Césaire's pâté de campagne, a generous country-style preparation with cornichons, pearl onions, capers and regional

French mustard. "Welcome," Callie said, more enthusiastic than she felt.

"My compliments to you, and to your chef," Samter said, lifting his napkin to his lips, which had traces of the grainy mustard. He stood, a gentleman, to shake her proffered hand. He was taller than she remembered, with a gray beard and cool, smart eyes.

"I'll tell him."

"Please, sit for a moment."

"Of course." Callie sat facing him.

He found her eyes. "Any word from your ex?"

She shook her head. Though his manner was low-key, behind his weathered face, Detective Samter was intense, especially for a Seattleite.

"This isn't making sense," he confessed, frowning. His eyes were on her, a hawk on a vole. "A guy doesn't just disappear from the hospital without a trace."

Callie bit her lower lip.

"May I speak frankly?" he said.

"Could I stop you?"

"Probably not." He looked away, finished off a cornichon, then looked her in the eye again. "I'm worried about you. You're not telling me what you know. I have enough of a sense about you to believe that there must be a darn good reason. And that scares me even more." He ran thumb and forefinger along his jaw. Callie recognized the coming-to-a-decision gesture. "So I'm going to make this offer. Tell me what you know, off the record, and I'll help however I can."

She wanted to tell him the whole story. She fingered her pearls. "Thanks, but no thanks," Callie said firmly.

"I'm running out of patience here. People say I'm your good cop and your bad cop rolled into one. I've been taking the high road with you."

"Are you threatening me?" she asked coolly.

"You bet."

She stood abruptly. "Enjoy your dinner." In the kitchen, she took slow breaths and prayed Cash's plan would wrap this up quickly.

◆◆◆

Avi and Christy were at their window table when the text came. Avi was eating the cassoulet, which he found excellent. The sausages, he explained, reminded him of the wild boar sausages he'd enjoyed so often in Argentina. Christy was just finishing the braised short ribs, which she had every time she came here. When asked, she'd say she just loved short ribs, she couldn't say why.

Avi dialed his cell phone, listened carefully to Maurie. He said only, "Wait," then broke the connection.

"Failure?" Christy surmised from his expression.

"Worse." He cut a piece of an elk sausage. "They have our people. They want to make a deal."

"A deal?" She looked around to make sure no one could hear. She smiled at Callie, who was making her way from the kitchen to the front entry. "Who the fuck do they think we are? Cretins? Idiots?"

Avi chewed his sausage. "Unusually good." He set down his knife and fork purposefully. "They propose meeting in New York City. Two days. They'll bring the Frenchman. They want us to back off until then."

"Two days?" She rolled her eyes. "Back off, huh? Here's what I know about that—" Christy took a beat to calm down. "You kill the snake that bit you."

Avi smiled, and then, with a slender forefinger, he began making circles on the linen tablecloth. This was going to be bad. "There's more. A lawyer in Amsterdam made inquiries about Ares,

And this man, her—what is your word?—gunslinger, yes. Maurie did the background work on this gunslinger. He's called Cash—I am not making this up. He made a name for himself as an import/export middleman—that is to say, he's smuggling without putting up his own money. He threatened to help Daniel finish his story. He says he can help him follow the money. This is, apparently, a very capable man who *knows where we live*."

Christy put her hand on his.

Avi covered her hand with his. "Maurie saved the best for last. This *Cash* says he knew Hasim. Maurie thought he was fishing."

"That changes everything."

"Yes, I'm afraid so."

"They have no idea, do they?"

"None. None whatsoever." Avi went back to his sausage. "There's an opportunity here."

"Start Casper." She pursed her lips. "Tonight."

"Casper's a closer." He shrugged, patted her hand. "He'll do what it takes. But there is risk. He'll attract attention."

She took hold of this, turning it over. When she was sure, she leaned in. "The only real risk is that these people learn that Hasim is still alive. Every minute this French peacock is out there, running his mouth, that risk increases. And with this Cash, he has expert help. A closer is what we need, what we need *right goddamned now*…" She smiled, giving Will a thumbs-up as he came by. "Pull the trigger," she added, almost a whisper. "Daniel and Cash. One price for both of them. Build in collateral damage."

Avi excused himself and went outside to talk with Maurie.

Christy watched him, lovingly, through the window. She kept her eyes on him as he rejoined their table.

"He's in play," Avi said.

"Good."

"He'll stir the pot, start things moving, tonight. Maurie con-curred—then once he's flushed out the Frenchman, we'll pay once for two kills. Collateral damage included."

Avi added, as he looked around the restaurant, "I'll miss the cassoulet here."

CHAPTER TEN

Cash gingerly negotiated the gentle curve of the loft staircase, steadying himself on the banister. It was 12:30 a.m. The bar was closed and Andre was wiping down the long brass surface, whistling some sea chantey. Jill sat on a barstool, mixing a fruity rum drink with herbs in it. Andre had told her how he'd learned about it in Haiti, and that they drank it at voodoo ceremonies. The only thing she knew for sure was that the Haitian herb drink made things glow, which was very cool.

Doc and Callie were at her table, drinking red wine. Doc, it turned out, had a good palate, and after she closed, Callie had started offering him her favorite wines to taste. It was, at least, a way to talk with him—even if he didn't say much. When he did talk, Doc was always thoughtful and precise about what he liked and why. Plainly, he cared about what he said and thought about it before he said it.

She'd learned that Doc and Andre worked around the clock when they were on a "project" for Cash. In between, however, Doc spent much of his downtime at the movies, and, she discovered, he also liked to talk about films from what he called the Golden Age—he said that, for him, it ran from *The Graduate* to *Heaven's Gate*, 1967 to 1980.

He rarely offered specifics about himself, but this evening, finally, in response to her direct questions, and her genuine interest, he told her about his scars. Doc explained that his bullet wounds were from a Taliban ambush during the war in Afghanistan.

Then, in his precise way, he explained how he got there. After Vietnam, he'd worked out a reenlistment contract, and the Marine Corps College Fund, in combination with the GI Bill, helped him earn a college degree. Afterward, he enrolled in Officer Candidates School. Callie was surprised to learn that Doc had been a Marine Corps lieutenant during the Gulf War. He'd made captain before being deployed to Afghanistan in 1991.

Doc even admitted, reluctantly, that he'd received the Silver Star for saving three soldiers who otherwise would have died, after he'd been wounded twice in an ambush. He'd been going back for a fourth man when two more bullets brought him down. Cash had carried him out. In the late nineties, Doc left the corps and went to work on a "project" with Cash.

Callie scolded herself for rushing to judgment about the man. His scars, his bearing, his reclusive nature, they weren't things to be afraid of. Doc was a seasoned warrior, a leader in combat, a man to rely on.

Callie was also surprised to learn that the horrible scar on his arm was from a bicycle accident in Los Angeles when he was eight years old. She'd imagined a knife fight or gruesome torture in captivity.

She saw Cash come in, waved him over. She touched Doc's arm and said, "Thank you for the conversation. It was helpful for me. I'd come to some wrongheaded conclusions, Captain."

Doc smiled, another first. "'Doc' is good."

She nodded. "Okay then, Doc."

Callie watched Cash making his way to their table. She felt a little better since Cash had been able to reach some kind of agreement with these people. She was hopeful, at least, that the earth was orbiting the sun again. Cash sat. His bruises were darker, red and purple, with lighter red patches around the stitches. The dark-purple areas around his eyes had new little yellow streaks.

"How are you feeling?" she asked.

Cash touched his face, his broken nose, sat down. "I'm okay." He looked at Doc, a question.

"On their way."

"Who?" Callie asked.

"Kelly and Gray."

Before she could ask, Doc explained, "They're packed in one of those big metal containers on a freighter bound for Mexico."

"What?"

"This trafficker moves illegals in...I didn't see why he wouldn't take people out."

Andre had that look; he was about to say something offensive.

She offered up a *please don't* look of her own, which made him wink before he said, "First time that egg-sucking leech ever took illegals *into* Mexico."

Callie ignored Andre, looked at Cash. "How do you manage this kind of thing?"

"Same way you order foie gras. You pay for it."

This wasn't working. She changed the subject. "So, do we have some breathing room?"

"I don't think so."

"I thought we had a truce."

"Uh-huh."

"I thought—"

"If it were me, I'd up the ante, strike tonight."

"Right." And nuke 'em to the Stone Age. She could feel her neck tightening.

"I'm hoping I'm wrong. But I want you out of here. You can stay on Doc's boat."

"What?"

"It's on Lake Union. Doc will set you up. Then I want Andre and Doc to sleep down here. Doc in the restaurant, Andre upstairs. I'll stay in the apartment. Tomorrow, I'm going to New York. I need some help."

"The Macher?" Andre asked.

"Yeah, it's been over a year since I saw him."

"Macher?" Callie asked.

"*Influential person, big shot*, in Yiddish," Andre explained. "His real name is Itzac, goes by Izzie."

"You understand Yiddish?"

Andre shot her a patronizing look. "Chérie...of course."

Callie frowned, turned to Cash. "Don't you think you're over-reacting a little? For God's sake, they said we had a deal."

"You're not paying me to argue."

"Right." She rubbed the nape of her neck, wishing now she'd talked to Detective Samter. She hadn't, though. She'd chosen Cash. Why? And why was she calling him that? She tried again, a little less strident. "Okay, please—why aren't we overreacting?"

"The conversation made me uneasy. When I talked with them they used high-tech scramblers. Whoever they are, they've put out more than half a million dollars to make Daniel disappear." He let that sink in. "Look, Amjad Hasim was among the most dangerous men I've ever met. I called an international lawyer in Amsterdam that I know. I asked him about Ares Limited, the company Daniel was checking out. He made some calls. He said it used to be a substantial trading company, import-export. Directed, apparently, from the Cayman Islands. It was liquidated more than a year ago. And now, there's no way at it. In short, it disappeared. They're very cautious, they're ruthless, and they've got money to burn. We have to assume the worst."

"Maybe the money doesn't mean anything to them?"

"It's too much money. That's my gut. Izzie knew Hasim. I met him, but the Macher did some deals with him. He owes me, and he'll help."

Doc, who had been listening quietly, nodded agreement, then stood. He looked at Andre behind the bar. *"Egg-sucking leech?"*

"You ever see that guy eat?" Andre nodded, emphatic. He had the trafficker nailed.

Callie watched Doc pucker his lips, try this egg sucking out. She gave up on both of them. She turned back to Cash. "Things don't always *have to* get worse," she observed, irritated. Tonight, working the restaurant, she'd had a glimpse of life as she knew it, and now these guys were dragging her back into the same awful black hole.

"I'm afraid things will get worse here, yes."

Callie pinched the bridge of her nose, took a slow breath. For the first time in her life, she wished she had a mantra or something. She looked at Cash, made an effort. "I'm thinking out loud. Follow this with me. You asked me to mace those people. You locked them in my cellar. For all I know, you tortured them. That was supposed to solve my problem. But no—now, yet again, things are getting worse. Every time you—what is your sports expression?—play offense, the problem gets bigger, harder to solve."

"With this kind of problem, things don't always go according to plan. Because you'd like it to be otherwise doesn't make it so."

"Please don't patronize me." He wasn't even listening. Her palms were starting to sweat. She tried again, "You're calling the shots. You confirmed that it's dangerous for Daniel if I talk to the police. You had my son leave the city. You kidnapped those people. Now you're telling me that I have to hide, you're taking over my restaurant. If you hadn't kidnapped them, maybe things would be better now?"

"Or maybe worse."

"I wonder if your predilection to see the worst is a self-fulfilling prophecy?"

"I wonder if your predilection to see the world as sunny, orderly, morally clear and governed by reasonable people ever cuts it outside of this restaurant?"

"Jesus." Callie looked away, composed herself. "Obviously, I'm not getting through." When he said nothing, she pinched the bridge of her nose again. "You're like this attack dog. Snarling and biting instinctively just because there's something out there to bite." She was up now, pacing from her table to the bar, then back. She leaned out over the railing, worked up, unsure what to do.

When she'd made her decision, she turned. "Okay, Terry, once again, I'll do as you ask. Every time I do that, though, I somehow come up short. I'm too slow, or too morally confused, or too Pollyannaish. Listen carefully—I'm following your advice. So damn it, this time, don't make me feel like it's not enough." She touched her cheek. It was warm, and she was sure there would be a blotch. Right. "I need a drink."

Andre had a knowing look. "I'm on that."

◆◆◆

Casper Pinder had a knack for blending in. He could go unnoticed at a formal diplomatic function, or at a shelter for the homeless. He stood five foot seven and weighed 140 pounds. His hair and eyes were brown, and he was thin, almost gaunt. He wore glasses as needed, and always dressed appropriately. His only distinguishing feature was a birthmark under his left arm.

He was nondescript, it was true, but that wasn't the reason for his chameleon-like adaptability. No, what made him so good at fitting in was thoughtful preparation, careful execution and his God-given talent. He had an easy way with people; he was a good listener, and confident enough to be self-effacing—Casper never drew attention to himself. On his best days, he was practically invisible.

Over the course of a project, Casper often became several different people. He had no difficulty shedding his skin, though almost always, his people used his affable nature to good advantage. He took pride in being an astute observer. Once he had the feel for a place, he'd think about who he should be, settle on a history. Finally, Casper would think through exactly how the person would look, how he'd feel about things, even how he'd move. His success, his art, if you will, was in the details. If necessary, he worked on it long before the job was done, then Casper might stay with it for several days afterward. He likened it to a movie director who insisted that the entire street be recreated in period, though his shot called for only one entryway.

Underneath his easygoing manner, beneath all of his many personas, Casper was, essentially, a ferocious, unforgiving man.

This was his legacy from his father, an Appalachian fire-and-brimstone preacher. Though Casper was not a religious man, at intense, challenging times, he turned to aspects of his father's teachings. When he needed to tap into normally inaccessible reserves of strength to accomplish a particularly difficult mission, he'd imagine himself as the instrument of a wrathful and vengeful God or a demon of Hell delivering souls to the fires of the vast bottomless pit. His father would have liked this deft, twisted construct, and would have understood the power that it imparted to him.

Tonight, he'd started out at the bar of Le Cochon Bronze. He wore jeans and a black crew-neck shirt under a blue, fleece-lined Patagonia shell. He'd grown a short black beard that he'd trimmed carefully. His shoes were sturdy, Timberland, with the Gore-Tex lining and hard-ridged rubber soles. He was ready to sail, go backpacking or eat dinner out. He liked working in Seattle. It was an easy place to go unnoticed. Casper liked that Seattleites were careful not to pry, overly polite and conflict avoidant. From what he'd seen, the Devil himself could join the Rainier Club, and if he wasn't too pushy and he paid his dues, no one would ever notice, or even ask just what it was he did.

He looked at his reflection in the mirror behind the bar. The stud in his left earlobe was a good bit for Seattle. Yeah. He touched it, thinking this was going to be hard. They'd brought him in late. The guy they were after, the journalist, was already hiding and surrounded by professionals. So he'd have to flush him out. He'd stir the pot, start things moving, and then he'd make his own reality. Until then, he was waiting, watching, killing time.

He smiled at the women next to him. They were drag queens, actually, who liked the bartender. He'd purposely sat next to them. He listened to them going on about Captain Smartypants, a gay vocal ensemble. They'd just come from a concert at Benaroya Hall. When they performed a whispered version of their favorite ribald lyrics, Casper nodded appreciatively, though he didn't care for the cheeky songs. And he didn't like the drinks with the umbrellas in them. They didn't belong in a place like this. Neither did the bartender. Nor the lanky guy with the wandering eye who lurked around the kitchen. He didn't like that guy. Un-unh.

After finishing a second Red Hook, Casper ate dinner. He'd asked for a quiet table, and he was seated toward the back, beside a window that overlooked a side street. He started with the seared foie gras—he wanted to try the pear sauce—and followed it with a recommendation from the waitress, the chef's new preparation of their bouillabaisse, featuring fresh, local lingcod. He found it splendid, as good as the bouillabaisse in Marseilles. He'd been tempted by the duck confit, one of the chef's signature dishes, but he decided that duck, browned, then stored for weeks in goose fat, was too rich for what might turn into a long evening. He was sampling the chocolate-covered profiteroles when his iPhone buzzed in his pocket.

He picked up the text message in the men's room, wood paneled with nice little white hand towels. On his way in, he'd noticed a basement door under the mahogany stairway. He'd thought the gentle curve of the stairway was a fine touch. Pocketing his phone, he decided he'd check the basement next. It was the perfect place to start things moving.

CHAPTER ELEVEN

The explosion tore a fifteen-by-twenty-foot hole in the dining room's wide-paneled mahogany floor. Tables and chairs were upended, tableware shattered. Bits and pieces of the wreckage were strewn on the floor, and some of the debris had fallen back down into the basement. The actual bar remained intact, but a cantilevered corner of the loft came unhinged in the blast, tilting down toward the dining room floor. Andre, who had been sleeping near the bar, had tumbled into a corner booth and, miraculously, walked away.

At first, Andre thought it was an earthquake. Then he saw that a fire had started in the basement. Smoke and tongues of flame were rising into the restaurant. The west wall was on fire. Andre hugged the south wall all the way to the kitchen. He didn't see Doc anywhere, but he found Cash coming down the back stairs. Together, they went looking for Doc. They found him in the front entry hall. He'd been shot at close range in the back of the head. They guessed that he'd been sitting in the restaurant when the arsonist came up from the basement. The killer was good. He'd taken Doc by surprise, no mean feat, and he'd used a silencer. Doc had certainly died instantly.

The basement door was unlocked. Whether someone forgot or the killer had opened it hardly mattered. Andre and Cash covered their faces with wet rags from the kitchen, then went down to the smoldering space.

In the basement, Cash found residual wax on a piece of yellow wood from a shelf in the furnace room. They suspected that disconnecting the fuel line from the furnace and leaving a burning candle on that shelf had caused the explosion. Since the commercial furnace used natural gas, the gas would have risen from the disconnected fuel line, accumulating at the ceiling. As more and more gas escaped, it would fill the furnace room, from the top down. By the time the leaking gas reached the burning candle, the arsonist would be long gone, and enough gas would have accumulated to ensure that the explosion would be formidable.

Cash called the fire department, then he and Andre removed the residual wax and Doc's body. They put Doc's body under a tarp in the back of Cash's pickup, then Cash called Will. He told him to come to the restaurant, deal with the firemen and the police, and wait for Callie's call.

The fire engines were there inside of five minutes. The explosion had blown out the new mullioned front window, leaving broken glass on the street. The firefighters pumped water through the blown-out window. By the time the fire was contained, the walls in the restaurant were charred and smoke-blackened; ash and smoke hung in the air, making it difficult to breathe. Six inches of water had pooled on the basement floor around the remains of the old furnace.

Le Cochon Bronze was closed until further notice.

◆◆◆

When the firefighters arrived, Cash and Andre disappeared. The men drove off in Cash's blue Dodge pickup, their friend's corpse under the tarp in back. They drove in silence straight to Doc's boat, the *Emily Cora*. She was a hardtop wooden yacht, a thirty-eight-foot Elco Cruisette cabin cruiser, originally built in 1938. Doc had carefully restored the boat, adding interior mahogany, and teak benches on the aft deck. The *Emily Cora* was temporarily moored on the eastern shore of Lake Union.

Cash woke Callie, who was sleeping below. "What's wrong?" she asked, putting on her robe, rubbing her eyes.

"Come on up."

"What?" she asked as soon as she was on the covered deck.

"Your furnace exploded. It wasn't an accident."

"How bad?" she asked.

"Bad. It blew the floor apart, started a fire. Doc was in the restaurant before it happened. He was shot in the back of the head."

"Oh no. No…" She started to cry. Cash held her; he didn't know what else to do.

"Please forgive me," Callie whispered, before she buried her face in his shoulder.

"It's not your fault," Cash said, meaning it.

She was weeping. He wondered if she was aware that her life, as she knew it, was over.

Andre came over.

Cash tried to step back.

Callie held him tight.

◆◆◆

They'd taken the *Emily Cora* out into Puget Sound. It was a clear night, and in the distance Callie recognized Restoration Point, the southeastern tip of Bainbridge Island. She remembered a holiday party there last winter.

Cash called Will, handed the phone to Callie, who was sitting beside him in the wheelhouse. She listened to him, taking stock of the damage, going over what needed to be done, then she assigned tasks. Her tone changed when Detective Samter came on the line.

"I'm on a boat in the South Sound," she explained, tense. "I don't know anything…It's three a.m.…I'm hours from the restaurant…I have no idea whatsoever if this is connected to Daniel. I don't even know what *this* is…Do we know it wasn't an accident?…I see…"

Cash mouthed, "Morning…"

"Can I meet you there first thing in the morning? If I hear from Daniel, you'll be the first to know…Eight a.m. In the meantime, if you need me for anything at all, you can reach me at this number…Yes…Thank you. Good night."

She handed Cash the phone, then closed her eyes, feeling frightened.

Beyond the point, the yacht veered southwest until they passed the sandspit at the northern end of Blake Island. As they turned south, Callie took one last look at the city. The downtown skyline, usually so familiar to her, was somehow otherworldly, little lights glowing like embers in an untended, distant fire.

Somewhere between Blake Island and the Kitsap Peninsula, they buried Doc at sea. Cash and Andre raised a glass to their friend. Their toasts were brief, but Callie watched in wonder at the depth of feeling on the faces of these hard men. Cash wore a worn Mariner's jacket; Andre had on some kind of French air force coat. Simply, respectfully, they laid their friend to rest in Puget Sound, like this was normal. When Doc was gone, Andre stepped up into the handsome wheelhouse and turned the *Emily Cora* toward Blake Island. Cash and Callie sat side by side on the open covered deck.

Everything, everything, had changed. Callie sensed that. And though she knew why, she had no idea what it meant. She realized, too, that this kind of intuitive, visceral knowledge was new and strange for her. It made her tense, and she was drifting, losing her bearings.

She tried to unwind. Mostly, she watched the cloudy night sky and listened to Cash. He was reminiscing, talking now about how he and Doc had moved carpets from Morocco to Spain to New York, years ago. Apparently, Doc had a thing for flamenco dancers. He used to disappear for days in Seville.

The way he said it made her realize how little she knew about Doc. Like her own conversation with Doc earlier—was it just hours ago?—it made her wonder what else she'd missed. "So you were close," she eventually volunteered.

"He was family."

There was a long silence. Callie watched the waves, black as night. "I'm afraid," she said.

"I am too."

"What are we going to do?"

"I can't let it go. As soon as you're safe, I'm going to New York City."

She saw him rub the back of his neck, a gesture he'd picked up from her.

"I still can't believe he's dead," Cash murmured.

Callie watched him now, his face still battered, colorful and misshapen. He seemed vulnerable in a way she'd never seen before, or noticed, anyway. It didn't make him edgy, though. She sighed. Every damned thing made her edgy. Life was changing too fast for her.

"What are they going to do?" she asked.

"I'm not sure. They put someone else on it, and this guy's not worried about breaking eggs. It's a big escalation—he's killing whoever's in his way, and he doesn't even try to make it look like an accident. No, they're past avoiding attention. I think they want to murder Daniel and anyone else who knows anything about his story. The money being spent must be substantial. I told them I'd help Daniel with his story. I told them

I knew Amjad Hasim. I must have touched a nerve. If we don't run, I think this person will kill us all." He frowned, listening to his own words.

"So?"

"We can run forever, or we can go after them. Find out what Daniel knows and get his damned story. It's got to be the story of the century with what they're willing to do to cover it up." He ran a hand through his sandy hair, which hung just over the collar of his jacket. "You can hide while I try to sort this out."

"I'd like to help. I'm not sure how—you're right about me; I don't do very well outside of my restaurant. But I'd like to try."

"Every time I think I see where you're going, you take this unexpected turn." He almost smiled. "Usually it's a U-turn."

"I'm not the most self-aware person in the world, if that's what you mean." She pulled back her hair, used a hairclip to hold it back, out of her eyes. She didn't get his point, and it made it hard for her to relax. "And I'm wound like a coil spring, in case you hadn't noticed."

"No, no, it's not that. What I mean is I think I understand why you're doing something, but then I have it all wrong. I was sure that you'd be done with me, that you'd go straight to the police. In fact, I was going to recommend it."

"I'll help. I mean that." She touched his hand.

He took her hand in both of his, a kindness. "I think you and I are—I dunno—bad chemistry. I listen to you and then I'm way too cautious, far too slow. Don't worry, we'll work out the money. And I'll give you back the deed to your restaurant. I'm sorry about what's happened. It's my fault. Go to that detective—"

She leaned in, touching her lips to his ever so briefly, quieting him. Then she lowered her head, suddenly aware of, and confused by, what she'd done.

Cash frowned, puzzled. "That's what I meant about U-turns."

Callie stepped back. "Sorry," she said. "I don't even know why I did that. It didn't mean anything." She turned away, embarrassed.

"Please don't worry about it…It's been a hard day."

"Right…Okay," she said, but she was already worried. Why had she kissed him? An overture? A thank-you? An unthinking goodbye to Doc? She had no idea.

No, Callie had no idea whatsoever why she'd done it or what it meant.

Andre, coming to ask a question, had watched in wonder. Then he exhaled and smiled.

When Callie looked at him, flustered, he asked, "Yo, bad kitty. Ready to check out my tattoo?"

"Not just yet," she answered, cold, already mortified about what she'd done.

CHAPTER TWELVE

The sun was up when Cash dropped Callie in the alley behind Le Cochon Bronze. From the kitchen, she could see right through her burned-out, blown-up restaurant. Wisps of smoke still hung in the air, and inside the space, the morning sun was hazy, reddish brown. Some of the dining area just wasn't there, and she could see where flames had blackened sizable areas of the walls. The smoky haze, the official-looking people milling about, and the randomly scattered, charred debris brought back TV news coverage of terrorist events. It was nothing like the warm, welcoming place she'd so lovingly created. She felt suddenly cold. This was where she'd been and done her best. But something had shifted. She'd lost her bearings. Today, she was unsettled, disoriented, here.

She wasn't sure what to expect. She had to be there to deal with Detective Samter, her contractor, the insurance people, the fire department, and so on. Cash had refused to drop her off until he saw Detective Samter, sitting at a table he'd resurrected near her blown-out front window. Cash had helped her work out what she'd say to the detective. Still, she was nervous.

They'd stayed up most of the night, making their plan. Cash decided he'd stay an extra day in Seattle. He'd drop Callie to meet with the detective, pick up Daniel, then everyone would hide on the boat, where they'd put together as detailed a picture as they could of Daniel's story. Somewhere among what Daniel had discovered, there was something he'd missed—something someone would kill all of them to protect. Cash and Andre were sure they could work with whatever Daniel had found, fill in some of those blanks.

They'd meet with Samter again with Daniel, as soon as they could organize that—the detective would demand that much, at least. And they'd tell him what they could. Cash thought that Samter would see that their interests were aligned—finding and bringing down the people behind this—and that once he heard their story, and learned about the back channels they had access to, he'd be a willing partner. If all went as planned, Cash would go on to New York City. He'd stay in touch with Samter, work with him as they learned more. Samter had access to all kinds of international databases that might be useful. Andre would hide Callie and Daniel.

When their conversation finally wound down, they went below and removed a panel in the galley that hid Doc's weapons cache. Cash and Andre took shotguns with shortened barrels, as well as handguns. Andre also took a state-of-the-art sniper's rifle. He brought it to the aft deck, where he mounted it on a bipod, then stowed it under the wooden bench seat.

Cash showed Callie how to use a handgun, which he insisted she carry in her purse at all times. Callie just nodded—yes, she'd do what he said—confused that she was taking direction from him, that she was even considering carrying a gun.

She'd kissed him the one time, and they'd gone on like it never happened. It had happened, though, remarkably—no—unfathomably, for her at least. It wasn't like she kept thinking about him. Or picked him apart, like she did with most men she found attractive. She'd picked him apart long ago, soon after he became her bartender. She wondered why she'd done that. She'd never found him attractive—he was charismatic, sure, but hardly her type.

And his presence, his physicality, even his touch, made her antsy. At the time, it had been easy to detail his shortcomings.

Callie remembered how he'd hit on her early on when he was tending bar at her restaurant. At the time, he was seeing at least two other women that she knew of. It never even crossed her mind to go out with her bartender. Her bartender? A former smuggler? She politely, but firmly, said no. It hadn't helped that he'd ended up with a twenty-three-year-old French sculptress who showed her work at a prestigious local gallery. The girl was a baby—a very sexy, precocious baby with red streaks in her blond hair, a chain hanging from her ear, and a gold ring in her left eyebrow. When they'd come to the restaurant for dinner on his night off, it made Callie uncomfortable. She winced at the memory.

She wondered if she'd lost her mind, kissing him like that. What had she been thinking?

Callie frowned, coming back to the here and now. Cash had explained that there was some risk, showing up at the restaurant. Doc's killer could be waiting, watching. He'd asked her to work it out with Detective Samter for the police to stay at the restaurant until at least noon, when he'd be back to pick her up. While she figured out what would become of her restaurant, Cash was going to move Daniel.

At the entry, Callie stepped out front to pat Lulu. She brushed some ashes and a piece of glass off Lulu's back. Her little bronze pig, at least, was fine—nose up, standing proud. Callie waved at Will, then headed toward Detective Samter. He was frowning, eyes closed, massaging his temples.

"Bad cop?" she asked when she arrived.

He opened his eyes, set his hand on the table deliberately and stood. He pulled up another chair for her, then sat back down, stern-faced. "You need a friend, lady. And I'm a good friend.

But unless you meet me halfway, I'm going to be the worst cop you ever met."

They'd anticipated that he'd be frustrated, even angry, with her. "I'm ready to talk."

"I'm listening" was all he said. The lines in his weathered face deepened as his cool gray eyes laser-focused on her.

She lowered her head, took a slow breath; she was learning. She looked up at him. "Here's what I know. Daniel came back to my apartment from the hospital. I told him he could stay at Will's friend's apartment." Callie pointed out Will, who was overseeing the cleanup. "After one night, he was moved. I don't know where." She shrugged. "I didn't want to know."

"So you lied to me."

Callie nodded. "It was a hard choice, but I had to. You said he wouldn't be safe in prison, and I couldn't get him to leave."

"And?"

"People came here. Asked about him. But by the time they showed up, I didn't know where he was. And I don't know about this." She waved her arm, encompassing what was left of her restaurant.

"People? What people?" His tone had an edge now.

"Young couple. Very well dressed. Looked like they were from LA." She sighed. "Will said they looked like movie people. I wouldn't know. Kelly and Gray, they called themselves."

"Did they threaten you?"

"Not exactly. It was like the movies, you know. Nothing direct. Nothing I could prove. But sinister. He'd say that my restaurant was underinsured. You know, veiled threats. I hired good help who backed them off."

Plainly disappointed, Samter said, "Why didn't you tell me any of this?"

The trick to this lying thing was to keep as much to the truth as possible; Cash was right about that. Still, it worried her that she was good at it. "Detective, from the start, Daniel made me promise not to bring the police in. Given his history and the danger he's in, you can understand all of the reasons why. I made that promise. And I keep my promises. It's who I am." She nodded. This, at least, was true. "Maybe I should have told you..." Her expression turned melancholy. "Sorry, I just couldn't."

He raised his thumb and forefinger, almost touching, in front of her face. "I'm this close to arresting *you*."

Way too close; this was scaring her. She took a calming breath. "Look, it's too late to fix what I did, and I'm telling you now."

Samter was frowning again. "Have you heard from Daniel?"

"No. Not yet."

"What does that mean?"

"I'm trying to reach him. I think I can do that by tonight. When I do, I'll arrange for you to talk with him. He'll tell you what he knows. That's what you wanted, isn't it?"

Disappointment morphed into something like suspicion. He was awfully intense for this town, she thought. "It's the only way you stay out of jail. I mean that."

"Yeah, I get that."

Samter leaned in. "You think this was an accident?" he asked.

"I don't know. What do you think?"

He was glaring at her now, a Terminator-like glare, as if he was processing what was going on in her head. When he was finished processing, he nodded. "I think your ex is on to something consequential. Important enough that dangerous people want to kill him. But they don't know where he is. And they're going to keep the pressure on *you* until they find out." He leaned in even closer. "I also think you know more than you're telling me. And we both know that it's pretty unlikely this was an accident."

Maybe she wasn't so good at lying after all. But here came the part she'd worked on. "Yes, I do know more than I'm telling you. But I'm going to ask you for twenty-four hours."

"To do what?"

She held his cool gray eyes. "Look, you can't imagine how uneasy—how anxious—it makes me to hide anything from you. If you knew me, you'd know that that's absolutely true." She hesitated. "But I have to find Daniel and talk with him first. I think I can find him tonight. Here's what I propose. When I find him, I'll arrange for you to meet with him. Right away. Latest, tomorrow morning. Off the record. At that meeting, you'll hear everything we know. Everything."

"And why would I agree to that?"

"Honestly, you have two choices: Agree to twenty-four hours and hear everything, or—well—arrest me and hear nothing." She shrugged, unsure where that came from. *Arrest me?* My God, had she actually said that? She felt a tremor in her right hand.

He sat back. "Lady, you're way out on a limb, and I'm more than a little worried that you've become too smart by half. And when I worry, I get agita…" He leaned in. "When, Ms. James, can I expect to hear from you?"

She put her unsteady hand under her right thigh to settle it. "Before nine tomorrow morning."

He watched her. "Something about this is off…and it's irritating."

Callie took another breath. "Let's try again. Twenty-four hours?"

"You have until midnight tonight to make that call. Arrange the meeting. I should be locking you up. But my uneasy gut says you *will arrange* this meeting. So reluctantly, I'm trusting my instincts. Until midnight tonight. Callie, you have one last shot with me. *Don't blow it.*" The detective stood. "Do you still have good people watching your back?"

Callie nodded.

The detective stood. "I'll keep a man here until I hear from you. Here's my number if you have even a hint of trouble before then." He set a card on the table.

"Thank you." Callie stood opposite him, hands clasped behind her back.

"I'm sorry about your place. Lucky no one was hurt."

"Yes," she lied, as he walked away.

◆◆◆

Callie felt safe. Detective Samter was gone, but another policeman was hanging around, and a firefighter was there, waiting to ask her questions. Her contractor, Tony, had a crew working already, and she spent a few minutes with him, figuring how long it would take to open her doors again. When he assured her it would be just a few months, a little light broke through the dark clouds hanging over her. But when she looked around her restaurant, she could see Doc lurking near her kitchen door, and she felt awful again.

Next, she and Will met with the firefighter. He was slight, clean-cut and cheerful. Yes, they'd do a thorough investigation, but so far there was no hard evidence of foul play.

Will introduced her to Max Stone, an independent insurance adjuster, then left them alone. Max had neatly parted hair. He wore a suit that probably came with two pairs of pants, a white shirt, and he had three silver ballpoint pens in his shirt pocket.

"Do you need me for anything now?" Callie wasn't ready for this. She was tired, and very low. Will could handle it.

Max handed her a form and one of his silver pens. "Please read this, and if it's okay, just sign at the bottom. We can talk after you review our estimate."

Callie skimmed the form. It confirmed the time of the accident and described the extent of the damage. He'd actually done a pretty good job of describing it, which only made her feel worse.

"Keep the pen, ma'am. It's our way of saying thanks for the business."

Callie looked at the silver pen with the soaring black bald eagle, the Stone family logo. They'd been in business for three generations, he explained. She nodded thanks, preoccupied now. She had to talk with Will; she'd been avoiding it. He was near the kitchen, dealing with the electrician.

Out of the blue, she missed Lew and wanted to hear his voice. But she knew better. If she tried to contact him, Cash would be angry, rightly angry with her, for endangering her son. And it would only worry Lew. She'd ask Cash to call Ed Rosen later, tell him there'd been an accident and not to tell Lew about it yet. He wouldn't mention Doc. Cash would tell him that they'd need to stay away for at least a few more days. He'd be in touch soon. Callie rubbed the back of her neck. She was tied up in knots.

She stopped to talk with Tony again, asking him to put whatever art she could still salvage in the kitchen. She'd have to organize the insurance claim. She looked at Will, handling everyone so effortlessly. She couldn't put it off any longer. Callie signaled him.

Will took her arm, led her to the kitchen. "I'll finish up here," he offered. "You need sleep."

"Bad news," she said.

"You can say that again." Will looked out toward the restaurant.

She put a hand on his arm. "Will, please sit," she said. And when he did, apprehensive—something about her tone—she adjusted his ever-present bow tie, buying time. "It was no accident.

Doc was shot and killed here last night. Cash and Andre carried him away."

Will dropped his head into his hands.

Callie looked around. She could smell the smoke, taste it. Everywhere she looked there were tiny pieces of her carefully constructed life. All the king's horses and all the king's men…

◆◆◆

At 11:00 a.m., Cash called Will, who brought Callie down to the alley, where he was waiting beside his truck. He spotted her in the doorway while he was patiently trying to manage a scruffy panhandler who wanted to sell him a shoeshine. When the man knelt and applied his rag to Cash's old boots, Cash firmly asked him to move on.

Cash was glad to see her. He'd been thinking about Callie. How she'd kissed him. It wasn't that he got romantic, or even a little sweaty, thinking about her. No, he didn't think about her in that way. And God knows, she wasn't really interested in him. She wouldn't even acknowledge what had happened. But it had. And the ice was thawing. Which could only help with what was coming.

In the truck, Cash asked her about the restaurant. He thought it made her feel better to talk about it, helped her unwind anyway. Her contractor had a crew on site already. Le Cochon Bronze, she told him, would open its doors again in ten to twelve weeks.

"You have a chance here to do something great," he said.

"Uh-oh. Like what?"

"Change the name of your restaurant."

"What's wrong with Le Cochon Bronze?"

"Nothing. It's just too fancy. Do you have any idea how many hours your bartender spends explaining how there's this bronze pig in the Pike Place Market, and 'le cochon bronze' is French for 'bronze pig,' and no, the market pig is Rachael and the restaurant pig is Lulu, and blah blah blah…"

"I like Le Cochon Bronze."

"How about just the Bronze Pig? You know, in English."

"Are you kidding? It's a French restaurant."

And that, Cash knew, was that.

She said her insurance would cover the costs of reopening, even if there had been foul play. The one thing that would cause a problem was if she became a suspect. But because of the success of her restaurant, and her history, the police and the insurance company agreed that she was not a suspect now, nor was this likely. Yes, her policy included business interruption coverage, so that she would be able to pay her staff during the time they were closed. She'd planned to do that anyway; it was the right thing to do.

As she talked, Cash drove in circles, doubling back several times before ending up on Third, two blocks east of where they'd started. Only now, they were headed north. He parked the truck at Portage Bay, near a rowing club. He held back a smile when she told him that it was the first time she'd ever seen the underside of the University Bridge. At the dock, a twenty-two-foot Bayliner with an eighty-horse Johnson was waiting.

As they navigated the Bayliner across Lake Union, then through the Lake Washington Ship Canal toward Puget Sound, Cash had her detail her conversation with the detective. He agreed that it had gone well enough, but reiterated that they absolutely had to set a meeting with him tonight, and they damn well better have something for him at that meeting. She talked about Will, about Doc, about her own sense of loss. It was somehow global. And she said she couldn't shake it.

"It's not like I understand it." Callie shook her head. "I just feel empty and low."

"Does that surprise you?"

"No. It's not that. I expected to feel lousy, you know, just shut down. The wind has been knocked out of me; I recognize that. But this is something different. Something new for me. It's like some kind of big change is starting. I can't think clearly about what's going on. With me, with the restaurant, with anything. It's like I can't focus. And the old tricks aren't working. I can't even shift into restaurant mode. I'm all over the place, floundering, out of control."

"What they did, it's a violation, a shock to your system. You need time to get your balance. Until then, cut yourself some slack."

"Sometimes I can't sleep, you know, and I don't know why. It's usually when things are going great. So I tell myself, just give it time, you'll figure it out. And I never, ever do." She rubbed the back of her neck. "I bet you sleep every night."

"Usually. I once fell asleep waiting in line for a movie."

"I envy you that."

"If I ran a fancy, high-pressure restaurant operation as well as you do, I wouldn't sleep at night either."

"That's the first nice thing you ever said to me." Callie worked on her neck, pensive.

Cash watched her. She had been violated—Doc, the destruction of her restaurant. Her sense of order and fair play had been upended. Callie needed to put some order to it. That's how she was. Some things, though, you never could master. You had to let them cool down. He'd learned about that in the Marines. At least she was talking more easily with him. And he wasn't holding back as much. Change the name of her restaurant? My God, had he actually suggested that?

"Who else did you talk with?" he finally asked. It was time to get back to work.

"Fireman, window guy, insurance adjuster, lawyer, my State Farm agent's assistant— I dunno—it's kind of a blur."

"Let's go over it."

She gave him the blow-by-blow. Then he patiently and methodically made her go through each and every conversation she'd had. Describe every person she'd met. When she snapped that she knew her contractor, he asked, "Was it him, or someone in his company?"

"I recognize my contractor," she assured him. She made an effort and explained, "I've worked with him for ten years."

Cash slowed the boat. These people were just too smart to let her walk away without a sure way to find her. "Stand up."

"What?"

"Someone figured out how to plant something that would send a signal."

He checked her, head to toe. When he was finished he added, "Let me see your purse."

"Why?"

"You're forgetting something." He dumped the contents of her purse on the seat, everything from Kleenex to checks to lipstick to the handgun he'd made her carry.

"That was organized," Callie muttered. She stared at the mess. "Satisfied?"

He picked out the Stone Insurance Adjusters, Inc. silver pen, unscrewed it. Inside, he found a tiny button-shaped microtransmitter set in the elongated top of the ballpoint pen. He showed it to her.

"Damn it," she said. "I wouldn't have thought of that in a million years."

"Yeah. He's good. What'd he look like?"

"The insurance guy? He looked just like what you'd expect—you know, clean-cut, ordinary. He certainly didn't seem scary or dangerous."

"The good ones never do." Cash pulled alongside a purse seiner moored at Fisherman's Terminal. He wedged the transmitter into an indentation in the hull of the commercial fishing vessel. "We'll lose him easily from here." He gave her a phone. "Call Will on my cell. Tell him about the insurance adjuster. He won't be back. But he should know."

Callie made the call but handed Cash the phone. "Please?" She looked up, wincing when she saw his battered face.

Cash explained the situation to Will, who understood. "Be careful," he added, then he turned off the phone. "We've got precious little time," he said to her. When Cash slowly pressed the red throttle forward, the Bayliner moved through Salmon Bay. Beyond the locks, the boat planed, then sped across Puget Sound.

Callie stood above the windshield and leaned into the wind. Her hair blew back, the wind washing the sadness and the worry from her face.

Cash watched her unwind, try a rueful smile.

◆◆◆

The *Emily Cora* was tied to a buoy on the secluded western side of Blake Island's little sandspit. It was drizzling, the sea and sky shifting through various shades of gray. In the summer, the buoys, anchored offshore to secure visiting boaters, were taken early. Depending on the tides, larger boats anchored offshore and smaller craft were pulled up onto the spit. People occasionally camped right on the beach. On this fall day, the other buoys were all free. On the spit, there were only three wet teenagers playing hooky, huddled around a beach fire.

Blake Island was a state park. It had a harbor on the eastern shore, designated picnic areas for boaters, trails and a large population of deer. Callie had once heard a story about a soldier who dropped a grenade down a well and destroyed the island's water supply. It didn't sound true to her. In any event, the island was not developed, and behind the sandspit they were out of sight.

Callie was surprised to find Daniel sitting on the covered aft deck. Cash, she realized, must have brought him to Doc's boat while she was at the restaurant, then Andre must have taken the boat here.

Daniel looked better. His face, at least, was not as swollen, or as bruised, as Cash's yellow-and-plum-colored eyesore. Daniel's leg was in a cast and his left arm still hung in a sling.

"I'm sorry," he said, surprising her even more.

"Jesus God. I wish I'd never seen you," she shot back.

"Ma chérie, like other unwanted things between us, this cannot be undone." He could maneuver his injured arm enough to show his left palm now, which he did, along with his right, to make his point.

"Are you aware that wherever you go you leave behind this great wake of pain and destruction?" Callie turned away. "Of all the gin joints in all the towns…"

Andre pointed a finger at her, appreciative. She thought he even winked. Daniel didn't get the *Casablanca* reference.

"Let's move on," Cash intervened. "I'm going after whoever's behind this. Daniel, I want your help."

"I want my freedom."

"Buddy, right about now, I have no time to negotiate. Listen carefully. You are responsible for what's happened. And now, you are going to help me any way that you can." This wasn't a question. He turned to face him. Daniel was sulking. Cash waited, an awkward silence, until Daniel nodded agreement. "And then, and only then, I may give you the story."

Daniel perked up at this. "So, then, it is a trade?"

"If I can figure this out, and stop these people—"

"I like this approach," Daniel interrupted, smiling at Callie as if he'd brokered a good deal.

"You're going to have to convince me before you write word one," she said.

"Why is this?"

"Because you're a menace to everyone around you. You aren't even aware that you put other people at risk. So, like a child, you need someone to set limits for you." Callie was standing over him, aware, finally, how very angry she was with him. She leaned in closer. "I'm taking that on. You're not hurting anyone else I know. Ever. I mean that." And she did. She knew, too, that this was her job—though she was surprised that she knew it.

"You are so very quick to lay the blame. Mon Dieu, you do not know many things. How old must you be before you can accept other people's mistakes? You are not the judge, not the jury—"

Callie slapped his face, a quick, sharp crack. She was even more surprised than he was. "Enough, Daniel. That's enough," she cautioned, ice cold *and* red hot.

Andre was watching her, plainly pleased. "There you go."

Daniel touched his red cheek. "Incroyable," he muttered.

"*Unbelievable?* I should have done that fourteen years ago," Callie said ruefully. And after a beat: "Daniel Odile-Grand, you should be *thanking* me." And she meant that. Under his posing, Daniel *was* child-like. He relied on other people to take care of him. Usually, they were younger women who idealized him. She'd had the job for a while. It had taken a whole year of therapy to put that together.

Cash broke the tension. "Callie, we can hide you in a safe place. Keep you out of it. I think you should step away."

"We've discussed this. I'll help however I can."

"This isn't what you hired me for. I can't be responsible for you."

"I understand." And she did.

Cash hesitated, waiting for her to say more. When she didn't, he asked, "Why are you doing this?"

"Because I'd rather help than do nothing."

"What does that mean?"

She thought about his question. "It's just—I dunno. It's right. A good man was killed in my restaurant. That's my home, it's where I live. I can't walk away from that." She raised a palm, a subconscious Daniel-like gesture. "I just can't."

Cash touched her forearm. "Your sense of *rightness* can lead you to bad decisions. Don't make that mistake again. Consider this carefully."

"At the top of my list of things that I don't like about myself is when I don't know what I'm feeling. Right now, my feelings are pretty much inaccessible. They're, at best, murky, like sludge. So when I do feel something and I'm clear about it—even if that feeling is as prosaic as knowing that a thing is right—I need to listen to that. Do you understand?"

"I think I do, but given our history it's hard for me to trust your sense of rightness."

"Damn it, Cash, as I said, there are things about myself that I don't especially like. In spite of them, I *do* like who I am. It's what gets me through the night. I'm doing this. It's who I am." She shrugged. "This decision is made."

He watched her, stern lines in his eggplant face.

"How can I help?" she asked.

Cash massaged his temples with his forefingers. "Okay...Let's see what Daniel knows, then we'll sort out who does what." He turned to her ex-husband. "From the beginning."

"Certainement." Daniel nodded, pleased to be center stage. "From the top, eh..." He sat up straight, adjusting this and that until he had everyone's attention. "So, we begin in the spring of two thousand fifteen...I was doing the story on the disappearance of weapons from the Soviet stockpile. Two nuclear suitcase bombs, developed by the Soviets in the sixties and seventies, went missing. You see, they were noticed missing after the breakup in nineteen eighty-nine. And then, it is said that they were improved, upgraded—vachement plus fort."

"Much, much stronger," Callie translated.

"Oui." Daniel nodded. "In two thousand fifteen, there was a rumored sale of an arsenal of weapons, including the two upgraded devices, for more than three hundred and fifty million dollars. Can you imagine?" When no one said anything, he went right on. "As you must see, this was the big league." He raised his palm. "An informant led me to Amjad Hasim, a Lebanese weapons dealer operating out of Amsterdam. I could prove nothing. On a hunch, I asked my friend, a computer—how do you say?—hacker?"

"There are hackers and crackers," Cash said.

"I do not understand."

"A hacker is a skilled computer programmer. A cracker tries to gain unauthorized entrance. A cybercriminal."

"Ah yes. My friend, she was, I fear, the cybercriminal. But she does this favor for me. You know?"

When Cash nodded, he continued. "So, this woman, she got into the Hasim bank accounts. The personal bank accounts, they were curiously inactive, except one large deposit—two hundred thousand dollars, sometimes two hundred fifty thousand—every quarter from a small bank in Amsterdam. After cracking into this bank, my friend, she discovers that this deposit is from a Global Trade account. Global Trade is a trading company with offices all over the world, including Amsterdam. Upon further investigation, she finds that Global Trade is owned by Ares Limited, another international trading company."

"And just what did you learn about Ares?" Cash asked.

"Not nearly enough. It was an offshore shelf corporation, held by the single corporate shareholder."

"What?" Callie asked. She'd forgotten just how good Daniel was at this kind of reporting. And she wanted to keep up.

Cash explained, "For a fee, certain offshore banks will provide a client with an existing corporation whose true ownership is not reported in public records. These corporations are set up by the bank and left 'on the shelf' for ready use if a client requests one. The client's name need never appear on any documentation."

"How do you know this?"

"I have several," he answered, stone-faced. "Which bank?"

"The Cayman Islands Bank of Trade."

"The client, I presume, was untraceable."

"Oui, absolument. The true owner is nowhere. Invisible."

"What does that mean?" Callie asked Cash.

"It means that Ares could do business worldwide and the beneficial owners would have complete anonymity. In two thousand sixteen, the Panama Papers detailed how a Panama-based law firm created over two hundred thousand offshore entities for wealthy clients. These documents revealed how rich people and companies all over the world have set up shelf corporations to avoid paying taxes or to hide questionable transactions."

"Is this legal?"

"Yes. Confidentiality of client information is protected in the Cayman Islands and other offshore secrecy jurisdictions by common law. Shelf corporations buying real estate with cash has become such a common form of money laundering that the Treasury Department just stepped in to regulate it in New York City and Miami-Dade County. In Manhattan, in all-cash purchases of three million dollars or more, the identities of the actual buyers must be reported. Just so you understand the enormity of the problem, in the second half of two thousand fifteen, in Manhattan alone, one thousand forty-five residential sales cost more than three million. In total, it was about six-point-five billion."

"And just how do you know this?" Callie asked, surprised. "Even the numbers?"

"It's my business to know this. You read *Gourmet* magazine, or maybe *Bon Appétit*. I read PropertyShark."

"I see…What was I thinking?"

Cash turned back to Daniel. "What did you do?"

"My friend, she could track it no further. We were stuck. Then, in two thousand sixteen, Amjad Hasim was killed in a car bombing. His part in my story died with him."

Cash nodded.

Daniel leaned in again. "A year goes by. Like this." He snapped his fingers. "I do my stories about le terrorisme. About ISIS. This is when I am paid the advance to do a story on money laundering. They were interested in terrorists and terrorism. How they moved money, bought weapons, and so on. This, as you know, is now hot." It came out *ot*. "I was looking for the angle—you know?" Daniel kept them waiting, eyebrows up. "It struck me that many of the Hasim weapons must have ended up in terrorist hands. And we had a lead on the money—we knew that Ares was based in the Cayman Islands. Having the new technology, and more experience, my friend—le hacker, le cracker, whatever the hell— she went back to various Ares accounts around the world. She was able to trace money going *from* Ares accounts in Russia, Austria and Morocco to the Cayman Islands Bank of Trade in two thousand fifteen and two thousand sixteen."

"And then?"

"Nothing." Daniel paused. "That is, until I had my big idea." He stopped.

"Yes?"

"We focused on money moving out from the Cayman Islands Bank of Trade. It took months. But we found there were several large transfers in two thousand sixteen to a correspondent account at Credit Suisse in Guernsey—"

"That's another secrecy jurisdiction," Cash explained to Callie.

"Exactement. From Guernsey, there were several transfers to the account of an investment company called InterCap, another offshore shelf corporation, this one in Saint Kitts and Nevis. These transfers were done without any client identifier on the wire documentation itself." Daniel sat back, pleased.

"And?"

"So my cracker, she is monitoring InterCap, and she picks up a regular data packet going from InterCap, Saint Kitts and Nevis, to a server in the Maritime Building in Seattle. This data packet, she comes three times every week to the same office. It is always encrypted…incompréhensible…But then, the data packet, she stops, comme ça—" Daniel snapped his fingers again.

"And?"

"That's all. We are not magicians. I was hoping to find out more about InterCap's wires, its business in Seattle, when you foolishly kidnapped me."

"But the wires to InterCap could have been from any client at the Cayman bank."

"Of course, this is possible."

"So you don't know anything else?"

"I know that they are trying to kill me for what I do know."

"Do you know anything about InterCap?"

"It, too, was liquidated two years ago. Just after the data packet, she stopped, InterCap disappeared. Poof...gone. Now, we can't even find it."

"You *are* a doofus," Andre muttered.

Cash stood, started pacing. "Okay. Andre, you and Callie check out Hasim. I know some people in Amsterdam who will help. If you're lucky, we can put together his last arms deal, follow the money. I'll get you started. Then I'll find out about InterCap, see what it did, who owned it, and so on. Daniel, I want you to leave us alone, but be available for questions. We'll reconvene tonight. Tomorrow I go to New York City. I called Izzie in Amsterdam. Andre, I gave him your cell, and he's expecting to talk with you today. He'll be able to help us with Hasim. He'll fly in to meet me in New York."

"I am the professional," Daniel explained. "You see—"

"We've got this," Cash interrupted. "You've done your part. Sit tight. Just be there if one of us has a question."

"*Sit tight?* What is this?"

They ignored Daniel, who let it go, though his expression was petulant. Callie touched his shoulder, surprising him, then moved on.

"What can I do?" she asked Cash.

"You help Andre. Listen in. Do what he asks." Cash stopped, looked at her. "As Andre turns over the rocks Amjad Hasim hid under, I want you to worry about what could go wrong. In spite of your predisposition to look on the bright side, I think you could be good at this."

"My what?"

"Bad choice of words. Sorry."

"That's another first."

"Callie, if you want to help, don't make a federal case out of every damned mistake I make. Okay?"

"Okay." She raised both palms. "I'll try."

"Keep your eye on what's off. What doesn't fit. Andre isn't even going to notice if he sets off a bomb. I'm pretty sure there's a world-class surprise at the bottom of this."

"This is what I am saying," Daniel insisted. "Mais oui."

No one responded.

Callie eventually turned to Andre. "Tell me what to do, then."

"Thatta girl," Andre said. "This could be about the worst movie you ever saw, a real cheeseball."

"I hope so," she replied, deadpan.

◆◆◆

Casper was nodding his head, thinking these guys were pretty good. He was walking on the deck of the seiner, where he was using a receiver to pinpoint the location of his transmitter. When he was satisfied it was on the hull, he looked out over Fisherman's Terminal. So many boats. He especially liked the huge bottomfish processing vessels, which went to the Bering Sea to make surimi. Okay, he'd rent a boat. He had one standing by. It was, after all, the Port of Seattle.

On the dock, he turned his receiver on again. They were very good, he decided, but were they good enough? He didn't think so. Casper said a silent prayer as he adjusted the frequency on his receiver. There it was. Yes. He smiled, his adrenaline kicking in.

The second device was working. They'd never looked for a second transmitter. That was human nature. He glanced heavenward, pleased.

◆◆◆

Avi, Christy and Maurie sat on their Bainbridge Island deck, looking toward Blake Island, and beyond to Mount Rainier. Christy was serving lemonade while Avi and Maurie considered strategy

"What's Casper's prognosis?"

"He believes that he will take Daniel and Cash, the smuggler, tonight. After dark. Between ten thirty and eleven."

"Where is the Frenchman?"

Maurie pointed southwest. "If you had a spotting scope, you might find their boat somewhere between Blake Island and the Kitsap Peninsula." Maurie cleared his throat.

"Who's on it?"

"Casper isn't certain."

Christy opened the door that led from their spacious deck to the living room. "I'll be back," she said.

Avi nodded and smiled to indicate he understood where she was going and why, then he turned to Maurie. "We will take further precautions."

"Such as?"

"Buenos Aires, San Diego. I want Salim Azar's financial history to be reviewed."

"Not to worry. I'll do that myself. As you know, we were very careful."

"*Very careful* is no longer adequate. Maurie, ask yourself, why is the Frenchman in Seattle? After turning this inside out, I can see only one possibility. I can only wonder if, somehow, he came upon our Seattle InterCap server. We shut down InterCap and the server after that network breach two years ago. It's the only conceivable piece of the puzzle that could bring him here. And it's yet another point that connects Hasim to the three of us."

Maurie spit into his spittoon, then he patted Avi's knee. "My friend, I think you are overreacting. Still, I will reconfirm— once again—that Salim Azar's financial life is in perfect order. Salim, as you know, has no direct connection to Ares, to InterCap, to any of this. His real estate interests from San Diego to Vancouver are owned by GRE, a legitimate US partnership. Salim receives regular distributions from GRE, which are then invested with Northwest Capital. He pays income tax on every dollar of income he recognizes from GRE and NWC."

Christy came back out with a telescope and night vision binoculars. The telescope was mounted on a tripod. Avi helped her adjust it. She trained it on the sandy beach on the spit at Blake Island. "All I see is some kids smoking dope beside a beach fire."

"Be patient," Avi advised.

"Patience is fine if you're in jail. Or herding cows," Christy said. "I'm not that gal."

◆◆◆

Long after the call with Izzie ended, Andre was still tapping his prosthetic leg. Cash watched his friend. He knew he tapped when he was organizing his thoughts. So Cash waited, going over his own notes.

So far, he'd come up short on InterCap. Nothing that helped at all. It had been an investment partnership. Its principal investor had been Fulcrum Ltd., a shelf corporation headquartered, of course, at yet another offshore bank. His lawyer friend was checking out InterCap's liquidation. It looked like they'd distributed assets, including partnership interests, to Fulcrum; Global Trade, another shelf corporation that had an ownership interest in Fulcrum; various holding companies; and so on. The trail was cold. The lawyer was not optimistic about finding anything more.

Andre tapped louder. He had something, Cash could tell. Andre, he knew, would reveal it when he was good and ready.

"It's sweet," Andre finally announced.

Cash just nodded, waiting.

"Hasim was wily as a fox. I'm guessing that no one still living knows for sure what went down. The only way I can put it together, he moved the weapons one direction, the money another. This is difficult to coordinate, and he did it carefully, expertly. No way to connect them. Daniel the doofus here did pretty good—"

"*Doofus?* What is this? A smart person?" Daniel asked.

"A smart Frenchman," Andre offered, straight-faced. "It was the wires you found to the Cayman Islands from Russia, Morocco and Austria that gave me the idea. And Cash, you were right about Izzie. He knew something about Hasim's route. Izzie didn't know how big the deal was, though."

"Did he know what it was?"

"If he did, he didn't say."

Cash nodded. Izzie had a finger in many of the biggest, intermittently illicit, transactions. He often brokered for buyers, and Hasim was a seller.

"According to Izzie, Hasim, or his people, shows the weapons in Orenburg, in South Russia, to prove he has them. Then he smuggles them through Kazakhstan, then Uzbekistan. At the Uzbek-Afghan border, the buyers take control for the final border crossing into Afghanistan. At that time, large parts of North Afghanistan were controlled by forces hostile to the Taliban, so it was easier to let the buyers handle it from there. At each stage—showing the goods, reaching Kazakhstan, Uzbekistan, and then at the Afghan border—he said there was to be a payment via a hawala network. I'm pretty sure that there was a balloon payment at the end. I'm still working on that."

"A hawala network?" Callie asked. "I mean, he had me taking notes while he talked, but it doesn't mean I understood this."

"They move money without wire transfers, without any paper trail at all. The agents are called hawaladars and often use a table at a teashop as an office with a notebook and a cell phone for equipment. They move money all over the world via telephone, relying on trust. Orders often go through Switzerland or Dubai. Many of the trades are simply existing debts. Suppose A in Los

Angeles does a deal to transfer one million dollars to B in Beirut. C in Switzerland may owe A one million, which he now settles with B. The hawaladars have been written up and regulated post-9/11," Cash said, "but they're still mostly operating under the radar."

"Yes, you might have read my article," Daniel offered.

"Missed that," Andre replied.

Cash went on. "Say that when the weapons reach Uzbekistan, a payment is due. The buyers have confirmation agents who can call in a hawala payment from anywhere in the world. They confirm the goods in Uzbekistan. A in Uzbekistan will call B in, say, Switzerland, who will call C in Austria, instructing them to deposit the money. Money that is already in Austria, awaiting use, will then be deployed to the appropriate Ares account."

"How do they account for it?" Callie asked.

"Often, they don't even report it. But Hasim was careful, so he'd have a story. Suppose the money is received in Russia, then there'd be an inflated bill of sale for, say, machine parts or electronics. If it comes to Austria, it might be for diamonds. And he would have done real diamond transactions—probably raw diamonds to polishers. Only they'd be small transactions, and this one would be a false bill of sale for tens of millions of dollars."

"Nice," Callie said.

Daniel had been listening, his mouth open. It was the longest time anyone had ever seen him speechless. Finally, he touched Cash's arm. "How is this possible? In the one day, you know more than I do?"

"Twenty years' experience."

"You? You are the arms dealer?"

"No. Mostly, we moved carpets from North Africa and the Middle East."

"Rugs?"

"Our specialty. They tripled in value by the time we got them to New York City. Some cigars, electronics, medical equipment, and so on. It put us in the same world as the bad guys."

"Did you smuggle drugs?" Daniel asked, suspicious.

Cash shrugged. "In two thousand ten, we moved a little hashish from the Bekka Valley in Lebanon. It was part of a complex transaction."

"And your principles?"

"There was only one: Don't do anything that could get us killed."

"None of Cash's friends ever died because of what he did," Callie pointed out. And Daniel shut up.

It was quiet then. The tide had turned, and as it went out, the sandy beach was growing larger. They watched the teenagers throwing driftwood on their fire.

Cash sat back, tired, frustrated and sore. They were stuck. The trail was so well covered that even if Andre's theory was right, they'd end up back in the Cayman Islands or St. Kitts and Nevis. He had to say, Daniel had done a good job of tracking the money. Whoever was behind this was just too careful. He needed to think.

"Let's take a break," Cash suggested. "Andre, how about a drink?"

"I'm in." He broke out a bottle of Bombay Blue Sapphire gin. "Any takers?" he asked the others.

"Where's the damned umbrella?" Callie wanted to know.

"Sugar, I never drink that caca," Andre said.

"Don't call me sugar."

"Just sayin' you're sweet. I didn't call you Twinkie or butterface."

"Butterface?"

Andre smiled his roguish smile. "Sugar, that's a woman with a fine, fetching body...*but her face?*"

"That's disgusting."

"Don't ask about Twinkie then," Cash cautioned.

Callie sighed. "Andre, I'd love a martini."

"Coming up." Andre stepped down to the galley below.

Callie checked her watch, frowned. "I've got to call that detective before midnight."

"Let's have that drink first, then we can call him, set it up for him to meet with Daniel first thing in the morning."

When Daniel started to protest, Callie pointed her finger at him and shot him a look that shut him up.

Andre came up the mahogany ladder that rose from the galley. He had a platter of martinis. He turned to Daniel. "Say, how about a Delta Blizzard for you, doofus?"

Daniel perked up. "A Mekong Delta Blizzard?"

"If that's how you like it, pal." Andre set the platter down on the teak bench, took out his pouch of herbs.

Callie saw the erotic netsuke then. Cash watched her put it together. She turned to him. He could see her working on it, prune-faced. Wanting to say something, holding it back. When she didn't say anything, he raised his glass to her, a toast. She glared at him, plainly pissed off. When he said, "Thank you," she relented, tilting her head, just a little. Cash thought she was handling this pretty well.

◆◆◆

Casper liked the boat, a well-worn twenty-eight-foot Osprey. He'd used Ospreys before, though this was the first time he'd had this particular model on the water. It had a forward cabin with two berths and was fitted with twin 315 hp Yanmar diesels, so this little sea boat could easily reach fifty-five miles per hour. There was room to store his gear, and he was protected from the weather. And in this boat, he looked like he belonged on Puget Sound.

He could be on his way to fish for salmon in Hood Canal, or just cruising the South Sound.

He had a good idea where they were, though he hadn't seen them yet. First, he was considering options. He'd thought about drifting in close at night. He had a rifle with a night scope, and titanium bullets that expanded on impact. The problem was that he hadn't seen Daniel Odile-Grand, and at night, he could make a mistake. Even if he got it right, he'd likely only have the one shot, and he'd need a second shot for Cash Logan, the hired help. Also, he didn't like the waiting. And then, he'd have to get in pretty close, and if he were somehow spotted, drifting out on the sound at night, they'd be on to him.

What did make sense, Casper decided, was to take them all out. He could plant explosives under the boat. He had C-4, a powerful plastic explosive. He could attach it to the hull of their boat, then detonate it once he was back on the Osprey. Their boat and everyone on it would morph into a towering inferno, its detritus scattered over, then swallowed up by, the cold currents of Puget Sound. Hellfire and brimstone, indeed.

He didn't like the idea of swimming in Puget Sound at night. But he had his wet suit and his scuba gear, and he knew how to use it. He could anchor his Osprey far enough away that they'd never see it. It was a good, thorough solution. No loose ends.

Casper checked the boat's nice little wall clock. Almost 10:00 p.m. Time to begin. He started the engine, checked the location of the transmitter, and turned the Osprey toward Blake Island's sandspit.

The trip to Blake Island was uneventful, and Casper slowed before he could be seen from the island. He turned off the Osprey's engines north of the sandspit. He checked his receiver. It was picking up the signal. Their boat hadn't moved in quite some time, and he guessed it was anchored. He had infrared binoculars and he trained them on the venerable Elco Cruisette, moored to one of the buoys. It was a fine old wooden boat, well maintained and newly painted. He wasn't surprised that they had an appreciation for fine things; the good ones usually did. He didn't see anyone, but he could see the lights on below, in the galley, perhaps, and yes, there was a light in one of the berths, too.

Looking closer, he thought he could make out three people on the covered deck in back, and another in the wheelhouse. He decided to make a wide pass around their boat, anchor his boat farther south, near the shore, walk north on Blake Island, then swim south, down to their boat. He'd have the current with him swimming south back to his own boat as well.

Casper took the Osprey southeast, finally anchoring his boat near the shore, perhaps four hundred yards south of the Elco Cruisette.

He packed his C-4—enough to make the boat and its passengers evaporate—put on his wet suit, adjusted his tank, then walked north. When he was above the Elco Cruisette, he waded into the cold black waters of Puget Sound.

CHAPTER THIRTEEN

Cash was sitting on the teak bench that ran along the port side of the old boat's covered deck. His back was against a post and his legs were stretched out on the bench. He checked his watch—10:30 p.m. Eventually, he had to get some sleep. He set his martini on the floor and swung his leg over his knee to begin taking off his boots.

He needed to get his mind around Hasim's significance. Why go to all of this trouble? Why was every loose end in this deal tied off so meticulously? Why was Daniel such a threat? His work boot laced up over his ankles, and the lace was caught on something. When he reached in to free it, he found the transmitter, hooked to the inside of his pants.

The shoeshiner. Damn it.

Cash sat up straight, listening carefully to the night. He heard the waves, the reassuring sound they made lapping against the side of their wooden boat. Nothing else at all.

Earlier, he thought he'd heard a distant motor. If a boat was out there now, its motor was no longer running. Clouds covered the moon, and fog was settling over the sound, so visibility was poor. He took a breath, considering what they might do.

They had no time, Cash knew. He signaled Andre to meet him below. When they reappeared on deck minutes later, Cash announced, "I screwed up. The panhandler in the alley, he hooked a transmitter to my pant leg."

Callie turned. "The shoeshine guy—"

"He knows where we are," Cash interrupted. "There isn't any time." Andre nodded as he quietly readied the Bayliner. Cash turned on several lights, while Andre brought the Bayliner alongside the *Emily Cora*.

Cash listened again for the distant motor, but the boat was gone, or else it was anchored somewhere out there in the fog. He checked the galley one last time. He'd propped up several cushions near a porthole and set Doc's Yankee cap on the top one. Then he'd turned on the lights, hoping it would be visible through the porthole. He'd set the transmitter on a shelf. Finally, he'd turned on the radio and the interior cabin lights, and even hung a jacket on a cleat on the covered deck.

He told Andre to take Callie and Daniel in the Bayliner five hundred yards north. He'd signal them when they could come back. Then, without another word, Cash stripped down, put on a wet suit and scuba gear, then dropped into the dark, cold waters of the sound.

With his underwater light, he located the C-4 right away, three nicely planted charges on the hull. He knew just what to do.

After the charges were on the ocean floor, defused, Cash called Andre on his cell phone. "All clear," he whispered.

When the Bayliner drifted alongside the *Emily Cora*, Cash helped them quietly board her. As they went below, he tied the Bayliner to the buoy, then he untied the *Emily Cora*, lifted her anchor and let the boat drift south.

◆◆◆

Casper climbed the ladder at the back of the Osprey. He set his tanks, mask, fins and other gear on the back deck. With his night vision infrared binoculars, he checked out his target. The boat was resting peacefully at its mooring, and the lights were on in the cabin. He moved toward the Osprey's forward cabin, where he'd left the detonator. Where was the Bayliner, he was wondering—had it drifted to the far side of the old wooden boat? He'd wait until the boat swung around again.

When he raised the binoculars again and turned back toward the Elco Croisette, the Bayliner was tied to the buoy, and the old wooden boat was gone.

◆◆◆

Cash eased the *Emily Cora* around the southern tip of Blake Island. When he was sure there were no other boats nearby, he increased their speed slightly, though the running lights were not on. He planned to circle the island and head north, to a boathouse Doc had rented near Kingston. As he rounded the southeast corner of the island, turning the *Emily Cora* north, Cash heard, then saw, the Osprey. It was running full out, maybe two hundred fifty yards behind them. He nodded at Andre, who was set up on the covered aft deck, his sniper's rifle loaded, mounted, ready. Cash turned on the running lights, raised the throttle to full speed, and they were off.

There was no way the *Emily Cora* was going to outrun the Osprey. The Osprey had a spotlight on them now, and when the Osprey narrowed the distance between them to sixty yards, the driver of the boat opened fire with a semiautomatic weapon. Because he was driving the boat while he was firing, and the distance was that far, the bullets only sprayed the water behind them. Andre was ready. At fifty-five yards, he fired three successive shots, aiming at the Osprey's fuel tank.

The explosion shot fire, water and boat debris into the night sky. It was as if an underwater geyser had erupted, spewing a fountain of fire and boat wreckage, and then it was over. One moment the Osprey was there, and then she was gone, leaving wisps of smoke and a burning fuel slick peppered with flotsam.

◆◆◆

Avi was pacing, a bad sign. Maurie was on the phone, leaving yet another message in some kind of code. He angrily spit into his spittoon, then wiped his chin with a checkered handkerchief that he stuffed back into his black suit pants. Christy was standing at the window looking out onto the South Sound with her night vision binoculars. "First I saw the spotlight. It came from a smaller, faster boat, then there was a flash—fiery, an explosion, I think— on the east side of Blake Island. They were supposed to disappear on the west side of the island. After, I couldn't find the smaller boat, and the bigger boat went north, toward Bainbridge. I lost it when it passed Restoration Point. Can you reach Casper?" she asked Maurie, anxious, almost shrill.

"No. Nothing."

"This is not good," Avi whispered to no one in particular. Then, even softer, "No, not so good."

"This is impossible. They can't be that able. It was luck...dumb luck...had to be," Maurie insisted. "They beat Casper? No one beats Casper."

Maurie's phone rang. He listened, then he asked, "Is this line secure?"

Maurie nodded to Avi and Christy, then he attached a scrambler and put the phone on speaker. "Talk," he said.

"They were ahead of me," Casper said. "Maybe two minutes, max. I'd like another shot."

"Where are you?"

"Blake Island. They blew up my boat. When the first shot hit the hull, I knew to jump overboard. I was able to get to shore. I'm at the marina. And I'm steaming...Like my merciless father, I'm preaching...wrath of God...let the Furies wreak their vengeance!"

"Wrath of God?" Christy hissed, then louder, "I'm not paying for this shit. What's this incompetent douchebag talking about?" She was as angry as he was.

Casper took her abuse, just barely, making a rasping sound.

Avi intervened, before Casper decided to unleash his vengeance on Christy.

"What do you propose?"

A deliberate breath. "Boone. He'll find them."

"Boone, the Tracker?" Maurie asked. "He'll cost a fortune."

"He owes me a favor. This one's on me." And after a quiet beat: "Look, you don't know me. All I know about you is a series of coded numbers. But whoever you are, please understand this...I do not tolerate failure. I'm a vicious, spiteful man, and I'm enraged. You can liken it to the rage of the Pharaoh after Moses' God passed over Egypt and struck down every firstborn man and beast. This is no longer a job, it's a calling. I am the Hell Roarer, the Foul Fiend, the Angel of the Bottomless Pit. And this is my life until you tell me to stop, until you're satisfied with my work."

"Hold on." Maurie put him on hold, cleared his throat, then he looked at his partners, a question.

"He's fucking crazy," Christy hissed.

"Boone *will* find them," Maurie said. "And Casper *has* to redeem himself."

"I care fuck all about *redemption.*"

Avi raised a hand. "Unleash the dogs of war."

♦♦♦

Callie put a forefinger on Cash's forearm, just a touch to get his attention. They were in the wheelhouse of Doc's boat, cruising toward their hiding place, a boathouse near Kingston. "I'd like to come with you to New York City," she said softly.

"No. It's not safe."

"It's safer being with you than not being with you. And besides, I've already made up my mind."

Cash turned to look at her. She had that unmistakable Callie-James-I'm-right-as-rain look. "What's come over you?"

"I'm not sure. I've been thinking about everything, and I'd much rather be with you in New York than hiding with Andre and Daniel in some old boathouse…It's—I dunno—some kind of sea change."

"And if I say no?"

"I'll come anyway."

"Could this be some kind of irrational delayed reaction—you know, like an aftershock?"

Callie shot him a look, one he knew all too well—*frosty*.

"Callie, it's not a good idea. It's dangerous, way out of your comfort zone, not where you want to be."

"I'm sticking with you. I feel like that's the place for me now." She raised her palms and eyebrows, an expression of vulnerability he'd never seen her use. "I may not know why I feel that but I do know what I know."

And just like that, Cash got why this was so important to her. He frowned—it was a new thing for him, understanding this woman without getting a headache. What he understood was that losing Doc, the explosion at her restaurant, the harrowing boat chase, the bear mace—everything—had cracked the dike and feelings were leeching through. Cash imagined that, over many years, the fragile interior region that housed Callie's emotional life had slowly shut down, atrophied, eventually growing numb, then lifeless. And now blood was starting to flow, nerve endings were beginning to work again. Emotionally, Callie was stirring, waking up, and he was, in some small way, happy to be around that—even part of it. And Cash already knew that he wanted to help her with this if he could.

Cash looked out at the water, suddenly aware, and pleased, that he cared for this unpredictable, unexpectedly brave woman.

This change in Callie brought back a long-buried memory. At twelve, he'd discovered his late father's vintage radio in the attic. It was an Addison model 5F from 1938. He plugged it in—nothing. For months, he tinkered with it, readjusting parts, wiring, everything. One day, inexplicably, music started to play. His father had died when he was three years old and Cash rarely thought about him. Remembering his dad, how he fixed his radio with a child's mix of love, hope and force of will, was, in some way he didn't understand, both a thank-you from Callie and a vote of confidence in her renaissance.

Cash glanced over at her, still pensive. "I need to think about this," he eventually said. "In the meantime, you owe Detective Samter a call." He handed her his cell phone. "He'll want to meet with Daniel ASAP. Tell him we'll meet him at a coffee shop near the ferry terminal on Bainbridge Island. Someplace off the main street. Tomorrow morning. Eight o'clock. After the meeting, we'll get on the ferry, go straight to the airport. Andre can take the doofus back to the boathouse."

Callie already had the detective's card in her hand. She dialed. "Detective, Callie James…Eleven fifty-five. Lighten up, I made your deadline…We'll meet on Bainbridge, tomorrow morning at eight. Daniel will be with us. Any out-of-the-way coffee shop you like near the ferry terminal…Yeah, I know the place. In the small building behind the parking lot. See you then." She hung up and turned to Cash. "So that's a yes on New York."

"Do I have a choice?"

"I don't think so." Callie leaned in. "But thank you. You won't be sorry."

Cash wasn't ready to bet his own money on that.

♦♦♦

Callie stepped into the coffee shop at 7:55 a.m. She saw Detective Samter sipping coffee at a corner table. He looked the same—lined, weathered face, cold gray eyes. But today, he was especially grim-faced, like a stern pit bull. She sat opposite him. "We need to agree on a game plan."

"What?"

"Daniel and I tell you what we know. You let him go back to his hiding place."

"No deals."

"No Daniel."

"You're starting to aggravate me, again. For Christ's sake, do you want me to arrest you?"

"Okay, let's start over." Callie looked him in the eyes, ready for this. "Detective, work with me. Suppose I sweeten the deal. Will you hear me out?"

"*Sweeten the deal?* Did I actually hear you say that?"

She cringed, worried that little crimson blotches might break out on her cheeks at any moment, then took a breath. "Suppose I ask the man I hired to protect my restaurant, the same man who's been checking out Daniel's story, to join us. He can tell you more about what's going on than anyone else. And it's a very big story—terrorists, stolen nuclear suitcase bombs, money laundering. When we're done, if you agree, he and I will go on to New York City to follow the story. Daniel will go back to a safe hiding place. We'll call you when we know anything more."

Samter didn't respond. Instead, he squinted, finding her gaze with his steely Terminator stare.

Callie held steady. "I'd recommend that you take my deal. You won't be sorry." And she was saying that a lot lately. Hmm.

The detective tilted his head, laser-focused, working this out in his mind. "Won't be sorry?…Okay, let's find out. Here's what I will do. I'll hear you all out, then I'll let you know what I'm going to do, and I expect you to tell me your plan. If your story convinces me that you can actually help me get to the bottom of this, I'll let you go on to New York. If I'm not convinced—" He raised a palm, scrunched his brow in a hard frown, a very bad cop, indeed.

"I can't convince you. But Cash is another—"

"Cash?"

"You'll meet him. You'll get it about him. Right away. He's very able, and he can navigate to and through dark places that you could never even find." Samter just sat there, stone-faced. Callie touched his forearm. "But Daniel? I can't bring him in here unless you'll let us hide him after—"

"Don't push your luck, lady. You will bring him in here. Period." Samter looked her over, hawk on a vole. "And what's come over you? What happened to the not-so-sure-of-herself, overwhelmed Callie James?"

"Events outside of my restaurant caught up with me, I guess. I'm not so afraid, at least. Anyway, it's a lot clearer to me now what's important. When you hear our story, I think you'll agree." She met his gaze again. "And truthfully, it's a big damn relief to be able to tell you what's happening." She smiled, pleased that she'd said "damn" to a policeman. She *was* happy to be talking with him, she knew that much.

He nodded. "Okay. Let's get started."

She went to the door, raised a hand, then came back in with Cash and Daniel.

♦♦♦

They talked for almost an hour. Daniel told the beginning, up to fleeing from the hospital. He wanted to hold forth, detailing his journalistic accomplishments, but when he made the *agh* sound, raising his hands and his eyebrows, for the third time, Cash simply but firmly took over. And remarkably, Daniel stayed quiet. Callie wondered—confounded by how this image ever got into her head—if Cash had a handful of Daniel's private parts in his fist under the table.

Cash laid it all out, clear, clean and smart. Detective Samter got it about Cash—Callie had been right about that—and he only interrupted to ask clarifying questions, smart clarifying questions.

Cash told him everything except the part where Doc was murdered and the part about opening fire on—blowing up—the hit man's boat. He explained that serious people wanted Daniel dead, and they'd overpaid heavyweight professionals to kill him and, apparently, them. He told Samter about Kelly and Gray, about their $500,000 fee, and finally, about how after catching this pair of killers and striking a deal with their boss, he'd found the transmitter and defused the C-4 on the hull of their boat.

Cash explained Daniel's story—Amjad Hasim, the size of the weapons transaction, how the weapons moved one way and the money another. No one knew exactly where the weapons went, or just what terrorist groups had the nuclear capacity to vaporize Manhattan.

Cash explained why he knew how to follow the story. He knew this world, he'd worked in it, and if he had time, he had a shot at piecing together at least a portion of what happened. If he could get to the people behind this, if he could discover what they were so afraid that Daniel might learn, he'd have a way to put them down, forever. This was, at this point, an all-or-nothing deal. If he failed, the three of them—he made a gesture that included Daniel, Callie and himself (Callie imagined Daniel let out a measured breath when Cash took his hand out from under the table)—were going to die.

When it was his turn, Detective Samter sat back, put his hands behind his head, his fingers laced together. "You clowns have broken more laws than I can count." And to Callie: "I can't believe that you maced two professional killers."

"I did that." Heat spotted her cheeks.

"And I wish I'd seen it." He nearly cracked a smile, caught himself. "Okay. As wild as it is, I believe your story, and maybe, just maybe, I'll go out on a limb for you." He turned to Cash. "Because you, apparently, can do things I can't do. And you seem to be good at those things."

Cash held the detective's gaze, unresponsive.

Callie looked at these two men sizing each other up. In some way she didn't get, the detective seemed ready to rely on Cash. Some kind of pattern recognition, she guessed.

"Bear in mind that I, too, can do things that you can't do. Here's how it's going to work. We'll pursue two distinct tracks. I'm bringing in a trusted friend, a higher-up I worked with on the National Joint Terrorism Task Force. So while you talk with the *bad guys*, I'll get whatever help I can from the *good guys*. Our objective will be the same—find out who's behind this and put them down. Like rabid dogs. We'll talk at least once a day. Agreed?"

Cash shook the detective's hand. They exchanged cell phone numbers.

"Keep her out of harm's way."

Cash nodded.

"And hide the doofus where he'll never be found."

"We have him in a boathouse in Kingston off—"

Samter raised a hand. "I don't want to know, so long as I can reach you and you can reach him."

Cash nodded again. Fine by him.

Callie was pleased—this had gone better than she'd expected. Cash had genuinely won the detective over. Yes, Cash had inspired confdence, and he'd been smart. The smuggler had been—well—impressive.

Daniel was the only one who was unhappy. Callie thought he looked like an oft-kicked junkyard dog.

CHAPTER FOURTEEN

Izzie, the Macher, was arriving from Amsterdam tonight, and Cash had arranged to meet him at his office in the Diamond District first thing in the morning. So he and Callie had an evening to themselves in the city. Cash hoped that he could distract her, at least, from the horrors of the past week. He was, however, mindful that professionals would be trying to find them, so they had to be both distracted and invisible.

The trick to becoming invisible in New York City was to go where no one would ever think to look for you, so Cash took Callie out for dinner at the saloon in the Oyster Bar on the lower level of Grand Central Terminal. You had to know how to find it. First, you looked for the six metal-framed glass doors under the marble arch at the bottom of the two-sided ramp on the Vanderbuilt side, opposite the lower-level train tracks.

All six doors opened into the sizeable restaurant. In the older, north or right side of the restaurant, people sat at serpentine white counters eating every known variety of seafood. The new bar sat in the middle, and to the south there were scores of square tables with checkered tablecloths. The ninety-eight-year-old Oyster Bar restaurant was a vast, lively room that was often crowded and always, always smelled like fish. Its best feature—the beautiful vaulted ceilings—was covered with Guastavino terra-cotta tiles set in a herringbone pattern.

Once inside, you had to turn north and hike to the right rear corner of the large space to find the simple wooden swinging door.

Cash bowed, extended a long arm and ushered Callie into the saloon.

Callie couldn't suppress an enthusiastic smile when she stepped inside and saw red-and-white-checkered tablecloths, warm, dark woods, chairs trimmed with rustic brass nailheads. To her right, a handsome, winding mahogany bar made an L along the north and east sides of the restaurant. Models and photos of multimasted sailing ships hung from the walls. Cash found two seats at the bar in the far right corner—under the mounted tarpon at the very top of the L—and ordered two Bombay Blue Sapphire gin martinis, extra dry, with olives, and a platter of sixteen oysters—pairs, four from the West Coast and four from the East Coast. Callie was surprised when he specified the oysters without even asking her.

The martinis arrived, each one with an extra inch of refill in a glass tumbler. "The angel's share," Cash explained. He raised his drink, a toast. "To you, Callie, to what you could become."

She clicked his glass with hers. "I'm not sure what you mean."

"You have a shot at extraordinary."

"You think so?"

"Possibly. But it's an entirely different kind of extraordinary than turning-me-over-to-the-cops-for-smuggling-erotic-netsuke-into-your-restaurant extraordinary."

"I deserve that. Jesus what an unforgiving, righteous gal I was." She raised a palm. "Your words. And you were right. I'm sorry." She touched his arm. "I was mean-spirited, foolish—just plain wrong—and I'll always regret that."

"Suppose we let that go." Cash raised his glass again.

She touched her glass to his. "Thank you."

"Speaking of regrets, honestly, I never anticipated that this past week would be so difficult—the anxiety, hiding Lew, the mace, the damage to your restaurant, the explosives on the boat…It was especially hard to lose Doc…" He let it drift.

She nodded, found his eyes. "I misjudged you early on…Conventional thinking sometimes blinds me—how you look, how you dress, what your job is. Long story short, you're not at all what you seem. I listened carefully to you with Detective Samter today. You're so smart, so able in the world. And in your way, though you'd never admit it, you try to get it right. Yes, you present whatever you're proposing as practical, a calculated, opportunistic thing. What I'm learning, though, is that with you that's also, as you see it—after carefully weighing pros and cons—the best for all involved. Or as I would say it, the *right thing*. How you get there is often confusing to me, but you do get there, way ahead of me, and, well, I admire you."

"Thank you…That's a two-way deal." Cash watched her, surprised by her expressiveness. "Truthfully, this past week, I underestimated you. You've been right there, as hard as that must have been for you. You kept defying my expectations. Just when I was ready to give up on you, you did the smart thing, the hard thing, under protest, but you did it. And now, I'm watching you in the eye of a serious storm, just when I'd expect you to cave in, fall apart. But no, you manage. You even stand tall. Callie, you have a fine, strong heart."

She smiled. "I'm a restaurateur. I never knew what to do outside my restaurant. I was always afraid."

"I didn't know that."

"It took a lot of work and a huge amount of energy to accomplish that deception. I mean you can't imagine what it was like for me to find you—ask for your help—at the Dragon. It was all I could do to look at you, to keep even a semblance of composure."

"And that's changing?"

"Yes, I think so. I hope so."

"How did this happen?"

"It's you, Terry." She looked at him, eyes serious. "In your tenacious, patient way, you dragged me—kicking and screaming— out into the world, step by baby step, and though it's every bit as frightening and even more unsettling than I imagined it, I'm okay with it. Yeah, I'm even getting my sea legs."

"Bravo, then, Callie James. To both of us."

She raised her glass. They toasted silently.

"Truthfully, Cash, at times I even like it out here."

"Well, it suits you." Cash watched her smile.

"I even like talking with you…And I was *never* a talker."

"I'm guessing we have some great, contentious conversations ahead of us."

"I like the idea of that."

"Likewise."

"Cash and Frosty, tête-à-tête."

He took her small, delicate hands in his big, busted-up mitts.

Their kiss was tender, sweet, Cash thought. After, there were tears in Callie's eyes.

◆◆◆

They woke up smiling, spread across the wide hotel room bed, wrapped in each other's arms. Callie went over it again, counting it, to be sure that they'd actually made love twice. The first time was memorable, the second, better than the first.

Cash grabbed the clock and broke their postcoital spell. "We're late. We're due at Izzie's in thirty-five minutes and I better shower."

"Yeah, you better." She kissed him. "Me, too, so hurry up."

They got out of the cab at a warehouse in the Diamond District with two minutes to spare. And then they were in the door and up the stairs.

And there he was, waiting warmly. "What's a beautiful girl like you doing with the schlemiel with the eggplant face?" the Macher asked Callie before shaking her hand.

Callie liked him already. "The schlemiel has been looking out for me lately. Good at it, too."

Cash put a big hand on his friend's shoulder. "Not so good. We lost Doc."

"This is a terrible loss…shoyderlekh," Izzie muttered, plainly upset. "Horrible, dreadful," he translated for Callie.

Itzac—she'd already decided to call him that—was five foot three, bald and wiry. Callie guessed he was at least eighty. He wore a stunning Loro Piana beige two-button vicuña wool sport coat over a black turtleneck, with black slacks and Italian black leather shoes. It was 7:00 a.m. and they were at his office—a small room in the back of a warehouse in the Diamond District. In the warehouse, containers were stacked floor to ceiling. Izzie took Cash's big hand in both of his little ones, looked up at him. "I'm so sorry for your loss…He was a good man, a good friend."

"He'll be missed," Cash said. "I'm hoping you can help me find the people who killed him."

"I'll help however I can. Not only am I in your debt, but I'm intrigued by your beautiful gentile lady friend who understands a little Yiddish."

Callie smiled. "Just a few words. I picked them up at my restaurant." She was surprised by how different Itzac was from Cash—so well dressed, so soft-spoken. If Cash were Robert Duvall, rough-around-the-edges charming, Itzac was Daniel Day-Lewis charming, a soft-spoken gentleman with a startling, colorful dash of Jewish street pizzazz. Not what she'd expected.

Cash had explained how Itzac had worked his way up—gambling to money laundering to becoming a broker in the biggest, most complex, sometimes illicit, transactions. He was one of the largest buyers and sellers of diamonds in the world. He was, according to Cash, "tougher than woodpecker lips" and even smarter than he was tough. He had a large network of international—including underworld—contacts, and he was feared and admired throughout the world of international trade.

"To business?" he asked Cash.

"Amjad Hasim?"

"I made my inquiries and learned something surprising indeed." Izzie smiled, ever so slightly. "Our colleague, the Turk, insisted that he saw him—alive—in California."

"No. Impossible. He's confirmed dead."

"My reaction precisely, but the Turk had proof."

Cash frowned, dubious.

"My friend, I put out the word. I made a point of offering a substantial, unspecified reward for any information about Amjad's last deal, and then we had the luck…the good fortune. The Turk called me on my private line. Collect. He said he had priceless information about Amjad. He added that I was the answer to his prayers. I had no idea what he was getting at, then he told me Amjad was alive and that he could prove it. I, in turn, insisted that he was mistaken. He explained how much it would cost to find out. I almost choked at the amount, then said I'd need indisputable proof." The Macher paused, took a breath.

"What did he have?" Cash asked, transfixed.

"The Turk said he never would have recognized him—new face, new hair, new body type—but he was in a bathhouse in Los Angeles eleven months ago, and he noticed the awful scar from his old burn. Apparently, Amjad was showering, and the door swung open. Freak accident. The Turk saw the grotesque burn scar on Amjad's left side, snaking down from his armpit. It's distinctive, one of a kind."

"Wouldn't he have had it surgically removed?"

"Amjad was being tortured with a blowtorch when he killed his torturer. The meshugge mamzer—the crazy bastard—bit right through the carotid artery in his torturer's neck. After, Amjad went through many skin grafts but the residual scar is irremovable. Except for when he showers, he keeps it covered with a specially made casing, so even his women don't see it. The Turk first saw the scar when he ran guns for Amjad in the late stages of his recovery. During a particularly rough patch, Amjad had the Turk help him dress it. Though the scar is only thirteen to fourteen inches long, apparently, the location and shape are unmistakable, and the scar is instantly recognizable."

"Can you be sure that the Turk wasn't lying?"

"The Turk's a thief, a gonif who eats like an animal—fressen—noisy, like a pig. But he's no fool. He managed a picture with his iPhone. Time stamped. He hid somewhere in the locker room, took the picture when Amjad was dressing—when he was covering the scar with the casing. Greed made the Turk do this—that's the only possible explanation. We had to agree to buy this picture before he would even tell what he knew. A small fortune in uncut stones. The Turk, he waits almost a year for the opportunity to sell his farkakt—and young lady, this one I do not translate—picture. He also produced medical records of Amjad's scar. It is, indeed, identical. He knew the value of what he had. After, the Turk disappeared." Izzic snapped his fingers, made a blowing sound. "Whoosh... In the wind."

"Anything else?"

"Nothing. No name, no location. Nothing."

"If Amjad's alive, the stakes couldn't be higher." Cash frowned again, working on this, moving pieces around in his head. "He's got a new identity," he said. "How do you manage that?"

"I'll find out. You're on the right track. We'll never find Amjad. We may, however, find the man who set him up as a different person. There are not many people who can successfully organize a new, absolutely untraceable identity, particularly for a notorious weapons dealer like Amjad. And Amjad would insist on, and pay for, the very best. I know a few people that I will talk to about this."

"How long will it take?" Cash asked.

"For you, two hours, max. I make my inquiries. Call me at nine thirty and I'll have names, a place to begin."

Itzac gave his card to Callie. "Here's my number. Anything you need. Anything at all. The schlemiel gets fresh, I take care of it. As we like to say in the Diamond District, mazl un brokhe—good luck and a blessing." He bowed and kissed her hand.

◆◆◆

Cash took Callie to Katz's Deli on the Lower East Side for breakfast. Callie knew good delis in Seattle, but this was in another class entirely. Unmistakable deli smells and sounds—heavy plates with hot pastrami and corned beef, lox, gefilte fish, chopped liver with onions, and so on, hurriedly set on tables; loud, brassy, all-business waitresses; busboys clearing quickly; people clamoring at the take-out counters or lined up to be seated—all contributed to the bustling, aromatic din that made Katz's a world unto itself.

Callie remembered the scene from *When Harry Met Sally* where Meg Ryan faked an orgasm while sitting with Billy Crystal in Katz's Deli. The spot was well marked now—a sign hung from the ceiling with a red arrow pointing down to the infamous table, which sat in the middle of the busy room.

Callie sat nearby, thinking that she hadn't had to fake anything last night. On the contrary, it had been an unforgettable, joyous night. She'd never, ever imagined that she could enjoy sex so much—especially with Cash—but she was remembering it now, and it was making her dizzy.

It wasn't about technique or trying new things or anything she could specify. What it was, with Cash, she somehow, inexplicably, felt totally safe. Her old Daniel Odile-Grand sex pals—guilt (about what she was doing), anxiety (about what he'd ask her to do) and shame (about doing it)—just didn't show up. Instinctively, she'd let herself go—a thing she'd never been able to do, never even knew about—and had felt more, more vividly, than she'd ever imagined possible. And in his gentle way, Cash had encouraged her to lose herself in their lovemaking. Remarkably, Callie was not at all aware of what she was doing. She blushed thinking about how she'd cried out, telling him how she loved him—*forever*—telling him exactly how to please her. Oh my God, had she actually done that?

And then, surprisingly, she was ahead of him, anticipating what he wanted. Hmm…go figure.

She took Cash's hand across the table, finding his eyes, and from the way he looked at her, she just knew that he was remembering it, too. It made her feel so damned good. Who would have known that this man could make her so happy? Who would have known that she could *ever* be this happy? Something new, something wondrous, had happened—the light was on, the curtains drawn—and she could identify waves of feeling breaking inside. She loved how she could pinpoint the shifting currents, crosscurrents and undercurrents, and even distinguish the swirling back eddies, the surging tides. Cash Logan, the bouncer from the Dragon? She gently fingered his bruised, battered face. She felt weak-kneed and breathless, like a schoolgirl.

A waitress approached, pad ready. "Whaddaya wanna ordah?"

"Order for me, please?" Callie asked, thinking: another rule broken.

Cash nodded. "We'll have lox-and-onion omelets, please, and we'll split the matzo ball soup, then finish with the kugel. Oh, and two vanilla egg creams to drink."

"Vanilla egg cream?" Callie asked.

"Vanilla syrup, milk and a spritz of seltzer. As Izzie puts it, 'heaven on earth.'"

"You've been here before."

"Izzie's a regular. He taught me deli food." And waving his big palm to encompass the sprawling deli: "And all about this."

"He likes you."

"I saved his life."

"Go on."

"It was more than ten years ago. I was buying rugs in Morocco and selling them to Izzie for three times what I paid. Diamonds were the method of payment. So I delivered the rugs, and the diamonds came from Izzie's guy in Amsterdam—half a million dollars worth of three, three-and-a-half millimeter round brilliant-cut melee diamonds in parcels."

"What?"

"Melee diamonds are small diamonds. They're sometimes called diamond chips, but jewelers don't like that term. Most of the diamonds mined, cut and produced in the world are melee. A single parcel of melee diamonds can be sold and resold three to four times a day, so they're like currency. I liked large parcels, thousands of stones, thousands of carats, worth at least fifty thousand dollars per parcel."

Callie sipped her egg cream. "Nice…" Another sip, smiling, then she nodded. "Okay. Got it. Go on."

"Here's where it got dicey. On a hunch, I had the diamonds inspected and learned that a quarter to a third of them were synthetic."

"Synthetic?"

"Produced in an artificial process, lab grown, not natural. In other words, forgeries. Worth twenty to thirty percent less."

"Ouch."

"Yeah. In those days, parcels weren't often inspected—the tools to inspect them were expensive, time intensive, and hard to get access to."

"So how did you do it?"

"I knew a guy. I was using the parcels for payments, and I was cutting them with synthetic stones myself."

"Ah ha…You are a scoundrel. A sexy scoundrel." She took his hand. "But a scoundrel nonetheless."

He kissed the back of her hand. "Could we let that go, babe?"

She squeezed his hand. "Yeah…sure."

"Okay, then…Anyway, getting shortchanged pissed me off, but I knew Izzie wasn't responsible. It was his diamond broker in Amsterdam, had to be. And if he was doing this to me, in a relatively small sale, I could only imagine what he was doing on some of Izzie's multimillion-dollar deals."

The waitress brought their matzo ball soup. Cash cut off a piece of the large matzo ball with his spoon, then scooped up some broth. He handed the spoon to Callie. "It's okay to slurp."

"Never. No way." She gracefully managed it. "Lovely," she exclaimed, and took a second spoonful. Cash was already working with another spoon. She winced at his slurping. "Please continue," she said, between spoonfuls.

Another slurp. "So I called Izzie, explained the situation. I told him that I didn't care that he was marking up my rugs to launder money. That I didn't even care that he'd shortchanged me, though I expected him to pay me what he still owed. I admitted that I'd come to like and trust him, doing business together, and I was worried that if his dealer was cutting his stones with synthetics, some of his customers might react less politely than his friend Cash."

"And?"

"Izzie started screaming, mostly Yiddish."

Callie finished off the soup. "I love this guy. Give me a taste."

"He called his dealer a khazer, that's a pig. A schmuck." He looked at her. She knew that one. "A mamzer, which means bastard, and so on. He had to go, but he insisted that I pay him a visit when I arrived in New York the following week."

"That's it?"

"No. When I went to see him, he was extremely gracious and grateful. He said I'd saved his life, then, for the first time, he let down his hair with me. Apparently, at that time, Izzie owed money to a powerful Ukrainian gangster. He'd brokered an arms deal with this gangster, a warlord, actually, and diamonds were the method of payment. Diamonds provided by Izzie's Amsterdam diamond broker."

Callie winced.

"Right…The Macher got to the Ukrainian warlord just in time. The warlord had discovered the synthetics and put out a hit on Izzie. Izzie made the warlord whole, and the hit was called off in the eleventh hour. His diamond broker disappeared in Amsterdam. Since then, the Macher and I have been fast friends."

"He's a good friend to have."

"Yes, the best."

Their omelets arrived and they dug in, famished.

◆◆◆

The call came as Cash was paying the check. He looked at his burner phone—Detective Samter. Cash took the call, put the phone to his ear.

"What's the name of your man's boat, the one in Kingston?" Samter asked.

"The *Emily Cora*."

"There was a horrific explosion in Kingston last night—enough explosives to take out all of the boathouses on one pier. Your man's boat, the *Emily Cora*, was in one of them. We're still searching through the wreckage, but we found a piece of flesh, some bone. Nothing easily identifiable. We're running some tests. I think they found your guys."

"Are you sure? My man's a pro."

"No one in or near that boathouse survived that blast."

"Shit. This changes everything."

Callie frowned.

"Yes. You better tell Callie. Prepare her for the worst. Call me in an hour, I'll know more then. Incidentally, my terrorism guy says Amjad Hasim's name opens doors that he's never been through. More later."

Cash hung up, took Callie's hand. "Brace yourself. They blew up the boathouse. Detective Samter believes that Andre and Daniel are dead, though he hasn't found their bodies yet."

Callie gasped. He moved to her side of the table, held her tight. "We can talk later. We have to get out of here, now," he said.

Callie was struggling to breathe. Cash left money on the table, put his arm around her waist and hurried her toward the door. There was a line waiting to be seated. Cash opened the door for her.

That's when he saw the van, idling in a no-parking zone. And three big men, moving toward them.

Without a word, Cash picked Callie up and literally threw her back into the restaurant. As he tried to follow, a stun baton came down on his back, and he went down. In the confusion at the door, the big guys picked him up and threw him into the van.

◆◆◆

Callie got up in time to see the van speed away. She wanted to scream.

She regained her composure, aware that the next few minutes really mattered. Detective Samter? Itzac? She dialed the Macher's number. "They took Cash. I'm at Katz's deli. He threw me in here before they knocked him out with some kind of stun gun."

"Don't move. We'll be there in minutes."

◆◆◆

Maurie held forth, pleased with the results he'd achieved so far. "Boone's in a class by himself, a maven," he explained. "Found them all in twenty-four hours. Casper says they have the smuggler, Cash Logan, locked down. Daniel and the bodyguard are surely dead, though we're waiting on final IDs of the bodies. This should happen today. Callie James is still at large, though they know where she is. The smuggler threw her back into the restaurant—Katz's, can you believe that?" He blew his nose into a blue-and-white-checkered handkerchief. "One of my favorite delis. The crowd made it impossible to grab her."

"Callie should be a manageable problem," Avi said.

Maurie cleared his throat. "Boone has her on his radar. Casper suggested taking her tonight."

Christy gave Maurie a thumbs-up at that notion. She was on the couch, feet propped on the coffee table, smoking a Marlboro, a sure sign that she was feeling better. "Casper's a born-again zealot, a bona fide douchebag. But okay, let him do the Lord's work—so long as he's delivering our goods. I have to say, I'll sleep well tonight. First night in a while." She reached out, took Avi's hand. "I'm getting too old for this."

Avi, who was sitting beside her, kissed her hand. "Does Casper have any way to get to us? Even a clue?" he asked Maurie.

"No, absolutely not. All he knows is a number code to contact us."

"Casper could disappear tomorrow, a precaution."

"Yes, of course. There will be, then, in total, five to eliminate."

"A gaggle of disappearing douchebags," Christy mused.

Avi smiled. "By tomorrow, this *hiccup* will be behind us. And, my dear, I'm especially glad that you've found your voice again, regained your stride."

She put out her cigarette, then leaned in, kissed him. "It's time we got back to what's important. Speaking of which, I have something special planned for your birthday."

"A clue?" Avi requested. "You know I don't like surprises."

"You remember last year? This is even better than that. Way better."

Avi turned to Maurie. "Is our business finished?"

"Yes. I'll let you know when we have confirmation from the boathouse and on Callie James."

"Excellent. Well done."

Excused, Maurie picked up his spittoon. At the door, he set it down and took a piece of candy from a soft leather pouch, a monogrammed gift from Christy and Avi. He put it under his tongue. Sucking certain candies helped control his hypersalivation. He turned, watching his partners, his bosses and, truthfully, his mentors. He liked to think about Avi and Christy. Compare himself to them. Understand them. To a rigorously logical person like him, though, their intricate emotional life and their understated, multifaceted interactions could be baffling. On some days, their relationship seemed to him to be illogical, even incomprehensible.

At these reflective times, Maurie always began by concisely summarizing what he understood about himself. This provided a point of departure, a reliable starting place for whatever came next. Today, he noted that he was undeniably ruthless, able to precisely calculate the costs and benefits of any transaction—business, personal or theoretical. The reason he could do this was because he was so smart in the accountant way—though he only admitted to five, he could actually multiply six numbers by six numbers in his head, always could. And he never got emotionally involved. He never felt anything, nor did he care what others thought of him.

If that made him an exceptionally efficient predator, if he were—say—a barracuda, then Avi and Christy were surely a pair of great white sharks. Mutant great whites—twenty feet long, five thousand pounds, with oversized human brains. They defined the top of the food chain. These were simply the smartest—smarter by far then he'd ever be, capable of extraordinary illogical progressions, flights of fancy that landed true, in the carpenter's sense of that word—certainly the most imaginative, and unquestionably the most dangerous, people he'd ever met, even working for the mob in LA. Here they were, brutally erasing a serious threat to their business, their well-being, masterfully orchestrating five murders without a single connection to them. But unlike him, they had feelings. Complicated, intense feelings. In some way he couldn't follow, they were hardwired to each other. And, he realized, getting away with murder excited them. Yes, inexplicably—to him, at least— they were giddy, like loopy, lovestruck teenagers.

Maurie shook his head, picked up his spittoon and walked toward his office, convinced he'd never understand their complex, diabolical relationship.

◆◆◆

The Macher came into Katz's flanked by four men. He was wearing a classic black fedora. He touched the brim and nodded to the cashier as he went right to Callie, who was hunched over a small table against the wall, pale and teary. She'd clasped her hands together to keep them from shaking. It wasn't working.

They encircled her, scooped her up, and hurried her to a black Mercedes, one of three double-parked in front. From the back seat, Itzac instructed his driver, who raised a window that separated the front and back seats. Then he took Callie's trembling hands. "We have very little time to save our friend's life."

"What can I do?" she asked, crying now.

"Tell me anything that happened since you left my office that could inform our thinking."

Still weeping and trembling, Callie told him about Detective Samter's call, about what he'd said about Andre and Daniel.

"Andre is a very able military tactician. Did they find bodies?"

She took a slow breath, then gasped. Finally, she said, "Not yet."

"Callie, collect yourself. You can do that," Itzac gently instructed. "As soon as you're ready, call this Detective Samter. Ask him if they've found the bodies yet. Do not, under any circumstances, tell him that they have Cash."

She wiped away her tears, took a deep breath. Cash needed her now, and she'd be there for him.

Callie called Samter, sufficiently composed to shift into restaurant mode. "Any news?"

"Nothing yet. You?"

"Nothing. Cash told me about Andre and Daniel. He's meeting with his friend. He said to tell you he'd call after the meeting… Yes…Okay." Callie broke the connection.

"Nicely done. Don't despair. We have a chance," Itzac explained. "I'm guessing that they won't kill Cash until the police find Andre and Daniel or have proof that they're dead. Andre has considerable experience and expertise in this sort of warfare, and they'd know that. He may have used the boathouse as a decoy while he and Daniel hid someplace else. They'll want to be sure. They'll torture Cash to find Daniel, if Daniel and Andre are still alive."

A tear spilled down Callie's cheek. The Macher paused to gently wipe it away with his handkerchief. "So now we have a very small window and an even smaller bull's-eye. I know someone here in New York City who can call your Detective Samter and convince him to hold back whatever he finds for a day, tops. At the same time, I'll do everything I can to find the guy who put together

Amjad's new identity. I have two contacts that can get you to the very best people for this. The cost is formidable. I've already told them that I have someone who will pay fifteen million dollars for a fresh, squeaky-clean start. No questions asked, but it must be foolproof."

Itzac checked his phone. "The most promising contact has texted that they no longer do this, but they may make an exception for me." He pressed an intercom button, then told the driver. "Moishe, get Nathan in Buenos Aires."

Callie never knew just how it happened, but something clicked in her mind, a specific connection with two well-liked customers who had asked her to have Will procure a particular case of wine for an uncle's birthday. The destination had been Buenos Aires. "Itzac," she whispered. "What's Nathan's last name? Ben-Meyer?" It just came out.

"How could you know this?"

"His nephew, Avi, is a regular at my restaurant."

"Avi Ben-Meyer? The international investor? I know these men." Itzac frowned. "They are not what they seem."

"Oh my God," she whispered, her heart ponding. Avi and Christy, the well-mannered diners, were nothing like they seemed. "If Cash taught me anything, this is no coincidence."

"These men are among a few in the world capable of providing Amjad a new identity and laundering his fortune."

They laundered money, they could give someone a new identity, and they'd kidnapped Cash. She knew this like a salmon knew where it was born. And just like that, she saw what she had to do. It scared her—suffocating, bone-scraping fear—though somehow, she knew that she would do it. *She had to do it.*

"I'm imagining, by the determined look on that sheyn gentile face that you already have a plan." As she frowned, thinking, Itzac added, "Sheyn means beautiful."

Callie squeezed his hand. "Yes, I know just what to do. But I have to get back to Seattle to do it."

"I can get you to Seattle in my plane"—he checked his watch—"by three p.m. Pacific. Tell me what you can."

She had no idea where her clarity was coming from. But she knew what she knew. "I don't want to tell you specifics yet. I will once I put it together. What I will say is that Cash taught me this. He calls it playing offense."

CHAPTER FIFTEEN

Cash had no idea where he was. They'd injected him with a sedative, and then driven him out of the city with a hood over his head. After he woke up, groggy, he guessed that they drove for another two hours, at least, before he was hurried into a house, still hooded, then led downstairs to a soundproof room in the basement. They'd seated him in a chair, then cuffed his wrists and, using a D-ring shackle, attached the cuffs above his head to a sturdy eyebolt screwed into the wall. When he was secure, they took off the hood.

He knew they intended to kill him because Boone had shown himself. He'd never met Boone, but Cash knew his story. Boone had started out as a recovery agent, a crackerjack bounty hunter. If you were on the run, he was your worst nightmare. He'd brought a bail skip back from Myanmar, when it was still called Burma and closed to Americans; found, then brought back, two deadly yakuza syndicate bosses from Kobe, by himself; found a Palestinian terrorist who'd eluded the Israelis; and so on. His prowess, his business and his sizable ego grew exponentially. Before long, the Tracker was the go-to guy for the big corporations, the Department of Defense, or anyone else who could afford his steep fee. He was the go-to guy when there was no other way to get a particularly difficult job done.

Since dropping out in the seventies, Boone had little or no use for conventional reality, society or status. He enjoyed a mischievous fantasy life, he shifted personas as it pleased him, and he liked making others uneasy. Not long ago, he'd found a rogue general who'd disappeared with army ordnance in the Middle East. Since then, he likened himself to Martin Sheen's Captain Willard in *Apocalypse Now*, the relentless assassin on a hallucinatory mission to find and terminate a mad renegade colonel. Lately, he liked to get under people's skin by reciting unsettling passages from Willard's voice-over narration in that movie.

Cash wondered who'd paid his fee to find them.

Boone came in soon after he was chained to the wall. The Tracker looked him over. Boone was a sixties throwback. A beard, long white hair, a colorful handkerchief wrapped around his forehead, and one hoop earring. Though Boone was fit and healthy, he had to be at least seventy years old.

He stood in front of Cash and recited, *"There's no way I can tell them...what really happened over there...I don't even know if I remember all of it. I can't remember how it ended, exactly—because when it ended I was insane."*

Boone laughed, a ghastly chuckle. "Recognize that, bad ass?"

"Captain Willard, *Apocalypse Now.*"

"Way cool." He gave Cash a thumbs-up.

Cash shrugged, looked him over; he could crank out this drivel, too. Maybe drop Robert Duvall's line, *I love the smell of napalm in the morning.* Cash decided to let it go; he didn't want to encourage this lethal miscreant.

Cash knew that under his sixties getup and feigned counter-culture attitude, behind his irritating playacting, Boone was first and foremost a world-class computer expert, a genuine master. He even did his own programming. He was a genius at hacking into and collecting people's private information, then using pattern recognition programs to find them. He developed his own pattern recognition software and used existing programs and pattern recognition algorithms with the deft touch and reliable outcomes of a virtuoso concert pianist. All of his software was patented, encrypted and totally off the radar. This was his true reality, where he lived, and no one could navigate it as effortlessly or expertly as Boone.

Boone shifted gears. "You were easy to find, *movie guy*— New York City, calls to Izzie the Macher in Amsterdam, New York restaurants he favors, and so on." He gloated. "Not what I would have expected, given your rep."

Cash cracked a smile. "If I'd know you were looking for me, it would have gone another way."

"Your friends"—and Boone actually sang this phrase—"*easy like Sunday mornings*...Only so many places you can hide a boat."

"Did you ID the bodies?"

"Not yet, but the police will surely do that today. Casper was still angry with you—and dude, that man nurses a grudge—so he planted enough explosives to take out all four boathouses on the pier. Even if they were hiding in a vault underneath the boathouse, they were nuked, annihilated." He snapped his fingers. "Poof, gone. All we need is for the police to find a finger, a toe, a stray hair, check the DNA. That defines your lifespan, bad ass."

"Casper the guy whose boat we blew up?"

"Wrong guy to cross. This isn't a job for him—he's delivering the wrath of an angry God."

"Uh-huh...You know my guy Andre, the one with Daniel?"

"Casper filled me in."

"He's hard to kill. If I were you, I'd watch my back, Boone."

"Always do...That's why you're the one cuffed to the ring. We'll bag your girlfriend today, make her eat grapes off the wall-paper, then this job is history."

"Like I said, watch your back." Cash decided that this guy was unhinged. When he turned to leave, Cash asked, "Why are you here?"

"Casper asked me to do him a favor. He hates you, you can't imagine."

"What favor?

"A slow and painful death," Boone said. "I wanted to check you out myself. Come up with an inspiration. I think I've got it…and, my man, it's choice. I'm jazzed, that's how sweet this is." Boone smiled, ghoulish. "Here's my idea—in Japan, they have this giant poisonous centipede, the mukade. It's as ugly and frightening as anything you'll ever see—fifteen inches long." He spread his index fingers. "A pair of modified legs, forcipules, come out of its head. The forcipules have sharp claws that connect to venom glands and are used to kill its prey. Every kid in Japan has terrifying nightmares about mukade. You ever hear of it?"

Cash nodded. He knew that mukade could grow to fifteen inches, were famously ugly, venomous, and had a horrific bite. Mukade, he remembered, were fiercely aggressive. They liked to kill and eat small reptiles. Mukade were so feared, they had become a symbol of evil in Japanese mythology. In mythology, mukade grew so huge and ferocious that even dragons lived in fear of them.

"What I bet you don't know is that they like body cavities. So I'm thinking, one in your nose, one in your ear and a third in your mouth, or maybe where the sun don't shine. Let that percolate, pal. I owe Casper, so I want to make him happy."

Boone left, humming the Turtles' "Happy Together."

Yeah, Cash thought, the guy belonged in the big glass aquarium at the Dragon where they kept the python.

He was still feeling groggy from the sedative. He drifted off, then woke up thinking about Callie and about how his luck had changed. Here he was, the Tracker's prisoner. And Boone was promising a slow and painful death by mukade. Andre and Daniel were likely dead. But he was feeling lucky. That was all Callie. Callie James…

Cash felt suddenly low, a rare feeling for him. He couldn't lose her. Not now.

◆◆◆

Moishe had driven them into a parking garage in a high-rise building. They drove up to the third floor, where they sped onto a waiting elevator. At the fifth floor, Itzac and Callie exited the car, and another man and woman took their places in the back seat of the Mercedes. Itzac sent Moishe and the Mercedes up to the tenth floor with instructions to wait five minutes, then exit on the second floor and drive to Grand Central Terminal. At Grand Central, the woman would use Callie's credit card to buy a train ticket to New Rochelle, where another car would be waiting.

On the fifth floor, Callie and Itzac stepped into a waiting pickup. Their new driver drove down the ramps and out of the parking garage from a little known basement exit. On their way out, Itzac spoke to the driver. "Samuel, have them prepare the plane at Teterboro."

As they approached the airport, Itzac gave Callie a burner phone that couldn't be traced, as well as a safe number at which to reach him when she was ready. He explained that the bad guys would follow the Mercedes and track the decoy to New Rochelle, but by tonight, latest, they'd surely be tracking her again. Time was of the essence. He'd be waiting at the number he'd given her until he heard from her. He leaned in, kissed her cheek, then whispered in her ear, "Godspeed, child. Mazl un brokhe."

◆◆◆

Callie had her feet up on the coffee table in the spacious cabin of the Boeing 767. She was the only passenger on the private jet.

She'd made her plan, written it down in sequence, made notes about what she'd need, and now she was ready to call Will.

"Sit down," she said when he answered the phone.

"Okay."

"I can't tell you what this is about, or what I'm going to do, but I need your help."

"What do you need?"

"Call Christy Ben-Meyer. Tell her the impossible-to-find imperial bottle of nineteen forty-seven Château Cheval Blanc that she's been looking for has just been located. Make up a story about how the friend who located it, a vineyard owner in eastern Washington, insists on delivering it in person. Tell her you're leaving town tonight, but you have arranged a meeting with your friend at his in-town apartment at five tonight. Tell her you'll pick her up at the ferry terminal. Then drive her to your actor friend's apartment."

"The place where we hid *the one*?"

"*The one*?"

"Oral sex? The doofus?"

"Okay, yes. But please save that…Just make this happen, lie as only you can do it, do *whatever* you have to do. *Anything.* I need for her to be at your friend's place at five o'clock, alone. Can you do that?"

"Of course. Not a problem. This wine is so rare that I can easily set the time and place if she wants to acquire it. But what is this about?"

"Can't say. It's what you'd call a real hairball. Ready for what I'll need?"

"Fire away."

"I sent you a text. Take a look."

After a minute, he came back on the line. "I see why you're not laughing at my jokes…Sweet pea, are you sure on this?"

"Yes, I've never been more sure about anything in my life. Just do it, please. Call me to confirm Christy. Pick me up wherever the private jets land at Boeing Field at three o'clock, and I'll explain what I can."

"Is this something I can go to jail for?"

"Absolutely. It could also get you killed."

"Sounds like you've come out of your shell. Sunshine, I'm in."

◆◆◆

Fifteen minutes later Will called back to say that Christy was confirmed. He went on to describe her gratitude and excitement about picking up the rare Bordeaux.

"Will she be alone?"

"I made up this story about the vineyard owner being very cautious about holding this rare, crazy-expensive wine. If he so much as sees a friend, or even another driver, he won't produce the wine. I explained to her that in two thousand ten, an imperial bottle of this wine sold at a Christie's auction in Geneva for three hundred and four thousand dollars, which is true. She offered to bring a cashier's check."

"I hope you told her that wouldn't be necessary."

"Dahlin', I may be a good ole Southern boy, but I'm no 'Billy Beer' Carter."

Callie smiled. "Right. See you at three."

◆◆◆

After checking her notes yet again, Callie called Itzac. "It's a go. I'm ready to tell you what I intend to do."

"Please."

She took a measured breath, then said, "I'm going to kidnap Christy Ben-Meyer, Avi Ben-Meyer's wife." She heard him inhale, almost a gasp. "Avi adores her...I'm going to trade her for Cash."

Itzac exhaled slowly, audibly. "My dear, this is excellent... Chapeau."

She imagined him tipping his black fedora.

"Lest there be any doubt, I spoke with his uncle, Nathan. He confirmed that he would make an exception to help with my request...Now, how can I help?"

"Once I have her—and I have an idea about how to do that—I'd like you to work out the mechanics of the exchange. I should have her at five o'clock Pacific."

"Yes, I will happily organize this exchange."

"Detective Samter is a good man, but we'll have to keep him out of this. I'm not sure just how to do that."

"He'd never allow it. You're ahead of me. What are you thinking?"

"I have one idea. What if we trade for Amjad, as well? I'm thinking Avi will do anything—*anything*—to get Christy back. If he gives us Amjad's new identity, we can give Amjad to Samter. It's the only thing I can think of that will keep Samter from losing it and throwing Cash and me in jail."

"Amjad, as well...I see. You are a bold and surprising young woman. With an unexpected flair for the high-stakes end game. Amjad, as well. Indeed..."

"Doable?"

"I think so. Amjad is blown. Avi will know this."

"Okay, then..."

"You must love my friend Cash very much."

"Yes, Itzac, I do love him very much. I understood this last night. I can't bear to lose him. Not now."

"Understood. As soon as I hear from you that your part is done, I will call Avi. You must send me a picture or, better yet, a video of her in captivity, a video that makes it *absolutely, unmistakably clear* that her life is at stake. I will tell him that the price for his wife's life is Cash *and* Amjad's new identity. Nonnegotiable. We must make this exchange tonight if we're going to get to Samter in time. You can call your detective with Amjad's new identity once Cash is with me. To make this deal, Christy and Avi must go free. I'll provide them safe passage to Argentina in a way that guarantees your safety. Leave that to me."

"Will Cash be safe until five?"

"No one can say with certainty, but I will make sure that your detective does not release any information about Andre and Daniel before I call Avi. I will also have my friend tell Detective Samter that he should expect to hear from you tonight."

"I'd like to be a fly on the wall when he gets that call…" Callie took a calming breath, then said, "Itzac, you're a wonderful man."

"Whatever happens, Cash was lucky to be with you."

"You're making me cry."

"Nu? So I should be the only one crying?"

◆◆◆

Boone had left a glass jar with three giant mukade on a table beside Cash. The Tracker was right, they were uglier than anything he'd ever seen.

Cash closed his eyes. He had to do something to divert his mind from these horrific insects. He turned away, stretched his sore arms, flexed his tense back, focusing on Callie. Callie James… Okay, it was working. Picturing her face, the corners of his mouth turned up and his spirits soared.

Callie James…Why did he feel so wholly in love with her?

He stood, arms extended behind him, as he considered his on-again, off-again history with women.

Women found him attractive, and he'd been with many of them. His relationships, however, rarely lasted as long as he expected. There was some part of himself that he held back, and women sensed this and eventually moved on or asked for more of a commitment than he could make. Over time, he realized that it wasn't a part—like a *piece*—but rather some portion of his unusual intensity. He understood that he was very accepting of other people and only offered as much as a woman looked for—some essential emotional minimum—to sustain the relationship. It wasn't a conscious decision. It was a strong, keenly sensitive person's way of protecting a partner from unwanted, possibly unsettling intensity. It's who he was. Everything that he did, he did well but sparingly. So in some way he didn't understand, he was choosing women who were less intense than he was.

Callie was the first woman he'd ever been with who demanded one hundred percent at all times. She was relentless, and even when she wasn't aware of it, every bit as intense as he was. He didn't hold anything back with her—yet she always wanted an explanation, an elaboration, an argument, or an answer to a difficult question. She'd never idealized him, that's for sure. And he never pretended with her. He couldn't put his finger on it, but the out-of-the-blue way this had happened between them, the strength of it, was something entirely new for him. Did he trust it? Yes, unequivocally. Did he know why? Yes, unequivocally again—it was because Callie James could never be untrue to herself.

Cash sat down, and turning back, he watched the horrible insects squirming in the jar.

No, he couldn't lose her. Not now.

◆◆◆

"Is it just my imagination or are we getting better at this?" Christy asked Avi. They were sprawled on the king-sized bed in the master suite with the view of Mount Rainier and the South Sound.

"You, my darling, have always been superb, and I believe I'm improving under your good example and tutelage."

"You silver-tongued devil."

"No, my darling, it's true."

"What can I say? You're not with Little Bo Peep."

The intercom rang. Avi sat up, pushed a button. "Maurie?"

They heard him clear his throat. "They've tracked Callie James. Casper wants the go-ahead for tonight."

"Done. Any word from Kingston?"

"Just a statement. There will be an update from the police this evening."

Christy got out of bed, put on her white silk robe. "Maurie, I'm going to town to pick up Avi's birthday gift. Tell Casper I want all four of them confirmed MIA by the time I get back."

♦♦♦

Will was waiting on the tarmac beside his BMW when Callie stepped off the private jet at Boeing Field. She hit the ground running. Minutes later they were on their way to East Lake, where Will's actor friend had his apartment.

"Did you get everything on the list?"

"Handcuffs, the Taser X26, a noose, rope, two heavy-duty eye-hooks—I've already screwed them into the ceiling beam, as requested—duct tape, a stool and a handgun."

"Thank you." Callie checked her watch. "What time does the ferry arrive?"

"She's on the three fifty. She'll arrive at four twenty-five."

"Okay. Drop me off by three forty-five. That should give me time to set up and you time to meet the ferry."

"What can you tell me?" Will asked.

"Are you sure you want to be part of this?"

"Sweetie, I'm already part of this. I want to know what *this* is."

"Fair enough. We don't have time for details, but basically, Christy and Avi Ben-Meyer have been behind all of our problems from the beginning. They paid to have Daniel killed. Their man blew up the restaurant and killed Doc, and now they've taken Cash. If it wasn't for him, I'd likely be dead now. They may have killed Andre and Daniel in a bombing at the boathouse in Kingston. That's not verified yet. Detective Samter is holding back what he knows until tonight. We're betting they won't kill Cash until they know Andre and Daniel are dead. So before they kill him, I'm going to kidnap Christy and trade her for Cash."

Will let loose a string of curses and swore that if his own mother told him this, he wouldn't believe her. When he managed to slow down, he asked her yet again, pointedly, "So...sweet pea, you're, uh, sure on this?"

"Sure as sunrise."

◆◆◆

Will parked under the viaduct, then met Christy as she walked off the ferry. He kissed her on one cheek, then the other.

"I'm so excited," Christy exclaimed. "Was it hard to find?" She took Will's arm.

"Needle in a haystack. Especially the six-liter imperial bottle. My friend, the vineyard owner in eastern Washington, had to reach out to Francis Ford Coppola himself, who bought Inglenook, to help him find it." Will opened the door to the BMW. Christy stepped into the front seat on the passenger side.

"Avi will be beside himself. He's been trying to find this wine for years. How much will it cost?"

"We made a good deal. One hundred ten thousand dollars."

"How do I pay for it?"

"We'll organize a wire transfer when you get the wine."

Ten minutes later, Will looped around the block for a second time to confirm that no one was following, then he parked the BMW in a parking garage behind the building.

"I have the key," Will explained. "My friend, Mike, is watching for us. As I explained, he's ultracautious about this extremely valuable cargo. He'll bring the wine up to the apartment in a minute."

He opened the back door and then led Christy up the stairs to apartment 2D. Will opened the apartment door, held it for her. Christy came through the door into the living room. Will closed the door behind her.

"Christy," Callie called from where she'd been standing behind the door.

When Christy turned, confused, Callie whispered, "You miserable bitch," and she fired two barbed, dart-like electrodes from her Taser into Christy's chest. The electrodes created a circuit in the body, essentially hijacking the central nervous system, causing neuromuscular incapacitation.

Christy fell to the floor, writhing in uncontrollable muscle spasms. When the writhing stopped and she'd curled into the fetal position, Callie and Will cuffed her hands behind her back.

When they were able to get her on her feet, Callie said, "We're trading you for Cash Logan and Amjad Hasim."

"What are you talking about?"

Callie slapped her, as hard as she was able. The blow tore Christy's lower lip, drawing blood, and bruised her cheek. Callie hadn't planned to do that—it was her second time, and she'd never hit anyone nearly so hard in her life—but red-hot rage was coursing through her veins. She was trembling, though her ever-present anxiety had receded, and she sure as hell didn't feel helpless.

"Are you crazy?" Christy cried out.

"Don't even try that. I know what you and Avi have done—to Daniel, to my restaurant, to my friend Doc. You almost killed us all on the boat. And now you have Cash, damn you!"

Christy's face changed; she got it—Callie had somehow put it together. "You low-life skanky cunt, I'll kill you myself." Christy spit in Callie's face.

Callie slapped her again, a fierce crack, astonished, yet again, by the rage she felt welling inside. And in that moment, she understood that her usual internal restraints—her rules and regulations—were no longer in place. It was as if an anvil had been cut loose from around her neck.

Blood dripped from Christy's lip, her left eye was partially closed, and tears streamed down her face.

Callie stepped closer. "If anything happens to Cash, if you hurt him again, I'll kill you, Christy Ben-Meyer. I swear that on my son's life."

Five minutes later Christy was standing on a stool in the center of the room. Her hands were cuffed behind her back. Her feet were bound. Her mouth was covered with duct tape. There was a noose around her neck that was tightly tied off to the pair of sturdy eyehooks that Will had screwed into the ceiling beam earlier. Christy's head was tilted back and up; the rope was that tight. Another rope was tied to the leg of the stool. If the stool were pulled out from under Christy's feet, she would hang.

Callie held a handgun to Christy's kneecap.

Will was shooting a video with Callie's iPhone.

Callie spoke to the camera. "Avi Ben-Meyer, I promise you that I will shoot out Christy's left kneecap in fifteen minutes if you haven't arranged the exchange with Itzac by then. In thirty minutes, I'll shoot out her other kneecap and hang her. Believe me on this—if Cash Logan is hurt in any way, I'll torture her without mercy before she dies." Callie nodded, done. She walked to a corner of the room, fighting for breath. Dear God! What had she just said? Torture Christy? Damn it, if they hurt Cash…She gasped—she'd never even known that she could have feelings like that.

Will placed a calming hand on her back, and he gave her the phone. Callie noted the time, then sent the video to Itzac.

◆◆◆

To keep his mukade fears at bay, Cash was replaying classic Callie James encounters in his mind's eye.

At the moment, he was remembering a night when he'd been tending bar for her, maybe two and a half years ago. It was late and they were closing up. Cash was singing "Tonight Is What It Means to Be Young," from *Streets of Fire*, a favorite old movie. He was crooning the chorus—*"Let the revels begin. Let the fire be started"*—when Callie came over and started reading him the riot act. She was angry at him for dating that twenty-three-year-old French sculptress—Justine—who he'd picked up while tending her bar.

"This is an upscale French restaurant, not some May–December dating site," Callie notified him, interrupting his singing and looking displeased, indeed.

Cash sighed, a twinkle in his eye. "I can't help it if your fancy French clientele finds me attractive."

"You could be her father."

"So?"

"So, that's not okay."

"Okay? What does *okay* have to do with this? I like her."

"Don't you have any sense of decorum?"

"What's decorum?"

"Correctness, appropriateness, dignity."

"Dating someone you like is all of those things. It just doesn't fit your restaurant rules."

Callie shot him a frosty look and left.

That Sunday, his day off, Cash brought Justine to Le Cochon Bronze for dinner. Callie seated them in the back corner.

After dinner, she came to their table, reluctantly, and asked them how they'd enjoyed their dinner. Justine complimented her and her restaurant in French, then surprisingly, she asked Callie, "Why is it that you disapprove of me—more specifically, disapprove of me dating this man?"

"Ma chère jeune fille, he's the bartender here, and he's old enough to be your father."

"So? Ma chère madame, he's also one of the most interesting, thoughtful people I've ever met. And how dare you judge him or me for our sexual preferences?"

Callie was speechless. She shot Cash one of her high-octane frosty looks; this one was a real scorcher.

Justine turned to Cash, batted her eyelashes, then, smiling a coy little-girl smile, said, "Can we have dessert…pretty please, Daddy?"

Cash was laughing, remembering the mortified look on Callie's face as the beet-borscht spots appeared, when Boone came back into the basement.

"We start soon. I'm waiting for the call," Boone explained. "I thought I'd give you a chance to focus on what you'll be working with." He held up the jar, shook it sharply, jostling the mukade, irritating them until they were writhing. "Killer, eh?"

◆◆◆

The Macher had arranged the call with Avi Ben-Meyer at 5:30 Pacific. He sent the video at 5:15 and called at 5:20.

"I'll want Cash delivered to my warehouse right away, unharmed. I'll want Amjad Hasim's new identity. If I have both of these things, Christy will be delivered to you in Seattle at a mutually agreed-on public place."

Avi was breathing heavily. "I don't understand. Why have you taken my wife?"

"We're both too smart for this, and Callie will start shooting in ten minutes if we don't work this out. Your life, as you know it, is over. Do we have a deal?"

"Cash for Christy. I don't know Amjad's new identity."

"No deal. Amjad is already blown. You get that…This is non-negotiable. Avi, listen very carefully. There's no time. No margin for error. Callie's in love with Cash Logan, and you've pushed her too far. You've awoken a ferocious sleeping dragon. Callie *will kill* Christy. I promise you that. And I will have a man there to guarantee it. Here's what you need to think about—would you like to spend the rest of your life with or without your wife?"

Avi didn't hesitate. "Cash will be at the warehouse by six fifteen Pacific. When Christy is delivered to a safe meeting place, I'll give you Amjad."

"At the same time. You know that you can rely on my word. At seven Pacific, Christy will be shown to you. At seven, you call me with Amjad's new name and a location, and I'll instruct my man to release your wife. The video I sent is encrypted. It cannot be copied or resent. I will delete it remotely when the exchange is complete…Do you understand what I'm telling you? You know my reach…I know who you are. I can keep you safe or make sure you're never safe again. If Amjad's new identity is not correct, or if there's any threat to Callie, I'll paint a bull's-eye on your back."

"We have a deal."

◆◆◆

Maurie came in when Avi buzzed the intercom. "We've been blindsided by Callie James," Avi said.

Maurie frowned. "What are you saying? How so?"

Avi handed him his phone, showed him the video.

Maurie put a hand on Avi's shoulder, squeezing gently. It was, he realized, the first time since his wife had died in an accident thirty years ago that he felt something so strongly. "We've had a good run, my friend," Maurie summed it up precisely. "What can I do?"

"Where's a good place in Seattle to pick up Christy?"

"In the alley behind the restaurant?"

"Good. Is Casper still an option?"

Maurie checked his watch, used a checkered handkerchief. "It's not too late. Yes, he is still available."

"Here's what I'd like to do."

$$\blacklozenge\blacklozenge\blacklozenge$$

Callie was sitting in the corner, trying to ride the waves of feeling that kept washing over her. Hatred and rage for Christy and Avi, sorrow for Doc, agonizing worry about Andre, even Daniel, then love for her son, Lew, and finally her fresh, fervent love for Cash would wash away everything else. And then she'd be afraid for him. The phone rang. Itzac.

"We have a deal," he said.

"Thank God," Callie whispered, giving Will a thumbs-up. He was standing next to Christy, afraid that she might pass out or stumble and hang herself.

"Your video was perfect."

"I didn't know I had it in me." She raised her hand; it was still trembling.

"I did…Here's how it's going to happen. Cash will be delivered to my warehouse, unharmed, before six fifteen Pacific. Avi will pick up Christy behind your restaurant at seven Pacific. This is the point of maximum danger, so I have sent two men to deliver her. So you know, one is Chinese, and they're already parked in the alley behind the apartment. They're in a black Ford Explorer."

"Why am I not surprised?"

"My dear, I've assumed responsibility for your safety and I intend to follow through. They'll hold Christy in a secure location until I let them know I have Cash. My men will take her to the meeting place, then let her go when Avi calls me with Amjad's new identity. I'll call you after they let Christy go. Get her ready. Cash arrives soon. I'm sure he'll want to talk with you. We'll both get on a plane for Seattle ASAP. I want him out of harm's way when the exchange goes down. Not to worry, it's just a precaution. And Detective Samter is expecting a call later tonight."

"Thank you, Itzac. What time will you be in Seattle?"

"If Cash arrives timely, and I'm sure he will, ETA is one a.m. Pacific. Are you okay? In that video, you looked as fierce as Cerberus, the three-headed hellhound with a mane of snakes that guards the gates to Hades."

"Well, I pretty much slapped Christy senseless. I wasn't expecting that." Nor had she expected to feel okay about it.

"She had it coming," Will volunteered.

"I heard that and I concur," Itzac added. "Enjoy the fire, Callie. It's soothing, and it's good for the soul."

"I'll try."

◆◆◆

Boone held a mukade in a pair of forceps. He placed it on Cash's upper arm. "Wicked, eh?" Boone smiled.

Eh? Cash wondered if this infuriating, big-brained freak was Canadian.

The mukade was crawling toward Cash's neck when Boone's cell phone rang. "Yes," he answered.

Cash could feel the mukade inching toward his ear.

Boone broke the connection. "I'm going to enjoy this, white man."

"White man?" Cash asked, instead of screaming at this crazy fuck.

Boone chuckled. Then, quoting Captain Willard, he said, *"Every minute I stay in this room, I get softer. And every minute Charlie squats in the bush, he gets stronger."*

Cash screamed, a harrowing cry, when he felt the mukade probing inside his ear.

◆◆◆

Will helped Callie bring Christy down the back stairs. Her hands were still cuffed behind her back, but other than that, she was not restrained. In the alley, Christy turned to Callie. "You are maggot food, a stone-dead, rancid cockwash," she hissed.

"Were you always this vile, spiteful psycho? Shut your filthy mouth, Christy," Callie snapped. "Before I wash it out with soap."

They handed her over to the waiting men, who injected her with a sedative and buckled her into the back seat of the Explorer. The men, Henry and Shen, had obviously done this before. When she was falling asleep, they held her head back and force-fed her a small portion of some kind of milky liquid. Callie watched them drive away.

◆◆◆

Boone chuckled his ghastly chuckle again. "You've got to be the luckiest white man alive," he announced as, with his forceps, he pulled the probing mukade from just inside Cash's ear.

Cash let out a measured breath when the Tracker dropped the squirming mukade back into the glass jar.

Boone put the hood over Cash's head, unhooked his cuffed hands from the eyebolt in the wall. "Let's bug out, bad ass."

◆◆◆

In less than half an hour, the van stopped in an alley in the city. A masked man Cash didn't know opened the side door, took off his hood, uncuffed his hands, then helped him onto the pavement. Cash was confused. They were behind Izzie's warehouse; he recognized the spot. He put it together quickly—when they'd taken him, they must have driven in wide circles for hours before heading back to the city. He looked at the early evening sky, as close as he'd ever been to believing in God. When he turned back, the van was gone. He checked his watch: It was 9:00 p.m. in New York City.

Cash rang the buzzer at the back of the warehouse. The door opened and Izzie spread his arms. Cash embraced his friend. "What did you do? How did you do this?"

"It wasn't me." Izzie took him straight to the car. His driver was waiting for them at the entrance to the alley. Before Cash could get in another question, Izzie was on the phone.

◆◆◆

Izzie stayed on the phone, making plans until they were on his plane, airborne. The Macher glanced at his phone, then set it down. "The rendezvous is set for seven Pacific, so we have perhaps ten minutes to catch you up."

"Please," Cash asked. "I have no idea what this rendezvous is, no clue what you're planning, not even a notion why I'm still alive."

Izzie handed Cash his cell phone, set up the video.

Cash watched the video, spellbound. At the end, there were tears in his eyes. Before he could speak, Izzie raised a hand to stop him.

"Callie put this together. Start to finish. Her analysis, her plan, her execution. She loves you more than life itself."

"My God, how?"

"I mentioned an Argentine lawyer, Nathan, as a person who might help someone find a new identity. Just like that, she knew his last name: Ben-Meyer. Then she told me his nephew, who I also know, was a regular at her restaurant."

"I know them. Avi and Christy Ben-Meyer."

"Without telling me her plan, Callie took one of my planes to Seattle, then, when she'd worked it out, she told me what she was going to do, specified what she needed from me, and finally, exactly as she'd laid it out, she kidnapped Christy. As we speak, we're trading Christy for you and Amjad Hasim's true identity. Also Callie's idea. She knew you had to have something to give to Detective Samter. She's a brilliant women and a force of nature. At the beginning, before she would give me any specifics, all that she would say was, and I quote, 'Cash taught me about this. He calls it playing offense.'"

♦♦♦

Will and Callie were sitting quietly in Will's friend's apartment when the phone rang.

Callie picked it up.

"Babe, I love you, you can't imagine."

Callie burst into tears, great heaving sobs—the floodgates were open.

"Are you okay?" Cash eventually asked.

When she stopped sobbing, Callie said, "This is the happiest moment of my life, Cash Logan." More tears, deep breaths. "I couldn't bear the thought of losing you."

"Same for me. That's all I could think about when they had me chained to the wall. I had to live to be with you...I saw the video. Izzie told me what you did. Callie, you saved my life."

"I love, love, love you. I have to call Samter, let Lew know that this is over, and then see the love of my life. I'd be thrilled to cook for you and Itzac tonight."

"I'll call Detective Samter. And I'll contact Ed Rosen about Lew. You've done enough."

"Thank you for that."

"Be safe, Callie. It's not over yet. I'll see you at the restaurant."

❖❖❖

Callie and Will were waiting anxiously in the apartment for Itzac's call, when Henry parked the Explorer in the alley behind Callie's restaurant.

It was 6:55 p.m. and Henry, Chen and Christy were the first to arrive. Five minutes later, a black Mercedes pulled into the alley and stopped, facing the Explorer less than seventy feet away. Avi Ben-Meyer stepped out, a cell phone in his hand. He wore a dark-blue suit and a light-blue tie. His hair was disheveled and he looked distraught.

Callie was already on her phone with Itzac, who had Henry on another phone. "Is he alone?" Itzac asked Henry.

"Yes."

"Show Christy," he instructed, then he picked up a third phone, where Avi was waiting.

Henry gestured to Shen, who rolled down the back window.

Avi stepped closer, to where he could see her. "Are you all right, my darling?" he called out.

Christy nodded, bleary-eyed.

There was a tense moment as Avi spoke into his phone.

As he listened, the Macher was taking notes. "I have Amjad's location and his new identity," Itzac eventually confirmed to Callie. Then to Henry, "Let Christy go."

Henry had Shen help Christy out of the back seat. He leaned her against the car and Henry uncuffed Christy's hands from behind her back.

Christy took measured steps until she reached Avi. She wrapped her arms around him.

Avi put Christy in the front passenger seat of the Mercedes, then he got in on the driver's side and the Mercedes pulled away.

"It's done," Itzac reported to Callie on the phone. "We're on the plane."

"I'm going to run some errands, then go home," Callie announced. "I may even take a nap. Can I talk with Cash?"

◆◆◆

Avi and Christy had switched cars, scanned her for bugs, and then Avi drove through Tacoma. They were avoiding the ferries, driving around to the Olympic Peninsula, where he had a private jet waiting.

"Callie James? I'm still in shock," Avi admitted.

"She was a fucking dragon lady," Christy said, rubbing her jaw. "I can't believe this…I'm too old to start over."

"We've always had a plan for this day. We have money, new identities, and a perfectly safe, quite lovely home in Portugal. We fly to Lisbon, use our new Canadian passports and enter as Dov and Lily Silverman, husband and wife. Untraceable. Global Real Estate owns property there and we're already on the books as the managing partners opening their new office."

"I'll miss Maurie, his black suits, his checkered handkerchiefs and his ever-present silver spittoon." As an afterthought, she added, "That clotheshorse could hawk a loogie."

"Hawk a loogie?"

"Throw down the phlegm. Spit like a champion."

"I'm glad you're feeling better." Avi took her hand. "Maurie's on his way to Buenos Aires, where he can retire comfortably. Nathan will help get him started. He's also got a new name, and more money than he'll ever need."

"And the bitch? She's like a piece of broken glass, stuck in my craw."

"Casper is—how do you say?—on it."

"Tell him to saw off her fucking head. I want proof of death."

"Will a photo satisfy my one and only?"

"Hell no."

An hour later, Callie and Will finished their errands—Callie wanted to replenish some staples for her personal use (she needed some semblance of normalcy), and she'd shopped for special items for their dinner tonight. Unexpectedly, shopping had been relaxing for her.

Will was going on about how formidable she'd been with Christy, how Le Callie Nouveau—a riff on Le Beaujolais Nouveau, the new Beaujolais—was like the great women of the South; he was comparing her to Scarlett O'Hara in *Gone with the Wind* when he turned down First toward the restaurant, and she shushed him.

A minute later, Callie was on the phone again with Cash—just talking to him was somehow reassuring. She was going over what she planned for dinner—she'd settled on the cassoulet—when Will finally pulled the BMW into the alley behind Le Cochon Bronze.

Callie got out of the car and opened the trunk, still on the phone with Cash. Will came around and took two bags out of the trunk. Callie closed it. "Did you reach Ed Rosen?" she asked Cash.

"Yes. They'll be back tonight. I told him to call me before dropping Lew at the restaurant."

"Why?"

"Remember the scorpion?"

For just a second, she thought: Oh shit, here we go again. "This is over—right?"

"I hope so, but I can't be one hundred percent certain until Avi and Christy are confirmed gone, out of the picture, and we have Amjad."

"No. Oh, no. And don't you dare call me a frog."

"How about *my* frog?"

"Ah…*my undying smart-ass.*" Callie turned toward her back door. "And what's worse, I'm getting used to it…I feel like years have gone by since I found you at the Dragon."

"I feel that, too."

Approaching the door, Callie started at a sharp crack. She turned back when she heard a loud scraping noise—something heavy falling on a roof across the alley—and then, without warning, a rifle tumbled to the ground in front of her. Soon after, a man rolled off the facing rooftop and landed face up. Callie recognized the insurance adjuster with the silver pens.

"What the hell?" Callie yelled into the phone. "There's a friggin' dead—"

"Got your back, babe," Cash said. "Eyes right."

Callie turned. And that's when Andre gracefully hopped off the restaurant's roof onto the awning above the kitchen door, then into the alley. He made a deft move with his prosthetic leg to break the fall and then balance himself. In his right hand, Andre held the sniper's rifle he'd taken from Doc's boat, on his face was a roguish smile.

Callie started to cry again. Tears streamed down her face as she embraced Andre. "I was afraid you were dead."

"Hard to kill, sugar."

•••

"So, boychik, are you ready to call your detective?" On the plane, Izzie poured Cash a drink.

Cash raised his glass to the Macher, then he called Detective Samter.

"Detective? When you hear what I have to say, you may want to reconsider 'fuck you'…You won't reconsider under any circumstances? What if I were to tell you that Amjad Hasim is still alive?…You're sending me to jail?…Callie, too?…What if I were to give you the people who set him up with a new identity?…Hard time forever?…Both of us can rot in prison?…What if I were to give you Amjad Hasim?…No, I'm not a weasel making shit up…"

◆◆◆

After helping Andre and Will hide the assassin's body in the damaged basement storeroom, Callie settled into her restaurant kitchen and called Cash back. "Is it over? Please, sweetheart, tell me it's over."

"Yes, it's over," Cash said evenly. "I spoke with Detective Samter. He's picking up Christy and Avi. Izzie's men put a specially designed undetectable transmitter in Christy while she was sedated."

"*In?* Itzac would never—"

"Dial down, babe. She swallowed it unknowingly in a liquid they had her drink when she was falling asleep. It'll beat the scanners. They'll never know it's there."

"I wondered what that was about."

"Christy and Avi are still driving—I'm guessing to a remote airport."

"How did the call go?"

"Samter was crazy mad, ranting. He swore that we'd spend the rest of our lives in jail, both of us…Then I gave him Amjad. That slowed him down. He jumped off to get his people to arrest Amjad, Christie and Avi. I have to call him back. He's going to have a lot of questions, and answering them will require a certain amount of, shall we say, contextualizing the truth—"

"You mean lying?"

"That might be a way of seeing it."

"Thank you. I don't know how much lying I could do right now."

"I told Samter about the man Andre killed on the rooftop."

"My insurance adjuster. We hid his body in the basement."

"I figured that. Samter said he'd take care of it."

"Did you find out who he really was?" Callie asked.

"His name was Casper. I learned that in captivity. He blew up your restaurant, killed Doc. He was also the man who tried to blow up our boat. He worked for Christy and Avi."

"Christy and Avi—they're still a mystery to me. Did they know we were willing to let them go?"

"Yes. Izzie made that deal, but only if they walked away without ever trying to hurt you. Now, all bets are off."

"It's odd that such smart people couldn't just let it go."

"They're a pair of scorpions. Izzie and I bet that they were going to try to kill you…It's just their nature."

"Please don't tell me another nonsensical animal story."

"*Nonsensical?* I love that story."

"Does that mean I have to love it, too? Forget loving it, do I have to even get it?"

"No, no, you don't."

"Okay, then, Come home soon."

"I gave Ed Rosen the go ahead to bring Lew to the restaurant. He's on his way."

"Perfect."

"We'll come straight to the restaurant, too. Could you cook the cassoulet tonight with Doc's game sausages?"

"I'd love that."

◆◆◆

Several hours later, Callie was in her kitchen prepping dinner with Will and Andre. Will was readying the foie gras with Césaire's signature pear sauce. Callie was gathering the ingredients for the cassoulet and discussing sides with Andre.

In the corner, at another prep table, Daniel was sitting next to Lew. They were talking, an intense, animated conversation.

Daniel was clearly enjoying his son, and Lew was beaming. Callie watched them for a long moment, thinking that as hard, as frightening, as crazy as this had been, she'd found the love of her life, and Lew had finally connected with his dad.

She could hear Lew telling his father about a girl he liked. This was new for him, Lew explained in his direct, honest way, and he wasn't sure what to do, or when. Daniel was listening carefully, asking questions. He thought it over, then suggested that girls were hard to know easily, and that Lew had lots of time. He should trust his instincts and go slowly. Watching her son, she quickly understood how much it meant to him to be able to talk to his dad.

She thought about what his dad had said. *Slowly?* That wasn't the Daniel she'd married.

That's when Detective Samter stepped into her restaurant kitchen. He took off his coat, sat at her prep table, stone-faced, and started right in. "You dodged a bullet."

"More than one. If only you knew." Was he angry? She couldn't tell.

"I underestimated you."

"Don't feel bad. I underestimated me for almost forty years…" She made a go-figure face. "Did you find Avi and Christy Ben-Meyer?"

"The Ben-Meyers were arrested at a private air field on the Olympic Peninsula. They'd driven around—through Tacoma—avoiding the ferries after leaving the restaurant. A private jet was waiting to take them out of the country. Portugal," he reported. "Thanks to your friends, we were waiting for them. We arrested them when they drove onto the field."

"A plane to Portugal, an escape just like in *Casablanca*." Andre smiled. "But in this cheeseball sequel to the classic, the sugar bitch and her silver panther get busted by the bacon."

When Samter actually chuckled, a quiet, rumbling laugh, Callie sighed, relieved.

Samter added, "You should have seen the look on his face when we closed in on them. And the foul mouth on that lady—that wasn't Ingrid Bergman–like at all."

Callie laughed out loud. "She's shameless...literally."

"Are you the one who messed up her face?"

"Moi? Impossible," she said, pronouncing *impossible* the French way. In the corner, Daniel had his arm around Lew. He shot her a thumbs-up.

"Right. I've talked twice to your friend Cash. Amjad Hasim, aka Salim Azar, is in custody in San Diego. My terrorism task force friend is a hero. I'm apparently in line for a promotion—so, hard as I try, I can't stay angry at you."

"If I were you, I'd be angry at me...and I'm sorry for cutting you out, but Cash wouldn't be alive if I'd done this any other way."

"I guessed that. Cash was somewhat vague about exactly what you did. We agreed that, under the circumstances, It would be best if I didn't know the details."

"Yes, in this case, less is definitely more. Suffice it to say that you wouldn't have let me do it had you known my plan."

"Cash did say that you saved his life, and that you insisted on delivering Amjad Hasim to me as part of that deal."

"All true."

"Bravo, Callie James." Samter bowed his head, a salute to her. When he raised it again, he was smiling.

Callie had never seen him smile; it was a warm and engaging smile, she thought.

His smile faded, back to business. "There's more...We've forced the Ben-Myers to cut a deal for their clients, their records, how they moved the money and how they reinvested the laundered money. It's already become a very important investigation."

"Good…Ed—can I call you that?"

"Of course."

"I hope that you make chief off of this. You've always been the good cop with me. Don't ever think I don't know and appreciate that. So once again, I apologize for disappearing on you, but Cash's life was at stake. Please forgive me."

"You're forgiven. I understand now why you'd want to save that man's life."

Callie kissed his cheek.

Detective Ed Samter took both of her hands. "Truth be told, you were right when you said, 'You won't be sorry.'"

◆◆◆

The kitchen had the look, smell and feel of a French holiday. They'd closed the door to the restaurant, which was under construction, and Callie had set the prep table for dinner. She'd used her best tableware, including painted plates she'd brought from Portugal. Callie had called her florist, who came in late and brought over flowers, beautiful bouquets that she'd set just so on the long maple table, and on the counter beside the cast-iron stove. The fragrant smells of cassoulet with duck confit, game sausages (wild boar, elk and venison), garlic, white beans and myriad spices; foie gras with pear sauce; roasted Squash Salad (with late harvest apple cider vinegar); truffle risotto; and Daniel Boulud's Potage Lyonnais (pumpkin, gruyere, jambon de Paris, caramelized onion, sourdough); and the beginnings of her own medley of pies for dessert, all contributed to the festive ambiance. Will had chosen the wines, and several bottles were already uncorked and being enjoyed by all.

Callie supervised everything, but Andre was handling the truffles, and Daniel had proudly taken on the Potage Lyonnais. Lew was at Callie's side, sampling the cassoulet and anything else that needed tasting. "My dad's all right," he whispered to her. "He invited me to Paris…Can I go?"

"Of course," she responded, thinking that she and Cash would take him in case Daniel didn't show up. Just thinking about showing Cash *her* Paris made her heart stir.

And there he was, coming through the door with Itzac. And then everyone was cheering, Callie was in his arms, and the place went wild, crazy wild.

EPILOGUE

It was 3:30 a.m. and they were all seated around the long maple prep table, finishing their meal. It had been a feast, and it was still being savored. The conversation had been intense and animated as Andre filled them in on his tactical ploys, how he'd used the well-insured boat as a decoy, even planted a hog carcass aboard; Izzie told and retold the story of Callie's chutzpah and audacity; Will walked them through the kidnapping and Callie's determination and toughness; Cash told them stories about Boone, the Tracker, then described the mukade; Daniel held forth on *causality*, explaining how if it wasn't for him, Amjad Hasim would still be at large.

The mood was festive. Andre raised a wine glass, then tapped his knife against it to get everyone's attention.

"This is a toast inspired by Daniel, the doofus," Andre offered. "From the classic *Casablanca*, an interaction between Bogart and the French captain Renault." He raised his glass to Daniel and began acting out Renault's part: *"What in heaven's name brought you to Casablanca?"*

Imitating Bogie: *"My health, I came to Casablanca for the waters."*

"The waters? What waters? We're in the desert."

"I was misinformed."

Amidst the laughter, everyone called out, "Doofus...doofus...doofus!"

Callie whispered in Lew's ear, "He thinks it means smart Frenchman, I'm not kidding. He earned it, believe me." And putting her arm around her son: "It's only a joke, hon. Truthfully, in spite of himself, your dad is starting to get it. I think you're helping him with that."

Daniel interrupted. "I know this movie, mais oui, oeuf course...but what is this *toast*? What is she meaning?"

"I think he's saying that your story will be exceptional, that our very own doofus is going to win a Pulitzer Prize," Cash explained.

"My story, yes...I am thinking that you, the Cash, you could be helping me with this. No?"

"Only if you promise to leave me out of it. You have to take all of the credit...all of it...everything, soup to nuts. I'll need your word on that."

"You have my word...This is as it should be, the right thing... Nuts to soup, the credit, she is mine...Finally, the fair deal."

Will turned Callie's way, leaned in and whispered, "He's the one."

"Shush."

"As surely as General Sherman was the scourge of the South, Daniel invented—"

"Stop it."

Will smiled, then raised a glass. "This is a toast to Callie. To begin, I want to talk about the new Beaujolai...It's proudly released every year on the third Thursday in November. The winemakers announce that 'Le Beaujolais Nouveau est arrive!' There are tastings and celebrations throughout France, throughout the world. It's the beginning of the holiday season. The harvest is in, and it's time to savor fall's bounty...Well, Le Callie Nouveau est arrive! Yes, the new Callie has arrived. Like the wonderful cherry-red Beaujolais Nouveau, she's rich, vibrant, fresh and vivacious. Like the wine, she represents hope for the New Year. So I raise a glass to Le Callie Nouveau, who's ready to savor life's bounty. She's strong, she's bold, she's unafraid. And she's just beginning to realize her astounding capacities. Merely thinking about Callie coming into her own takes my breath away. Don't boss her, don't cross her…Bravo, Callie James."

The ping of wine glasses touching after a stirring toast filled the room, followed by a rousing chorus of "Bravo, Callie!"

Daniel raised a glass. "I propose this toast—to my story, the story of the century."

Andre booed. Others made faces, cried out catcalls, lowered their glasses.

Daniel went on, unfazed. "Which I'm dedicating to my son…" And raising his glass again, he added, "To Lew, the finest son a man could hope for. He is the great good fortune, the best thing that could happen—especially to a narcissistic *doofus* like his dad."

This was greeted by enthusiastic cheers, even applause.

Lew borrowed his mom's glass, held it high. "To my dad."

Daniel came around, picked up his son, held him tight, then set him down. "I leave now, to write my story while she is still fresh. The Cash, I will call you tomorrow to be my *helper*. Lew, I see you soon à Paris." He raised his glass. "Au revoir et merci." He turned to Callie. "Callie…mon Dieu, merci beaucoup."

Callie watched him go, thinking she'd never seen him like this.

The Macher stood, raised his glass. "To Cash and Callie. I begin in Yiddish." He looked to Andre, who nodded.

Callie smiled at Cash; she couldn't help it. Cash was next to her, his arm around her waist. He squeezed gently.

"A mentsh tracht und Gott lacht."

"A person plans and God laughs," Andre translated.

"Cash, a Choshever mentsh."

"Cash, a man of worth and dignity."

"Callie, a vundern zikh."

"Callie, a wonder, a marvel."

"L'chayim."

"To life."

"L'chayim," said in unison around the table.

Callie stepped to the head of the table, raised her glass. "First, to my son, Lew. I could not be a prouder, happier mom." She sat beside him, poured him a sip of wine, touched her glass to his.

Callie stood again. "And to my new family…" She raised her glass to each of them in turn. As she touched her glass to each of theirs, she found the person's eyes, then bowed her head.

Callie turned, finally, to Cash, "And to you, Cash Logan, the finest man I know. Utterly, utterly unlike the scorpion in your fable. If the scorpion is vicious and evil, you are kind and gentle and good. I misjudged you, punished you unfairly, then refused to see you clearly. Yet, you never gave up on me. Thank you for making me talk, for believing that I could live in the world. Thank you for my new life."

Cash walked to her, touched his glass to hers. Kissed her.

He raised his glass again. "First, to Doc. I know he's here at the table tonight. Let's take a moment…"

Glasses pinged, then heads bowed for a moment of silence.

And finally, Cash said, "To Callie…In the way that only she could do it, Callie James—Frosty—has taught me to love…"

Andre turned on Doc's boom box. It played a haunting, lovely version of Louis Armstrong singing "As Time Goes By."

"You must remember this, a kiss is just a kiss…"

They all listened, lost in the moment.

Then Cash swept Callie up in his arms, and there was pandemonium, a thunderous, joyous uproar, in Callie's country kitchen.

ABOUT THE AUTHOR

Burt Weissbourd is a novelist, screenwriter, and producer of feature films whose novels include *Danger in Plain Sight*, the first Callie James novel; the Corey Logan trilogy (*Inside Passage*, *Teaser*, and *Minos*); and *In Velvet*, a thriller set in Yellowstone National Park. Weissbourd grew up in Chicago and graduated cum laude from Yale University, with honors in psychology. During his student years, he volunteered at the Museum of Modern Art in Paris and taught English to college students in Thailand. After he graduated, he wrote, directed, and produced educational films, then began a finance program at the Northwestern University Graduate School of Business, which he left to start his own film production company in Los Angeles. From 1977 until 1986, he developed screenplays working with screenwriters including Frederic Raphael (*Two for the Road*), Alvin Sargent (*Ordinary People*), Andy Lewis (*Klute*), Stewart Stern (*Rebel Without a Cause*) and many others. (Film credits are for identifying the writers, he did not work on these specific films). He also worked with actors including Robert Redford, Lily Tomlin, Goldie Hawn, Sally Field, Diane Keaton, and Al Pacino. During this time he produced films such as *Ghost Story*, based on the novel by Peter Straub and starring Fred Astaire, and *Raggedy Man*, starring Sissy Spacek and Sam Shepard. He's a voting member of the Academy of Motion Picture Arts and Sciences. In 1987, he founded an investment business, which he still runs. An avid fly fisherman, he's often in Montana.

Weissbourd has lived in Los Angeles; Bainbridge Island, WA; Seattle; and New York City. He currently lives on Long Island with his wife, Dorothy. He has three adult children and two grandsons.

ACKNOWLEDGMENTS

Jacob Epstein, Judi Gress, Brendan Kiley, Patricia Kingsley, Mike Reynvaan, Robert Lovenhelm, John McCaffrey, Ron Mardigian, Emily Weissbourd, Dorothy Escribano Weissbourd